Vintage
Volume One

Lisa Suzanne

Printed in the United States of America.

ISBN-13: 978-1511477376
ISBN-10: 1511477377

This book is a work of fiction. Any similarities to real people, living or dead, is purely coincidental. All characters and events in this work are figments of the author's imagination.

All songs ment
songwriters.

Cover Art by L

praise for Lisa Suzanne's books

How He Really Feels (He Feels, Book 1)
"I could not put this book down. I think I read this in one day... It is a book for those die heart romance fans like me."

–Jackie, Fire and Ice Book Reviews

What He Really Feels (He Feels, Book 2)
"What He Really Feels is beautiful story. It's filled with emotions and heartache and healing. It's raw and real. It has moments where you want to hug them, strangle them and hug them again. It's got it all."

– Jodie and Bree, Fab Fun & Tantalizing Reads

Since He Really Feels (He Feels, Book 3)
"I loved the whole cast of characters and how the stories evolved. I would definitely recommend this book and the whole series as a 'must read'."

–Crystal, Those Crazy Book Chicks

Separation Anxiety
"...this book has everything. It's sweet, emotional without making you ball tears, funny, HOT without being too dirty and even has a bit of mystery in the story. LOVE!!!!"

–Gretchen, Battery Operated Book Blog

Side Effects
"Side Effects Warning of Reading This Book: will cause extreme fits of laughter, will cause panties to melt clean off, will cause frustration and yelling out loud, will cause family/friends to believe you are a lunatic for yelling out loud, and MOST IMPORTANTLY: will be one of the best damn books you read this year."

–Cassia, Deliciously Wicked Books

Second Opinion
"Lisa Suzanne is a go to author for me and I can't wait to read more from her."

–Nicole, Author Groupies

also by Lisa Suzanne

The He Feels Trilogy:

How He Really Feels (He Feels, Book 1)

What He Really Feels (He Feels, Book 2)

Since He Really Feels (He Feels, Book 3)

The Love Sick Series of Connected Standalone Novels:

Separation Anxiety

Side Effects

Second Opinion

dedication

For my "Rock" Star

Thank you for your endless support.

prologue

I'm in trouble, Roxy. You're better off without me. I won't be back, but I will think of you every single second of every single day. Stay in this house if you want. If I stay, I put you at risk. If I tell you more, I put you at risk. This is a forever kind of goodbye. Please don't hate me. I couldn't take it.

one

Four hundred of my dad's closest friends held their glasses in the air after the best man gave his speech.

I glanced at my new stepmother, Jadyn Snow, adult film star.

Who the fuck marries a porn star?

A rock star, that's who.

Dear old Dad.

I had only attended the wedding because I loved and respected my father. I'd contemplated not attending, but my dad had texted me the night before. *CC, I would love if you could accept my new wife into your life. I'm glad you decided to come.*

At the rehearsal dinner, I considered keeping a tally of how many times I heard my dad's bride-to-be talk about money, fame, or my dad's band, Black Shadow. What she really cared about became pretty evident as I listened to her talk to their guests.

That's why I was having a hard time raising my glass in the air to toast this couple's wedded bliss.

It was his third wedding in the last ten years, and this one was even bigger and more extravagant than the last.

This marriage wouldn't last any longer than the others, but at least this time he'd been smart enough to make his blushing bride sign a prenup.

My dad took the microphone after his best man finished his speech.

"First I must toast to my beautiful bride." He looked over at her, and it was clear he had genuine feelings for her. Maybe I just didn't know her well enough to appreciate that she really loved him, but somehow I doubted that. He held his glass up. "I love you, Jade. I can't wait to spend every day showing you how much. And to everyone else, especially my baby girl CC, thank you for being part of our day. We love you all. Now let's get fucked up!"

The crowd roared with laughter while I fingered a lock of my hair self-consciously. It got stuck in a knotty layer of hairspray. I tended to be low-maintenance. My almost-black hair naturally dried straight, but the stylist insisted on curly waves for the day, and then she'd lacquered those waves until they were shinier than the sun.

I felt like all eyes in the room were on me when my dad said my name, and I wanted a hole in the ground to swallow me up.

Although money and fame certainly had its perks, I hadn't asked for the attention that was forced on me because my dad was a famous rock star.

"Why does your dad call you CC?" A male voice from a nearby table spoke to me. I turned my attention to the voice.

He looked familiar, but I didn't know his name. He was in a band, maybe, or on some television show. I didn't keep up with celebrities.

"My middle name. Cecilia. He wanted it to be my first name."

"Your mother insisted on Roxanna?"

I nodded. Roxanna Cecilia Price was my full name. I looked nothing like a Roxanna, but my parents assured me that my name was musical. I was named after the muses of two famous songs—"Roxanne" and "Cecilia." I wanted a normal name. I wanted to be called Anne or Jen or Megan or Katie. But instead, I was Roxanna Cecilia. The name was too big for my skinny frame.

"Roxy, we need you for more pictures." Delilah, my dad's wedding planner, pulled my attention from my short conversation.

I'd had my picture taken more times just driving up to the hotel than I'd had in the entire last year. This circus of an event had brought out Hollywood's elite. Paparazzi clicked away, each hoping for a glimpse of any one of the celebrities attending, not to mention the groom himself.

Those pictures would be worth a fortune.

Growing up the daughter of Gideon Price wasn't all it was cracked up to be. Most kids grow up wishing that their parents were cool, rich, and famous. I had all of that, and I grew up wishing my parents were just normal.

My mom had slept with my dad when his band stopped in Miami on a tour. It was a one night stand, a ploy by my mother to find a way to set herself up for the rest of her life.

It worked.

My dad felt a sense of responsibility toward me, and he tried to work things out with my mom.

It didn't work.

Sometimes it was hard growing up with the knowledge that I came from what only should have been a one night stand, but my dad always made me feel loved.

While my mom wasn't a real part of my life, my relationship with my dad was the opposite. Even though he led an extremely busy life in the spotlight, and even though everyone wanted a part of him, he always put me first. He was my closest friend…my only friend, really.

After Delilah's pictures and a visit to the ladies' room, I was heading down a long hallway back to the ballroom when I heard voices. I glanced toward the doorway. It looked like a conference room, but the lights were out. The door was just barely cracked open.

"Do you think he'll show up today?" I stopped in my tracks when I recognized the voice. It was Jadyn, my new stepmother. My dad's bride.

"Maybe. We have everything in place for today." It was a male voice—one I didn't recognize.

"Don't call me. I'll get in touch with you." I heard rustling, like someone was about to walk out of the room, so I slipped away before I was caught eavesdropping.

What the hell was that about?

I'd ask my dad.

While I didn't want to needlessly upset him on his wedding day, I wanted to protect my father the way he'd always protected me. I had no idea what Jadyn had been whispering about. Maybe he already knew, but maybe he didn't.

I had to walk past the hotel lobby to get back to the reception, and I saw my dad standing near the doors leading into the ballroom. He was facing the entrance of the hotel, his gaze narrow and focused. I followed his line of sight.

Men in black suits, who I assumed were part of my dad's security detail, appeared to be tackling a man just on the other side of the glass doors. I couldn't make out who it was from my distance, but there was certainly a commotion happening out front.

I watched as George, the trusted head of my dad's security team, strode across the lobby. He met my dad's eyes, and George nodded once. My dad nodded back in George's direction before his eyes landed on me.

He looked anxious, but he smiled warmly at me as our eyes met. Clearly he was covering up the fact that something was happening out front, and it was enough to cause me to forget that Jadyn had just been mysteriously whispering with someone in what she thought was a secluded area. My dad waved me over and threw his arm around my shoulders. The two of us headed back into the ballroom.

He had people to entertain, so I went back to my table. I felt alone in the middle of four hundred people. I had no date for this event. He had left me nearly a year earlier.

I only had one constant that I held onto.

My job at Vintage.

two

"Roxy, when you punch in, can you hang up the posters Flashing Light's manager dropped off?"

I nodded up at Tim, my manager at Vintage. I'd had a nice long weekend off work for my dad's wedding, but it was Tuesday and I was back at the store.

Vintage had once been exclusively a record store before digital media emerged. To keep the store going, Barry, the owner, started selling vintage clothes and posters and books. He'd installed a small café that was perfect for breaks, and it offered a place for people to hang out.

A small crowd started gathering in the café where I was sitting before my shift started. Their t-shirts told me that they were waiting around for the band coming in to sign albums later that night. Barry didn't allow lines inside the store any earlier than three o'clock, but the purchase of any café item was one way to get in early. The band wasn't scheduled to arrive until eight, so these idiots had a long wait in front of them.

I finished my Coke and then headed to the break room to punch in and start my day. Monotony was my life. Punch in. Fold t-shirts. Alphabetize albums. Slurp down a Coke during my break. Set up the tables, chairs, and ropes that created the queue when artists came in. Punch out.

Vintage was the one thing that made me feel like a normal person.

I started by hanging up the posters the band's manager had dropped off. I took a minute to study the four men on the poster. They looked like the type of crew I'd hang out with back when I used to have friends, back before my ex,

Damien, had left in the middle of the night with a note telling me to move on.

Their faces were shadowed in the picture, but staring at a poster seemed more interesting than folding t-shirts. Their album was on the corner of the poster. I looked at the image for a minute, trying to decipher what it was. It was red and black and had some abstract image that made me think of blood. The album was titled *Try*.

Tim told me the band moved to LA from Chicago a few months earlier, but their career had skyrocketed quickly. They were set to open for some other band on a US tour, but they were making the rounds of the local dives before heading out.

Try. I was curious about their sound, and I knew playing their music would make the fans who had gathered in the store happy.

I found a copy of their album under the counter where the registers were located, and I slipped it into the disc player that broadcast through the store. I pressed play and heard the first note of the first song. A cheer rose up through the crowd.

The first track was titled "Trial and Error." The song started slowly as a bass drum echoed quietly in the background before it hit loudly, and then a guitar joined in. The singer belted out the first verse, and then I heard another voice backing up the lead over the bridge and through the refrain.

I can't keep trying
You're killing me slowly
I can't keep dying
But I'm dying for you
You told me I'm a sucker
Just a crazy motherfucker

I'm done with this life
You're handing me the knife
We tried, we tried, we tried
But all we got was an error

The words came from someone who was hurt, tormented by something that had happened to him. I knew that feeling because I'd lived it myself.

The next song played, and the next, and the next. I found myself swaying to their beats as I folded shirts and prepped the store for the chaos that would surely ensue later that evening.

The disc started over from the beginning. Ten songs. Too short in my opinion.

They were a mix of rock and metal. I liked their sound, but there was a voice behind the vocals, a sound that spoke to me. I couldn't put my finger on it, but as *Try* started playing for the second time, I knew there was something special about this band.

Tim's voice cut into my internal analysis of the album. I snapped to attention.

"Roxy, can you bring another box of CDs from the break room and set them out on the table?"

Barry decided fans could only stand in line if they purchased a CD. It was a great marketing strategy even if it completely ripped off the fans. The store would do well, and Flashing Light would certainly get their cut.

I walked to the break room to gather the box he'd mentioned, still thinking about the music.

Somehow those songs had wrapped around me. I felt it in my skin, in my bones. In my chest.

I *felt* it.

Irritation lanced through me because Tim had taken away the feelings by sending me back to the break room to gather albums.

I took a minute in the break room to compose myself. That album had temporarily snapped me out of the detachment I had allowed to engulf me for much of the past year.

Music never had that sort of effect on me. I worked in a music store. I was the daughter of a musician. I was well aware of the powerful effects music could have on people, but I'd never felt it. Not once in my life.

I didn't really care about the music scene. I had only applied to Vintage my senior year of high school because I thought it was cool to work somewhere named Vintage.

Truth be told, I resented the fans who screamed and acted like a bunch of maniacs. It was revolting to hear a woman tell someone she'd never met how much loved him. She didn't know him. She didn't know if he had a wife and kids waiting at home. All she knew was that he had money and he played music.

That was all my mother had known about my father. Maybe that was why I resented the fans so much.

Maybe that was why I resented musicians so much, too. The majority gave into the fawning fans. It took a strong man to reject the advances of a beautiful woman throwing herself at him.

And that was just one of the many reasons why I never wanted to date a musician.

I wasn't interested in dating anybody, actually. I had moved past my ex, but relationships were too much work. Besides, everyone I'd gotten close to in my life either left me or had been taken from me. Only one person had always been there for me—my dad.

I was better off alone. I was still working on relying only on myself when I'd become so emotionally dependent on Damien that I lost sight of who I was.

After he'd left, I'd deleted my social media accounts. I'd changed my phone number. The only person I gave my new number to was my dad. I didn't even tell my mom, not that she'd tried to get in touch with me in months anyway.

I didn't want the friends Damien and I had known to ask me about the end of us. I didn't have the answers they were looking for. Besides, every single one of them was only using me for my connections. In fact, pretty much everyone in my entire life had only ever used me for my connections... starting with my own mother before I was even conceived.

I was just the ticket to something bigger and better. I was the ticket to Gideon Price.

A customer pulled me out of my thoughts as I stacked CDs on the table. "Do you have any Flashing Light shirts for sale?" she asked.

I shook my head. "Sorry. We have CDs, but no shirts."

She walked away in disappointment without so much as a thank you.

"Sure, no problem," I muttered to myself when she was out of hearing distance.

We were fully staffed, which meant all ten Vintage employees were on duty in some capacity. My job that night was to straighten merchandise...at my request. I didn't want to deal with registers. I didn't want to watch the line. I didn't want to stand by the door watching for line jumpers or shoplifters. I just wanted to mill around the store like I always did, and because Tim had always nursed a crush on me, that's what I got to do.

I'd been listening to Flashing Light for five hours, and I wasn't tired of it. Playing the album on repeat made the fans happy, but it also pulled at something inside of me.

I had opened the booklet inserted inside the CD case at one point.

Aaron "Fitz" Fitzgerald –Vocals
Vinnie D'Angelo – Drums
Parker James – Guitar
Garrett Harper – Bass

It wasn't the lead singer whose voice spoke to me. There was some other voice in there, the one whose voice wouldn't stop playing in my head.

I read through the entire insert. The guitarist seemed to have written most of the songs. It was his words that were washing over me, his words that were whirling around in my mind.

What was it about this song, this disc, this band, these artists, that bass drum, that guitar, that backup voice?

That voice.

It was the first thing I'd really felt in months.

three

I needed a ten minute break, a quick getaway from the throngs of screaming women clad in tight jeans and tighter shirts before the band arrived and the real insanity began.

The café was overcrowded with fans. The entire store was, actually. So instead of my usual Coke in the café, I headed to the break room for a few minutes of meditative peace.

The back door was open. It led out to the alley where I took my smoke breaks—or, rather, where I occasionally smoked a cigarette just to have an excuse to get out of the store for a while.

I made my way over to shut it when I heard voices.

It had to be the guys from the band.

I sat at the break room table, an old table that looked like it had once sat in someone's kitchen. It was filled with grooves and scratches, a table that had clearly lived a long life. I strained to hear the conversation outside. Of course the first words that caught my attention were: "I heard Gideon Price's daughter works in this store."

It wasn't the back-up's voice. It wasn't the lead singer's voice either. I didn't recognize the voice.

There was a grunt in reply, as if whoever voice number one was speaking to didn't really care who worked in the store. I liked that about him.

"Maybe we can figure out who she is and she can talk to her dad," voice number one said.

"The fuck good is that gonna do?" I heard his voice. He was muttering, but it was in the same timbre as the back-up. It was him. I recognized it immediately.

"You never know, Parker." Parker. Guitarist Parker. Songwriter Parker. "Do you think it's that hot piece of ass with the dark hair and the luscious tits?"

"Jesus, Vinnie. Have a little respect."

Vinnie laughed. I remembered reading that he was the drummer. "This coming from you? Don't pretend like you don't want to bang the shit out of her in this alley."

"Don't talk about her like that." Parker's voice was forceful. He was pissed at the way his bandmate was talking about me.

I didn't blame him. I was pissed, too.

"Why are you being so defensive?" Vinnie asked.

"I'm not. Yeah, she's hot. Yeah, I'd fuck her. But what does it matter?"

Guitarist Songwriter Back-Up Vocalist Parker wanted to fuck me.

"Since when do you pass up pussy?"

"Since when did she offer hers to me?"

He had a point, but now that I'd heard him defending me to his friend, I was ready to serve it up on a platter to him.

"Since when did you need an offer?"

Guitarist Parker changed the subject. "We should probably get in there and sign some shit."

I heard some rustling. Maybe a cigarette thrown down and ground out with a shoe. I heard footsteps, and then the two of them appeared in the doorway. Both of them had their heads down as they walked into the break room, and the moment I saw Parker in person for the first time, I knew which one was him.

His appearance matched his voice. He looked like heat and sex. He glowed with a light that shouldn't have been surrounding him given the dark hair that peeked out from the cap he wore backward on his head, his dark eyes and facial scruff, his black shirt and black jeans and black Nikes, the black ink of tattoos snaking down his arms. His voice alone had made me feel emotions that I'd blocked for a year, but the visual image matched that voice. He was goddamn sexy and I felt my blood boil just looking at him.

Vinnie, on the other hand, didn't have a light surrounding him. He was tall—taller than Parker—and thin with defined muscles in his arms. His dark hair was a little on the longish side, and he tossed his head to the side as he walked through the door to allow the fringe across his forehead to fall into a perfect sweep to the side.

"This is gonna be a long ass six weeks if you're gonna act like a pussy every time we talk about a woman," Vinnie complained.

They looked up at the same time. When they saw me, they both froze.

I pressed my lips into a thin, fake smile, trying to communicate without words that I had heard everything. I forced myself to maintain my cool in the presence of Guitarist Parker. I was used to putting on an act for people, anyway.

I maintained my dignity when what I really wanted was to pull off my clothes so Parker could fuck me on top of the old kitchen table.

It didn't really matter either way. I'd never see either of them again after that night. But it was kind of entertaining to watch them suffer.

They glanced at each other and back to me, and I raised my eyebrows.

"My father doesn't give a shit about new bands," I said. I stood and faced Vinnie. "Neither do I. And just for the record, I would never let you bang the shit out of me." I looked over at Parker, a ripple of adrenaline firing up my spine. "You? Maybe."

I turned and exited the break room, a smile of triumph on my lips.

It was the first time I had really, truly smiled in a while. My face stretched into a wide grin once the door to the break room closed behind me. I brought my fingers to my lips in wonder.

I couldn't get over the torrent of wild emotions crashing through me, emotions I had essentially shut off. I forgot what it was like to have highs and lows when everything was set on even for so long.

It was Guitarist Parker. He made me feel again.

And for that, I owed him.

I just wasn't sure what I was going to do to pay him my debt.

I stood in the hallway leading from the break room to the main area of the store to catch my breath for a minute when I felt a hand on my shoulder. It was warm. It felt like summer or maybe sex in the rain.

I wasn't really sure what that felt like, but I knew who it was before I turned around.

"I'm sorry about Vinnie." My eyes met Parker's when I whipped around at his voice. Typically band members were ushered to the table for the signing and ushered out just as quickly. They didn't have time to spare on long conversations with their adoring legions.

But Parker had made an exception. He'd come after me.

The question was *why* he'd done that.

The insecure part of my brain told me that it was because of my dad. But a tiny speck of confidence reminded me of what he had said to Vinnie only moments earlier. I'd caught a conversation neither of them could have had any idea I'd been listening to. Guitarist Parker had stood up for me anyway.

Just as I was about to respond with something clever, something that would hook him in, something that would allow me to repay my debt to him, I realized that I couldn't.

I couldn't understand the waves of emotion coursing through my system as I faced Parker. I'd never felt so pulled to a man—to anyone—before in my life.

It wasn't just because he was attractive. He was.

But it was so much more than physical beauty.

I was attracted to something inside of him, something that connected me to him. I was pulled toward him. I could see myself becoming addicted to him, and that obsession was unhealthy. I'd lived it once before, and I couldn't go through it again.

Besides, he was a musician.

I didn't date musicians.

I wanted nothing to do with musicians.

Even if a little part of me was curious what he was like when he was in his element. What he looked like shredding a guitar on stage in front of a crowd.

He had to be sexy as hell on stage.

But I couldn't get involved.

I was far too vulnerable to be with someone who could potentially only want to be with me because of my dad.

So instead of saying anything at all, I simply nodded my head once and turned away from him, walking toward the store and the monotony of folding t-shirts.

For some reason, Katie popped into my head. After my best friend had been taken from me, I'd had a hard time getting close to people. But when Damien left, he shattered me. It was too painful to deal with the roaring ache of loneliness, so I'd gotten in the habit of shutting off everything around me.

Emptiness had surrounded me, gathered me up in its arms and sheltered me. It had become my companion, my comfort after I'd lost everything.

And then he walked into my store.

He was like a ray of sunshine in my dark existence. If I was rain and thunder and clouds, storms, then he was warmth on my skin and a balmy breeze. But much like oil and water or truth and lies or fire and gasoline or order and chaos, darkness and light had little chance of surviving together.

Flashing Light was scheduled to sign for two hours. Eight to ten. They'd barely even started, and I was already counting the seconds until they left.

I was used to my monotonous life. I didn't like events that threw off the curve. I didn't like upsetting the balance.

I couldn't help my traitorous eyes darting over in his direction. His fans loved him. The ladies were swooning and flirting and acting like immature fools.

All four men in the band were attractive, but Parker stood out the most. It was the dark shadow of a beard, the way he wore his hat like he just didn't have a care in the world, the confidence that oozed from him.

Vinnie sat next to him, and instead of a sexy confidence, he showcased an ugly arrogance. He knew he wasn't hard to look at, and he used that when he flirted with the women asking for his signature. The other two, Fitz and Garrett, I assumed, were more like Parker than Vinnie. One had sandy hair and piercing blue eyes. Just by quick observation based on the things he said and the way people reacted to him, he had to be the lead singer, Fitz. The other, Garrett, had longer blond hair and green eyes.

My eyes returned to Parker.

I couldn't help it.

I was intensely attracted to him.

But it would never happen.

People were buying vintage t-shirts like they were going out of style. The store was busier than I'd ever seen it. I was glad for Barry and his pocketbook, but I missed the quiet hipsters that typically shopped our place.

I went back to the break room to check our inventory. Three boxes marked "TSHIRTS" were stacked on top of one another. I yanked on the top box and let it crash to the ground in front of me. I used my box cutter to slit the tape over the top. I slipped the box cutter into my back pocket and bent over the box to see what was inside. I was sorting through the t-shirts when I heard a voice as I bent over the box.

"Well if that isn't an invitation, I'm not sure what is."

I straightened and whirled around at the voice. It was Drummer Vinnie. The one who'd been making lewd comments about me. The one Parker had stood up to in order to defend me.

I felt my face heat. I didn't like the idea of being alone in the break room with Vinnie. He seemed somehow…dangerous. After what had happened to my best friend, I tended to side with my instincts about people.

"I wouldn't invite you to the last party on earth."

"Ouch. She's got fangs."

"And she isn't afraid to use them." It wasn't true. I was suddenly terrified, and I hated Parker for one hot second for making me feel emotions so strongly again. Before my shift had started that day, before I'd heard Flashing Light for the first time, that lush voice that called to something deep inside of me, I wouldn't have been so scared. I'd been used to blocking out my emotions, and I could've faced Vinnie head-on. But now I had fear, and he sensed it.

He laughed, a fake, harsh, tinny noise that grated on my ears.

He walked toward me. Stalked toward me.

I was uncomfortable, but I was working hard not to show it. I couldn't let him see that I was weak. It would only allow him to take advantage of me.

When he was mere feet from me, he stopped.

I held a t-shirt in my hand and held my eyes steady to his. I slowly lowered my hand, trying to appear nonchalant. I felt the cool handle sticking out of my back pocket.

If this asshole took one step closer, I was going to use my box cutter as a weapon.

"Vinnie, leave her alone."

The breath that had been expanding my chest flew out in a whoosh as my eyes darted from Vinnie's and fell straight onto Parker's.

He saved me. My savior had come to protect me.

If my instincts told me that Vinnie was dangerous, they also told me that Parker was safe.

"I was just messing with her," Vinnie said, another harsh laugh echoing through the break room as he turned from me and headed to the alley door for a cigarette break.

Once he was out the door, Parker moved toward me. "Are you okay?" he asked when he stood across from me, as close as Vinnie had been, his voice soft.

I found it funny how the wrong man standing in front of me could trigger my fight response, while the right man standing in front of me could trigger my emotional response.

"I—I'm fine," I said, the strength gone from my stuttering voice.

"You're trembling," he said, looking at my hands absently wringing the t-shirt I held.

He took another step and reached toward me.

My natural reaction was to fold myself into him as he wrapped his arms around me. My cheek met his chest. I breathed him in. He smelled like whiskey and cigarettes and some expensive cologne that reminded me of a field filled with sunshine after a violent thunderstorm.

He gently stroked a hand down my hair, smoothing it before running his fingertips down my back. "I'm sorry Vinnie's an asshole."

"It's fine," I said, pulling out of his embrace.

"No, it isn't." He reached for me again, but I backed away and returned to my box of t-shirts.

I couldn't do this. Not with Parker.

Not only was he a musician, but I knew he was good. I couldn't get tangled up in him. He'd only leave me, or he'd be taken from me.

And based on the emotions that had been running rampant through me since I'd heard the first song on the Flashing Light album, I knew I was incapable of handling our imminent end.

"It's not the first time some asshole from a band thinks he's too good to follow the rules, and it won't be the last."

"Will you at least tell me your name?"

"Roxanna." I realized I should've asked him his name, but I already knew.

"Roxanna?" I could feel his eyes on me even though I wasn't looking at him. "That name doesn't fit you."

I shrugged. "Tell that to my parents."

He laughed, and it seemed like the room got a little brighter just with the sound. "What's your middle name?"

"Cecilia."

"Roxanna Cecilia. If that's not the daughter of a musician, I don't know what is."

"I hate my name."

"What do you want it to be?"

"Something simpler."

"How about Jimi?"

"Jimi?"

He nodded toward my shirt. I'd thrown on a Jimi Hendrix t-shirt and a pair of jeans that morning. It was sort of an undeclared uniform that employees of Vintage had to wear a vintage t-shirt to work.

"Sure. Jimi it is." Like it mattered. This guy was in my store for one night, but I'd at least have the memories of our conversations to hold after he was gone.

"Okay, Jimi. I just came back for a break with Vinnie."

"Do what you need to do."

"You'll be around?" He took a step closer to me.

"Yeah. I'm here until close."

"What are you doing after close?" he asked. He reached out and briefly fingered a stray lock of my hair.

I ignored the shudder that rolled through me at his touch. "Going home."

"You probably shouldn't do that alone." His voice projected confidence. He seemed like the kind of guy who was used to getting what he wanted.

I rolled my eyes. "Good line." I turned my attention back to my t-shirts.

"What time is close?"

"Eleven. But with cleaning up after you, I'll probably be here until after midnight."

"Perfect. I have a short set to play at eleven, but I can be back here around midnight."

"You have no reason to come back here."

He took off the hat he wore backwards and set it on the table with the grooves. He ran his hands through his thick, luscious, messy, dark hair. I found myself wanting to do that for him.

I stared down at the hat for a second, memorizing it. It was black. The word "Sox" was embroidered in black letters, black on black. It was the Chicago White Sox logo.

"Looks like I forgot my lucky hat. I can't go on tour for six weeks without it."

I couldn't help my smile. I didn't want him to see it, so I ducked back into the box of t-shirts. I didn't want him to know how he affected me. I didn't want him to know that when he'd touched my hair, an air of intimacy and eroticism accompanied the gesture. I didn't want him to know that just feeling like he cared—that miniscule act of caring that came so easily to some people—was enough to send a shudder of desire through me.

And I certainly didn't want him to know how goddamn sexy I thought he was.

I'd forgotten what desire, true desire for another person, felt like. It had been far too long. I needed to pull myself out of the despair that I'd been in, but I still wasn't sure how to get out.

All I knew was that Parker couldn't be my answer.

He turned to head out the door to join Vinnie, or maybe to yell at him for scaring me, and then he paused. He turned back toward me. "Why is a beautiful girl like you with all the money and connections in the world working in a place like this?" His voice was soft.

I glanced up at him. His brows were knit together with curiosity, like he was trying to figure me out. I grabbed a stack of t-shirts from the box into my arms, and then I said, "Because I can."

I heard a chuckle behind me as I walked out of the room, the image of his hat on the grooved table burned into my memory.

four

I could feel his eyes on me.

I kept doing my job, all the mundane tasks that I did every day. I wanted to look over at him, wanted to see his dark eyes light up as they met mine, but it was all wrong.

I knew nothing about this man aside from his name and the fact that he was in a band, yet we were somehow connected. I'd known it from the second I heard the first whisper of a lyric on his album. My soul was linked with his, and meeting him in person only confirmed that.

Virtually everyone listens to music. Some feel a connection while others don't, but most are realistic enough to know that they'd never really have a chance to meet the voices emitting from the speakers.

My situation was different.

Because of my dad, I had access to just about every musician on the planet. If Parker James hadn't walked into Vintage that night for a signing with his band, if I hadn't pressed play on his album that morning, if life was completely different...

Something told me I'd still have crossed paths with him at some point.

It was inevitable.

But just because we had met didn't mean that it had to go any further than that.

I was lost in thought when dark eyes met mine over a rack of books. I shuddered and averted my eyes back to the books I was rearranging.

"Why are you trying so hard to ignore me?" he asked bluntly.

"I'm just doing my job." My voice sounded tired, which was the exact tone I was trying to portray. It was an act, but I didn't want him to get the wrong idea. I didn't want him to think I was interested. Even if I was. "And you probably shouldn't be over here. Your legions of fans will attack."

"Look at me." It was not a request, and I was startled enough by the force in his voice to follow his direction. "I've never seen eyes as blue as yours. I could write a fucking song about it."

"You don't seem like the romantic type."

"I'm not," he said. He laughed humorlessly. "I'm an asshole. If you only knew."

"Then tell me."

Some blonde grabbed Parker's arm. "Can I get a picture with you?" she gushed.

"Sure, sweetheart," he said. I could hear the arrogant insincerity in his voice, but obviously Blondie couldn't. "Wait in line. I'll be right over."

"No, I mean now." She tugged his arm toward her. I glanced up and saw a friend waiting with her cell phone camera-ready.

"I'm in the middle of something." He pulled his elbow away roughly. "I'll be right over." He turned back toward me, and I watched her dejected face fall. She didn't walk away.

"Give me your number," he said to me. It was another demand.

I shook my head. "No."

"Why not?" he challenged.

I motioned between the two of us. "Because this isn't going to be a thing." I was done arranging the books, but I didn't want to stop talking to him.

I forcefully reminded myself that I refused get involved with a musician. I couldn't.

But this guy I'd met less than an hour earlier certainly had my undivided attention.

The fan's friend finally pulled her back toward the line, and I watched her walk away before I spoke again. "I can't get mixed up with you."

"Let me be the judge of that." There was that arrogance again.

"You were about to tell me about how you're not the romantic type." I thought maybe changing the subject would distract him from the dangerous conversation we were having.

Turns out I was wrong.

"That girl that just wanted to take a picture with me? If I hadn't run into you tonight, I'd probably be out back shoving my dick in her mouth during my next break."

He said it for shock value. I didn't doubt that was exactly what he typically did, but he certainly hadn't shown that side of himself to me. The side I'd seen was gentle. Borderline sweet. He'd defended me without knowing me to his friend. That counted for something in my book.

This was all an act. It was his bravado, his way of pretending like he was macho. It wasn't him. The real Parker was the one who told Vinnie to stop talking shit about me.

"Don't you need to get back to your band?" I asked, not sure what else to say.

"Don't you even want to know why?"

"Why what?"

"Why I'm not shoving my dick down her throat?"

Of course I wanted to hear what he had to say. Of course I wanted to know why. But logic overruled emotion as I realized that the only reason he was paying me any attention at all was because Gideon Price was my father. "You can do whatever you want with your dick, Parker. It's not my business."

"Maybe it should be your business, Jimi." His voice was low and dangerous. It was a clear invitation, one I wanted to accept, but I wasn't going to.

"So you can shove it down my throat? No thanks." I walked away from him and toward the registers.

Tim and Virginia were working up front. Of the ten people Vintage employed, I really only talked to Tim and Virginia. I wouldn't call Virginia a friend, exactly, but she was the kind of person I could get a drink with after work. She acted like we were best friends, but the truth of the matter was that she didn't know me.

No one really did.

I'd learned that people used you for what they needed, and when they were done with you, they threw you away. I didn't need that in my life, so I stayed away from relationships in general.

Parker halted my progress by grabbing my arm and pulling me toward him. He stepped in close to me, so close that I could feel his breath whispering against my lips as he spoke. I stared at his lips, willing myself to maintain some self-control as he spoke. "You can't deny there's something between us."

Every part of me wanted to move my head an inch forward so our lips would meet. I wanted his warmth, his comfort, his roughness, his severity. I wanted to know everything about who he was. I wanted to know why he desired my company over the blonde. I wanted to give him my number as requested, to invite him into my house, my bed, my soul.

All this from knowing the man for literally less than two hours.

I couldn't imagine the kind of brutal torture we could do to each other if we had the time.

But he was leaving for a tour, and I was a realist.

"You're right. I can't deny it. I won't. But it doesn't matter."

"Of course it does," he whispered, his breath warm against my mouth. A quiet, intimate moment passed while his dark eyes bore candidly into mine. Standing this close to him, I could see tiny flecks of gold in his brown eyes. From far away, his eyes looked like dark chocolate. Up close, they looked lighter, like dark chocolate mixed with bronze and whiskey.

No one existed around us as my eyes took in every detail of his. The store became muted in the background, exceptionally silent in a moment that belonged solely to us, the eroticism of it mixed with lust and desire. A tingle of need danced down my spine. I'd never craved a kiss before, but I suddenly felt like I'd die if his lips didn't touch mine. I saw everything in his eyes that I needed to see. He'd suffered. He'd been down a hard road. Yet he brought this light with him, a light that suddenly I knew only I could see in him.

His eyes flicked away from mine and down to my lips for a few brief seconds. I was about to assault his mouth with mine when our stolen moment in the middle of the store was interrupted by perhaps my least favorite person in the universe, Drummer Vinnie.

"James, we need you back at the table. Bitches are getting out of control without you there."

The spell was broken as he dropped my arm and his eyes moved from mine over to Vinnie.

"I'm coming," he said, his voice that had whispered intimately to me only a few seconds earlier at full blast again.

He glanced briefly back at me. Torture and pain that I didn't understand passed through his eyes before he turned from me and walked wordlessly away.

I drew in a shuddering breath, more affected by the moment than I cared to admit.

He was a stranger. A complete, total fucking stranger.

And I was pretty sure a piece of me had fallen in love with him in that moment that was only ours.

five

"I'm sorry, but we have to cut the line off here," I heard Tim say to some customers waiting for their chance to meet the members of Flashing Light. The store was a mess, and I was just doing my best to keep the top layer of everything looking nice enough for people to consider purchasing. It had been a successful night for sales, but it felt like the longest two hours of my life.

A rise of protest greeted him, and I wondered how pasty and lanky Tim was going to deal with it. Luckily, Flashing Light's manager was there to back him up.

"Flashing Light has a set tonight at Live Oak at eleven," their burly manager said to the crowd. "Head over there so you don't miss it." A few people toward the back left the line peacefully, presumably to head over to the bar he'd just named. It was only a few blocks away. Walking distance. A few stayed, hoping to get their chance to meet the band.

When the line started getting shorter and the manager forced the back half of the line out the door, I felt a sudden loss.

I couldn't ignore the pull I felt to Parker, but he was leaving for six weeks.

I didn't want to be the reason he didn't do whatever the fuck it was that boys did the first time they were on a tour.

Besides, I had to think of my own sanity. I couldn't possibly sit at home wondering what he was doing for those weeks.

Or how many girls were getting the pleasure of his dick in their mouths, as he'd so eloquently put it.

He'd be leaving my store soon, and I couldn't handle another goodbye. It was stupid, perhaps, but I had lost too much over the past year. I hardly knew the guy and I didn't understand the feelings I was having. All I knew was that I was feeling again.

So instead of saying goodbye, I locked myself in a bathroom stall. He'd have to leave to get to his set, and he wouldn't know where I was. It was weak. But, admittedly, I was fragile.

I put the lid down and sat on top of it. The floor was sticky. The bathroom needed a good cleaning, but Virginia was on toilets that night, not me.

I did everything I could to focus on the ordinary, but thoughts of Parker snuck their way in. A single tear leaked from my eye, and I laughed as I wiped away the moisture. I hadn't even cried when Damien had left me without an explanation, so I wasn't sure why I was crying now.

I felt like a crazy person locked in an institution inside of that stall. Laughing and crying at the same time.

I checked the clock on my cell phone. I'd been in there for at least fifteen minutes.

It should have been enough time. The band should have left.

"Rox? You in here?" Virginia's voice shattered the silence.

"Yeah."

"You okay?"

"Yeah."

"You just need some quiet time?"

"Yeah. Is it quiet out there?"

"The band's gone. So are all of the loud bitches with the huge tits."

"Thank God," I said, unlocking the stall door and letting myself out. My eyes met hers, and I couldn't help but think how lucky she was.

She was gorgeous with her big brown doe eyes and straight nose and black hair cut into a blunt bob. Her hair was a different color every other week, but what made her lucky was the fact that she could just be anonymous. She didn't have to ever worry that someone only wanted to befriend her because of who her dad was.

She looked past me into the stall with the lid down over the seat. "You've just been sitting in here?"

"I skipped my usual breaks today. I deserved it," I said, faking like I was checking myself out in the mirror when in fact I didn't give two shits what I looked like. I just didn't want to look at Virginia's prying eyes.

"The store is a disaster. We've got a lot of clean up ahead of us."

"Better get started, then," I muttered, pushing my way out the door.

It was half past eleven when I started to feel the nerves tingling up my spine. Parker had told me that he would return around midnight.

I wanted to see him again.

Really.

But I couldn't do it—not to myself, and certainly not to Parker.

I took the coward's way out. Or maybe I was being a hero.

It didn't make a damn bit of difference. I wasn't going to face him again.

"Tim, I have a raging headache. Is it okay if I go home?" I asked. "I'll come in thirty minutes early in the morning to restock shirts."

"Don't worry about it, Rox. Go home. Feel better."

"Thanks," I whispered, rubbing my temple with my fingertip to make my fake headache appear real.

I bolted out, got into the black Porche Cayenne my dad had insisted on buying me for my twenty-first birthday, and sped off toward home.

I watched my rearview mirror, noticing a car behind me following closer than I liked. I signaled at my exit, and the car followed me. I drove through town toward home, and that car was immediately behind me the entire way.

Nerves bundled in my abdomen. They always did when I watched someone behind me get off at the same exit as me and follow me for any length of time. Eventually the people I thought were following me usually turned off at another street, but this one didn't.

I made a series of random turns, hoping to lose them. I wasn't dumb enough to drive home when someone was following me at nearly midnight.

My heart raced as the car continued to tail me.

I pulled my phone out of my purse to call someone for help.

Maybe I was just being ridiculous. But maybe I wasn't. Maybe my safety was at stake.

It was too dark to see who it was or to determine what type of car it was. I kept driving, trying to figure out who I should call.

Normally I would call my dad, but he was on his honeymoon in between tour dates. My mother was in another country.

I'd lost every friend I ever had.

I had no one.

I could call Tim. Surely he'd still be at the store. Surely he'd help me.

I could drive back to Vintage to see if this person continued to follow me.

"Hilton" screamed in red letters at me up ahead. I made a sharp and sudden turn into the driveway leading up to the entrance, checking my mirror. The car who'd been tailing me continued going straight. I pulled into the entryway of the hotel, an area someone had once told me was called a porte cochere, and I took a deep breath and closed my eyes as I tried to steady the rampant beating of my heart.

The exhale of my breathing exercise was cut short by a loud knock at my passenger side window. I jumped in my seat and then I lowered the window. "Good evening, ma'am. Checking in?"

"N—no," I stuttered.

"Can I help you?"

"I'm sorry. I'm in the wrong place and just needed to stop for a second."

"Can I get you directions somewhere?" He was young and earnest and kind.

"No, but thank you."

He nodded. "G'night, ma'am. Drive safe."

He walked back into the building, and I chalked up one point in the Hilton column as I drove toward home.

My eyes were glued to my mirror for any sign of someone following me, but I was safe.

For now, at least.

I finally pulled in front of the building housing the condo where I lived in Beverly Hills, a three million dollar gift from dear old Dad. My heart rate was mostly back to normal and I was mostly over the fear that had engulfed me.

My thoughts shifted to my condo. Part of me was tired of relying on my dad to provide for me. It led to an existence of little appreciation for hard work. Maybe that was why I loved my job at Vintage. It made me feel like a regular person instead of the rich princess I was raised to be.

The daughter of a rock god wasn't the only label that defined me.

And that was why I couldn't face Parker. I couldn't get involved with a musician. I couldn't move from the princess of rock to the girlfriend of rock.

It wasn't me.

I tossed my keys on my kitchen table, noting the smooth surface. This kitchen table was a far cry from the one in the break room. This one didn't remind me of Vintage, but it did bring up memories of my ex. And Katie.

Katie had left me first, but she'd left me in a much different way than Damien had.

It all added up to the same thing, though. I was the common denominator. Anyone who got too close eventually left me, and I couldn't take any more loss in my life.

six

I woke up in a cold sweat, my heart pounding in my chest.

It had been weeks since my last nightmare. I hadn't realized how important a full night's sleep uninterrupted by nightmares was until I had another nightmare.

Sleeping had been the one time when I couldn't block out my emotions.

Sometimes my dreams were terrifying, and other times they weren't. But they were always vivid.

When I was awake, I could consciously block out emotions. But when I was asleep, that was a different story. I couldn't control what my subconscious wanted me to feel.

And apparently that night, my subconscious wanted me to feel fear.

Panic.

Devastating grief.

I sat up in bed, panting. These were the moments when I hated living alone.

Images of the crime scene were burned into my memory.

It was a dark memory that would never fully leave me. It was the most painful loss of my life, and watching her parents break down when the police informed them of the tragic news was something that would haunt me for the rest of my life.

Katie and I had been best friends since I was born. She was four years older than me, the daughter of Mikey Reynolds, drummer of Black Shadow and my dad's best friend. We were raised together, but the difference was that Katie's mom stuck around. Katie's mom, Fern, and Mikey were married at the young age of eighteen, and they had Katie

Lisa Suzanne

when Fern turned nineteen. I had always envied the relationship they shared.

Fern treated me like a second daughter. She loved me, and I loved having someone to turn to as a mother figure since my own was essentially nonexistent. But it wasn't the same.

But when Katie was murdered, Fern couldn't take the loss. She divorced Mikey, and the last I heard, she'd holed up with some banker in Florida and bought a bunch of cats. She was never the same.

It had been a brutal crime scene, one that still haunted my dreams.

In fact, the images of the crime scene were so burned into my mind that I had started experiencing insomnia shortly afterward.

It was the pictures of the crime scene that burned in my memory. Photo after photo shown during the trial replayed in my head and maybe always would.

My doctor prescribed sleeping pills and told me to write my feelings in a journal or diary.

So it was either stay awake all night or wake up from a nightmare.

The nightmare was the lesser of two evils. The nightmares were sporadic. Lying in bed and staring at the ceiling for eight hours a night did nothing for me except force me to replay the scenes of horror in my mind.

Katie had met Chad outside the building where her Psychology class was held. Ironic, considering Chad turned out to be an insane lunatic.

She was a freshman at UCLA majoring in marketing. She had ambitions. I was a freshman in high school. I aimed for graduating from school and getting the hell away from my mother. My goal was realized; hers never was. Chad had taken it from her.

We talked every single day. I missed her company since we'd spent every night at each other's houses for as long as I could remember. Katie was the one person in the world who understood what it was like growing up the daughter of a rock star. Our friendship was built upon the strong foundation of that common trait. We understood each other in a way that no one else ever could.

She started talking about Chad almost from the first day she arrived on campus. I'd met him a few times, and he always seemed a bit off to me. Something shady lurked behind his eyes, but I was naïve enough to ignore my intuition because my best friend had fallen in love. I chalked it up to jealousy. He got to spend time with her while I was forced into the background, a place I'd never held with her.

They started dating exclusively. She started sleeping with him.

And then one day, Fern didn't hear from her. She ignored her mother's intuition that something was amiss, figuring her daughter was busy living the life of a college freshman.

Another day passed. It was unlike Katie to miss her daily call to her mother, but it was even more unlike her to miss her daily call to her best friend.

When Fern called me and voiced her concerns, a strange terror burned in my abdomen. I immediately knew that something was wrong.

Fern and I went together to her dorm. Her parents had paid for her to have a single room at her request, so there was no roommate to account for her whereabouts.

No one had seen her in a few days. No one, it seemed, could account for her absence.

Fern called the police, and Chad was questioned. He had an airtight alibi and a fantastic ability to act.

He convinced us all that he was as worried as we were.

Her body was recovered days later. She'd been found west of Topanga State Park. Her neck was badly bruised with finger marks, clear evidence that she'd been strangled to death. I couldn't listen to the police reports anymore, couldn't deal with the trial, but I'd been by Fern's side through it all. I'd tuned out as much of it as I could, focused on the indifference instead of the emotions. It was when I first learned how to block out emotions.

It took years before Chad was convicted. He maintained his innocence until he cracked under the pressure of a high profile trial. It turns out his goal had been to get into the good graces of the Reynolds family by showing how much he loved Katie even after her death.

But it had been cold-blooded murder. He had taken away my best friend, Fern and Mikey's beloved daughter, a selfless and loving woman who would be forever missed.

I would never get over the loss of my best friend.

It wasn't until I had met Damien that I'd even been able to smile again. But then he left me, too.

And I hadn't smiled again until earlier that night. Parker had put that smile back on my face, but I couldn't stop thinking about the divisibility of three.

Bad things always happen in threes.

I'd lost Katie.

I'd lost Damien.

I couldn't get close to another person, because I'd only lose him, too.

He'd be the third.

seven

I had a second dream that night.

This one was different from the first.

It was that voice.

That voice was like honey cascading down the side of a cliff like a waterfall and landing in a pool of warmth at the bottom of a ravine. I stood at the bottom of the ravine waiting for him, listening to his voice echoing off of the walls around me. And then he appeared, and he ravaged me in ways I'd never been ravaged before. His hands were everywhere on me, caressing and memorizing every part of my skin.

I woke groggily at the sound of my alarm. I was extremely turned on.

It was an hour before I could convince myself to get out of bed. That feeling of Parker touching me in a place that I hadn't touched in months except when absolutely necessary warmed me, washed over me, comforted me.

It was something I'd needed, especially after the nightmare I'd woken up to first.

I slid my fingers into my panties and felt the moisture from a place that had been aridly dry for a year. I pushed one finger inside my pussy and pulled my fingers out, spreading the wetness up and over my clit. I felt the old, familiar sensation of quaking in my thighs as I stroked my clit softly, adding pressure to push myself into a climax that my body hadn't felt in far too long.

As I stood under the hot spray of the shower a little later, I couldn't help but think that it had been Parker who had pushed me into sexually pleasuring myself that morning. I hadn't even thought about sex, much less had an interest in it, in a very long time. And if he'd been able to dredge up those feelings, I couldn't imagine what else he could do. I couldn't begin to imagine what actually being with him would be like.

When I walked into Vintage that morning, the store had been transformed. Apparently Virginia and Tim had stayed well past midnight straightening everything. Even the café had a bright sparkle to it. It looked like it should have been called "Modern" instead of "Vintage."

"This is for you," Tim said, handing me Parker's hat. "He came back looking for you."

Tim's eyes screamed of jealousy. I didn't know how to handle his emotions on top of my erratic and excessive feelings.

As much as I didn't want to feel anything, a tingle ran up my spine when my fingertips held his hat in my hands. "Thanks," I said, tossing the hat on the counter in a display of indifference that I certainly didn't feel.

"There's a note inside. I didn't look at it, but he asked me to make sure you got it."

More unwelcome tingles raced around my body.

I turned the hat over and pulled out a scrap of paper. I recognized it as the back of the receipt tape from the Vintage register. The writing was a messy scrawl.

Jimi-
You said you'd be here. I'm disappointed. Call me. 312-555-3157
-Parker

I folded the paper and stuck it in my jeans pocket. I knew I wouldn't use the number. I couldn't.

But that didn't stop me from wanting to.

eight

Seconds bled into minutes. Minutes bled into hours. Hours bled into days.

It's funny how six minutes can feel like the longest six minutes of your life, but six weeks can pass in the blink of an eye.

Day to day, the hours felt long. I felt the suffering, the want, the desire. I wrote in my journal. Often. I tried to recreate the feelings I'd felt that night I'd met him.

I looked up his tour schedule. I thought mailing his hat to his next location.

Part of me didn't want him to come into the store when he got back, but I knew he would regardless of whether or not I had his hat. It was inevitable.

I stared at the note he left me a million times. I thought about calling. I thought about sending a text. But I knew I never would.

If something happened between us, it would be because of his persistence. It wouldn't be because of me.

I tried to forget about him, but it was useless.

And then I looked at the calendar and realized six weeks had passed since I had first met Parker.

I thought I'd forget him as one day faded into two and two faded into three, but I hadn't.

I didn't turn on his music. I erased all signs of him and the Flashing Light signing from the store.

The only thing I had left of him was his hat and a slip of paper. The hat sat prominently on my family room table, mocking me every time I walked past it. I couldn't find it in myself to move that hat.

I often wondered—obsessively, really—what he was doing, whether he was thinking about me. If he was shoving his dick down some girl's throat.

It was his first time on the road. I couldn't expect him to save himself for me. It was stupid to think he would even consider that. He had a life to live, and I had made the choice not to use the number on the slip of paper he'd left for me.

Maybe if I had, things would be different.

Maybe I'd feel better about where I stood with him.

There was nothing between us except one shared moment in the middle of my store, those seconds when our eyes connected and I felt something I'd never experienced before. He had to have felt it, too.

He had to have.

No matter what I tried, he wouldn't get out of my head. So eventually I stopped trying. I stopped ignoring what I felt. Maybe it's true that absence makes the heart grow fonder, because over the six weeks that had passed, he'd become larger than life in my mind.

The darkness in his eyes was somehow darker. The light that burned around him was somehow brighter. I'd even dreamed about what he looked like beneath the black shirt and black pants and black shoes. I imagined a hard body littered with tattoos, veins filled with life surging above his skin, comfort in his solid chest, the smoothness of his skin under my fingers.

It was easy to imagine after I'd Googled him and seen his perfect body without a shirt.

The one image that stuck out to me most was his chest. Comfort.

That was different.

That was something I hadn't felt in a long, long time.

And in the few warm seconds Parker had held me in his arms, that was exactly what I'd felt. Comfort.

I didn't deserve it, and I hadn't been looking for it, yet there it was.

Enveloping me like a blanket. Soft, sturdy, heated.

While part of me assumed he'd just forget about me and I'd eventually forget about him, a deeper part of my conscience knew that he would show up at Vintage as soon as the tour was over.

So when he walked into my store after his six weeks away, I wasn't surprised.

I felt his warmth behind me before I saw him.

It was mid-afternoon, the quiet lull forcing me into the mundane checklist of my daily tasks. My list started with the bookcases and straightened each book, checking for alphabetical order. Then I moved onto t-shirts, folding them and stacking them into equal piles. Then I moved over to the music, where I first alphabetized records and then moved onto the compact discs.

I was in the middle of t-shirts when he walked in.

Instinctively I knew he was there, because somehow we shared this unreal connection that I'd never shared with another human being. Ever.

"You never called."

His voice was loud and clear in the quiet of the store. He stood behind me, but I knew exactly who he was. His voice was burned into my memory. I was pretty sure it would be for the rest of my life. There was no escaping the warmth that wrapped around me when I heard it.

Tim was in my line of vision, and I saw his face whip up when he heard Parker's voice, too. He knew exactly who it was talking to me, and from the sour look on his face, he didn't like it.

But I couldn't find it in myself to care what Tim thought. He represented the indifference that had clouded over me for far too long. Parker was emotion. Bright, light, white emotion. It was too strong to ignore.

"How was your tour?" I asked, refusing to meet his eyes as I continued folding shirts.

I knew if I met his eyes, I'd be lost again. He'd take me into his soul, and a part of me would be lost forever to him.

"Would've been better if I knew you were here waiting for me."

"Who says I wasn't?"

"You. By refusing to call me. Look at me."

The potency in his voice forced my eyes toward him.

My memory hadn't done him justice.

He took my breath away.

He looked even better than I had remembered. Handsome and sexy rolled into one package that was making my mouth dry.

Nerves carried through my veins, spreading into my chest. It was uncomfortable and unfamiliar. I didn't know how to act around him, and that had never been a problem for me before.

He wore almost the same thing as the last time I'd seen him, except for the hat.

Because I had his hat.

His eyes were heated. He looked angry. "Why didn't you call?"

"Because I can't get mixed up with you."

"Why not?"

I shrugged. I had about a million reasons, but I couldn't seem to remember any of them when he looked at me that way.

"You don't know?" he asked. His voice was soft, a sharp contrast to the hard look in his dark eyes.

"Because you're a musician," I said flippantly, as if that explained it all. I took the easy road, the simplest answer. I didn't know how to admit to him that I already had feelings for him when I didn't know anything about him. It was too strange, too strong of a pull to be real.

And I didn't know how to tell him that I was terrified for his safety. He couldn't get mixed up with me any more than I could get mixed up with him.

"I'll change jobs."

I laughed. I couldn't help it. "Don't be ridiculous. I'm not worth that."

"Your sense of self-worth is disappointing, Jimi. I expected more out of someone so beautiful."

"You can't say things like that to me." I turned away from him, focusing on the ordinary to rid myself of the quaking going on inside of me.

"Why not?"

I didn't answer.

He sighed. "Jimi—"

"Why are you here?" I asked abruptly, interrupting whatever he was going to say.

He looked momentarily surprised, the desire and heat in his eyes temporarily slipping. I liked that I caught him off guard. He was so used to people giving him whatever he wanted that I was proving to be a challenge.

He seemed to like that about me.

My guard was up, but it was slipping. I wasn't going to be able to resist him much longer. I didn't want to. I wanted to fold myself into him. I wanted his warmth surrounding every part of me. I wanted his eyes to look lovingly into mine. I wanted to share the pain of my past and wallow in his. I wanted to writhe naked on top of him. I wanted his hard cock pushing into me, pushing me past my limits, pushing me into a soul-shattering orgasm that I'd never recover from.

That was what was going to happen if I gave into what I was feeling.

But the stubbornness in me knew I couldn't.

I had to protect both of us.

The life of a successful musician wasn't easy. It was six weeks or three months or more on tour. That meant time away from loved ones. I was all too familiar with that concept. I just didn't want that life for myself. I wanted a normal relationship with someone who worked a normal job someday down the road when I felt ready to let someone into my life again.

Parker's band had real talent. I knew their big break was just minutes away. It was in my blood to be able to recognize those things.

I'd grown up around that life, and it was too hard to say goodbye all the time.

But more than that, I couldn't allow him to get to know me—the real me—because it would only hurt him in the end. Everyone I got close to ended up hurt, so if I was strong, if I kept my guard up and kept pushing him away, he'd be safe.

"I'm here because something started that night of the signing, Jimi. I'm here because I couldn't get your goddamn beautiful face out of my head for the past six weeks."

His hand found my chin and he forced me to look up at him again. "I'm here because I turned away every slut that paid any attention my way in the hopes that you'd give me a chance when I got back. I denied every single one of them because I wanted to be strong for you. I don't understand what the fuck is happening to me, because that's not who I am."

He paused, his eyes latching onto mine. I saw the bitter anger he held behind them, and I knew it wasn't because of me. He was going through a change, dealing with something, and he wasn't sure how to handle it. "You want the truth? I'll tell you the ugly truth. I wanted to fuck every single one of them until they were begging me to stop. I wanted to shove my cock down all of their throats until they made me come. I wanted to fuck and forget. Fuck and forget. That has been my lifestyle, my mantra, for as long as I can remember. And then I met you. And now I'm all sorts of fucked in the head because of it."

Jesus.

I listened to his words, not thinking for a minute that they were actually about me. But I saw the simmering anger. I saw the confusion written in his eyes. I saw everything he was trying to hide, like he'd stripped naked in front of me for only me to see.

And when he was naked, exposed, vulnerable, my heart latched a little tighter onto him.

I couldn't turn him away any more than I could accept what he was saying.

I was stuck in some limbo zone, fighting internally with how to accept his words.

Because if I accepted it, if I let him in, I would slowly drive him away from me until all that was left was a shell of a man who had to leave me in the middle of the night because he couldn't deal with the trouble he'd made.

I knew he wasn't my ex, but damn if I knew how to protect Parker. Because protecting him had become the most important thing in the world to me in the span of the three minutes he'd been standing in front of me.

And maybe the best protection would be holding him close. Keeping him safe. Keep your friends close but your enemies closer, right? Maybe my enemy was myself, and maybe if I gave myself over to Parker and held him close, that would be the best way to keep him safe.

It was worth a shot.

I had nothing to lose.

Parker was the one who had everything to lose.

"What do you want me to say, Parker?" I finally asked, breaking the spell that held our eyes captive to one another.

"I want you to give me a chance. Give me your number. Let me take you out. Let me kiss you like I've wanted to kiss you since the day I first saw you. Prove to me that waiting for you—that passing up all of the women I could've had over the past six weeks—was worth it."

If that wasn't a sick and demented way to earn your way into somebody's good graces, I didn't know what was.

But damn if it didn't work anyway.

"I get off work tonight at eight," I finally said, my voice small.

"Eight?" he asked incredulously, like I'd handed him the hidden secrets of the world.

I nodded once.

"I'll be back at 7:57," he said, his voice full of authority that managed to kill a part of me at the same time it sparked everything inside of me. "Just in case you decide to sneak out early."

I chuckled, and he walked out of my store.

nine

The day lagged in a jagged haze of nothingness. I spent more time trying to figure out what I really wanted to do with my life than I did anything else that day.

Normally I loved my job. I'd never really aspired to anything else.

But some strange thought crept into my head that there had to be more out there for me than working at Vintage for the rest of my life. I couldn't seem to push out Parker's words from the night we'd met when he had asked me why I worked there. I didn't need to work. Surely my talents could be used somewhere else. I'd been complimented on my singing talent. I had my mother's flair for fashion.

But I didn't want to be my father or follow in his footsteps. And Lord knows I wanted nothing to do with my mother's footsteps.

I think the reason why I couldn't settle on any single ambition was that my God-given talents were those of my parents. I wanted my own life built my own way. I just wasn't sure what that looked like anymore. And even as I thought it, I knew I'd use the money my father had given me to get to the ultimate end goal. Wherever that was.

But as I stood in the break room of Vintage, staring down at that old, grooved kitchen table, I had a feeling my future wouldn't be folding t-shirts for much longer.

My personality and my family background made me more of an employer than an employee. I didn't have the credentials to own a business, but I had the money to. I'd just never wanted to before.

Was it Parker that was doing this to me?

I wasn't sure, but I was definitely thinking in a new way and feeling a lot of new things.

Things I'd never felt before.

It was actually 7:52 when I felt his presence in the store again. Ordinarily my days at Vintage passed in a whirl because I enjoyed it, but I was anticipating this meeting. Every passing tick of the clock felt longer than the last.

I felt him first, and then I saw him before he saw me this time. I'd been checking out a customer at the register when he'd slipped into the store, and I saw him looking around for me. I took a moment to drink him in while the man I was helping ran his debit card through the reader.

Every part of him screamed that he was a musician. Strong arms that looked like they could shred the shit out of a guitar. Hands that worked hard strumming strings and caressing microphones. He was dressed in all black again, except he was missing his trademark backwards hat. My guess was because he wanted the one he'd left with me. He was hoping he'd get it back. I saw the tattoos peeking out from his short-sleeved shirt again. I was curious about his selection of ink. I'd seen it courtesy of my Google searches, but I wondered why he'd chosen the images he had.

I had a feeling I'd find out someday.

"You're early," I called from behind the register. His head whipped around in my direction.

A smile tipped up the corners of his mouth. "And you're gorgeous."

I felt heat creep up my neck, an unfamiliar sensation. I wasn't used to feeling out of my element, but Parker managed to constantly do that to me.

I put the man's purchase into a bag and handed him his receipt. "I thought so, too," the man said to Parker. "But I'm guessing you've got a better shot than me."

I stood mortified, shuffling some paperwork on the counter behind me to gain my bearings. The man was absolutely right. He had no chance. Not when Parker was looking at me with all of that heat in his eyes.

They said more words to each other, but I tuned them out. I couldn't hear over the roaring embarrassment in my ears, anyway.

"Seven minutes." His voice was low and close to my ear. I wasn't sure when he'd moved in so close behind me, but I could feel his heat.

And fuck did it turn me on.

I'd known the guy for all of a couple of hours with six long weeks peppered in, but he seemed like the kind of guy who would walk into a place and my clothes would supernaturally fall off.

In fact, I was sort of surprised I still had clothes on.

"Until what?" I finally asked, turning around to face him.

Big mistake.

Because I almost took my clothes off in the middle of Vintage.

His eyes were full of lust. That's all this was. This was a game of desire, and he was winning.

"Until we get the fuck out of here."

"And then what?"

"I think we both know where this is going." His voice was sinful. Dangerous.

But so fucking warm.

"I'd love it if you could spell it out for me."

"I'm going to do things to you that I've thought about doing for six endless weeks."

"And what might that be?"

He closed his eyes and took a deep breath as if he was trying to hold himself back from something. He glanced up at the clock. "Six minutes. You'll find out in six minutes."

My heart stuttered a bit on his quote about "six minutes." It reminded me of my thoughts earlier that day about six minutes feeling longer than the six weeks he'd been gone.

And this six minutes was going to be the death of me.

"Who says I'm going to let you do those things to me?"

"You do. With the way you're eye-fucking me."

I laughed. I couldn't really argue that. He seemed to instinctively know that we were on the same page.

A customer came up to the register to check out. She set a Madonna record in front of me, a collector's item, and her friend looked at Parker the same way I did.

She was eye-fucking him, too.

And I didn't like it.

His eyes were still on me, watching my every move as I rang up the purchase.

"Excuse me," the friend of my customer said. She was looking at Parker, but he was still staring intently at me.

"Are you Parker James?" she asked.

I glanced over at him, and he slowly turned to look at the girl. "I am."

"Oh my God! I'm such a huge fan!" She was gushing. Annoyingly. Obnoxiously.

"Thank you." It was a simple statement, and he turned his attention back to me. My hands shook slightly as I bagged the record.

"Can I get a picture with you?"

He sighed and leaned in close to me, touching his lips to my temple. A shudder ran the length of my body at his touch and the implication of it. He was showing this fan that he wasn't interested in anything more than a picture. I respected that. It made me actually believe his words about his lack of action during his tour. He'd given me no reason to think he had lied, but I was a disbeliever by nature.

"Sure," he said, stepping around the counter to fulfill his duties as the lead guitarist in an up-and-coming band.

A smile tipped my lips watching him. He maintained his distance even though she didn't. He was respectful but direct, making it clear from the way his eyes kept moving in my direction that he only had eyes for one woman in the store that night.

It lit something inside of me that I'd never felt before. It made me feel cherished, treasured.

I'd never been treasured before. I'd been used, neglected, ignored, recycled, mistreated, possessed, obsessed, infatuated. But I'd never felt that special value of someone revering me. Wanting me. Loving me.

Parker gave me that, and he didn't even know me. In some ways, he'd given me more in the couple of minutes we'd interacted than Damien had given me the entire time we'd been together.

Damien and I met in high school. He was a year older than me, a senior when I was a junior. He'd transferred in from another school, and we passed each other in the hallway on his first day. His piercing blue eyes had met mine, and I'd felt a strong pull to him like nothing I'd ever felt before him.

That's how I knew that this connection to Parker was real.

I'd felt a pull at first sight before with Damien. But it was different. With him, it was all about friendship first. Feelings came later. Addiction came later.

But with Parker, the emotions I'd been missing for so long came first. They came before I'd ever even seen his face. They surged through me when I'd heard his voice in the alley defending me, and they'd implanted in my blood the moment our eyes met across the room.

My first words to him had been sexual, so it didn't surprise me that he had certain expectations. I wanted it, too. I wanted to give myself over to him—eventually—even though I knew we would be bad for each other.

I'd be honest with him, and if he decided to risk it anyway, there wouldn't be anything I could do to stop him.

I wished I was stronger than I was. I wished I could protect him.

But I was only human. My humanity had no chance against his sex appeal.

"Time's up, Jimi."

I glanced over at the clock. Eight o'clock on the dot.

"Let me just run in back and punch out. I'll meet you back here in a minute."

He nodded, allowing me to do my thing.

I headed to the break room and stamped my timecard through the machine. I yelled a hasty goodbye to Tim.

Poor Tim. He looked longingly in my direction. He had no idea that he just wasn't cut out for me. He had no idea that I was leaving with another man and that I wanted to let Parker fuck me for the rest of the night.

I grabbed my purse and my keys out of the drawer where I stored them in the back room and headed toward the front to meet Parker.

"Where do you want to go?" I asked when we walked out the front door together. I felt his hand on the small of my back, and more unfamiliar emotions rocketed through me.

"I know a place. It's a little bit of a dive."

"Sounds perfect."

"You drive a Porsche?" he asked as we approached my car.

I nodded. "What do you drive?"

He nodded in the direction of the car parked directly next to mine. A GMC Jimmy. It looked like it had to be twenty years old.

"Ironic," I said, a hint of a smile turning up my lips.

He moved in close to me, so close that his body was flush against mine while my entire back side pressed against the door of my Porsche. His eyes never left mine.

"Quite ironic, Jimi," he said, his voice soft and his breath whispering against my lips. His eyes flicked for one second down to my lips, and he moved in even closer.

"Where are we going?" I asked, breaking the spell between us.

Parker cleared his throat and backed away from me. "Follow me. It's not far. A little Mexican place in Culver City. You know where Washington is?"

I nodded. I wasn't thrilled with the idea of Culver City, but chances were slim that I'd run into the only man I knew who lived there.

I followed Parker's old SUV through the streets of LA until we wound up in front of a taco shop. We both managed to find spots in the small lot behind the building. He met me just behind my car and pulled my hand into his as we walked toward the entrance.

A little shiver pierced my torso.

I should avoid him at all costs. I knew that. I'd only end up hurt again in the end.

Even his goddamn warm hand in mine was comforting.

There was no way I'd be able to stay away.

ten

"Who gets a cheeseburger at a taco place?"

Parker glared up at me over the top of his Coors Light. "I do."

"Strange."

"Best burgers in LA. But I guess you'll never know since you're a walking cliché with your tacos."

I held up my drink. "Don't forget my margarita."

He smiled.

I was biting into the best shrimp taco I'd ever tasted in my life when the chimes over the door jingled. I glanced in that direction.

An immediate chill floated through the air despite the warmth Parker made me feel.

Three men walked through the doorway. They were all big, burly men. Individually, they would have been intimidating. But together, the three men walking through that door scared the hell out of me.

Mostly because I recognized one of them.

I shifted my gaze down to my plate. I felt my hands trembling, so I placed them on either side of me.

Please don't see me. Please don't see me. Please don't see me.

"What's wrong?" Parker asked, alarm in his voice as he set down his cheeseburger. I felt his eyes on me from across the table, but I knew if I looked up, if I made any movement at all, I'd draw attention to myself. So I stayed still as I felt the eyes of the three men at the door roam around the restaurant.

What the fuck were the chances that I'd run into the one person I didn't want to see who I knew lived in Culver City?

Please don't see me. Please don't see me. Please don't see me.

I kept repeating my mantra, hoping for its effectiveness.

Unfortunately, it didn't work.

"Roxanna Price!" My name boomed out of his slimy mouth. He walked over to our table. I kept my eyes lowered. "How's little CC doing?"

"Fine," I said, my voice quiet.

"And how's the old man?"

"Fine."

"Fine. Fine? You got anything else to say, girl?"

I shrugged.

"You need anything else?" Parker asked, eyeing the man hovering over our table.

Fuck.

"Parker, don't." My voice was sharp.

He didn't know what Randy was capable of. I wasn't sure I even fully understood it, but I knew that pissing him off was the worst route to take.

"Look at the macho man defending his little girl." He looked at me. "You dating this pussy?" He jerked a thumb toward Parker.

I took a deep breath and looked up at him. Randy Marino was a heavy-set, middle-aged asshole who happened to be a bookie.

He and my dad had grown up together. I didn't know what sort of illegal business dealings they'd had together, but Randy had been around a lot when I was a kid.

He'd always been a dick, but one of the "highlights" of our history was when he hit on me when I was seventeen fucking years old.

My dad had been in town, and I didn't want to stay with my mom. My dad had a few friends over, Randy included. They'd been playing cards in the basement. My dad had converted the entire basement into a gaming area, complete with a bar. He had asked me to stay upstairs. I knew there were women down there. Even though I hadn't seen them come in, I'd heard the noises. I knew they were gambling high stakes, drinking, and smoking something that didn't smell like a cigarette. I wasn't naïve.

Plus the distinctive smell of pot had wafted upstairs.

I'd stayed out of the way. My dad and his friends had been busy in the basement, so I figured I was in the clear. I'd wanted a beer, and I knew my dad kept it in the refrigerator, so I checked the hall, found it empty, and darted to the kitchen to grab a couple of bottles for myself.

After I'd procured two bottles and turned around, Randy stood behind me. He was fucked up. He reeked of alcohol and marijuana, and his eyes were bloodshot and unfocused. The look in his eyes told me that he was probably high on something other than pot.

A frisson of fear had run through me, but he was harmless. He had to be. I had to believe he was, because believing the alternative was too scary.

"Pretty CC, pretty CC," he had sung to me.

I'd wanted to puke in his face.

He had been standing close to me. Too close. I'd been uncomfortable and scared, but I wasn't sure what to do. So I held the bottles in my hands, staring daggers at him.

"So pretty in your little black tank top and shorts. You shouldn't be wearing shorts that short with all of these men here. They might think you're putting that pretty little body on display for them."

He'd taken an unsteady step toward me and reached out to run his fat fingers down my cheek. "Are you putting that pretty little body on display?"

I'd closed my eyes as the blood pounded in my ears. In that moment, I had feared for my life, for my safety.

He'd never hurt me.

My dad would kill him if he hurt me.

Literally.

Deep down I knew he couldn't be serious.

It was the drugs combined with the alcohol. It had to be.

Instead of responding, I'd darted around him. His reactions had been too slow to stop me. I'd leapt up the stairs. I'd slammed my door and locked it, throwing the bottles on the floor and crying into my pillow, shaken and scared for the rest of the night.

I hadn't been fine.

I still wasn't fine.

But at this point in my life, Randy hitting on me in my dad's kitchen while he was fucked beyond recognition was just one more shitty experience stacked on so many others. I wondered if he even remembered what he'd said to me that night.

It didn't matter if he remembered.

I did.

And seeing Randy here in this taco shop with Parker put the fear of that night right back into me.

"Well?" Randy pressed. I was snapped out of the traumatic events of the past.

"We're not dating," I said. It wasn't really a lie, even if it wasn't exactly the truth. And if nothing else, it would protect Parker from the asshole in front of me. If I couldn't save him from me, at least I could attempt saving him from Randy.

Parker shot me a look. "Yes we are," Parker said to Randy.

Randy's eyes bored into me. "Tell your dad I said hello."

I wished I had the guts to tell him to say hello his damn self. Or to tell him to go to hell.

But I didn't. I ignored him and prayed he'd go away.

He gave me one last lascivious gaze, his eyes wandering down to my chest, before he turned and joined the other two men he was with at a booth not far from ours.

I was silent.

I knew if I spoke, Randy would hear. I didn't want my getting-to-know-you dinner with Parker to be blemished by the traumatic secrets of my past.

"Who is that guy?" Parker asked softly.

I shook my head. I'd fill him in later.

"Are you okay?"

I glanced up at him, not sure he'd actually spoken the words since his voice was so quiet.

I shrugged. I wasn't sure.

We finished our meal quickly and quietly. I felt Randy's eyes on me the entire time. I couldn't figure out if he was harmless or if he wanted something. The prickling of my nerves told me it was the latter, but I was putting on a show in front of Parker. And Randy, if I was being honest.

The second we were back outside, the inquisition began.

"Who the fuck was that?" Parker asked.

"Someone my dad knows."

"I gathered that when he told you to say hi to him." His voice was dry and humorless.

"I don't want to talk about him."

Parker ran a hand over the scruff on his cheek, clearly annoyed. I cleared my throat and tucked some hair behind my ear, also annoyed.

It got awkward. I blamed Randy.

"How does your dad know him?" he asked, trying another tact.

"They grew up together. Randy's a bookie and an asshole."

"Sounds like a gem. Want me to kick his ass?"

"Yes. More than anything. But he's not worth your time."

"You were scared when he walked in."

I nodded slowly. "Yes."

"Why? What did he do to you?"

I shrugged. He reached out for me, pulling me against him. He wrapped his arms around me, and it felt good. I just stood there unmoving. I liked being in his arms. And not hugging back felt like less of a commitment. Like this wasn't going to turn into something more than I could handle.

Even though just the way he held me told me otherwise.

My cheek met his heart. He just continued to hold me, and right when it got to be too much, right when I was about to lift my arms to wrap them around him too, he let go.

His hands found my biceps, and he pushed me back away from him, but not before pressing his lips softly to my temple. It wasn't the first time he'd done that, but last time it had been in front of someone else, a way to show that he wasn't available in the way some girl had wanted him to be.

This time was just for me. Just for us.

"Where do you want to go?" he asked, his eyes dark and heated.

I shrugged. "I don't care."

Truthfully I didn't. I just wanted to get away from Randy.

"I live with three other guys. So not my place."

I could tell from the way he was looking at me that he wanted to come to my place. But I wasn't ready for that quite yet. I was intensely private, and I wasn't ready to share something as personal as my home with someone I hardly knew.

Plus I still didn't completely trust his intentions.

I didn't know why he wanted me.

I had to admit that we had an intense attraction to one another. My soul was bound to his because he'd made me feel again after so much time spent in oblivion.

But that didn't mean I could trust him.

I had to look out for myself, especially when it came to a musician. I had to ensure that he wanted *me*, not my father.

"Not my place, either," I finally said.

"Where do you live?"

"Beverly Hills."

"Fancy."

I rolled my eyes. "My dad bought my place."

"Of course he did."

"What's that supposed to mean?"

"Let's be realistic here, Jimi. You work retail in a record store. You think you could afford a place in the Hills with that paycheck?"

I shrugged as I clicked the unlock button on my key fob.

He had a point, but I'd never really had any true concept of the worth of a dollar. I'd never had to. I'd been given anything I ever asked for because money clearly bought my love.

"I know a place between here and Beverly Hills. Sound okay?"

I nodded before getting into the car to follow him. He drove safely, slowly, ensuring I was behind him the entire time.

We were ten minutes from my place when he pulled off the highway. I knew exactly where we were, and he pulled in front of a strip mall.

I parked in the spot right next to his, and just like when we'd gotten out of our cars earlier, he grabbed my hand and led me.

We walked up to a frozen yogurt shop. Going to a place like this seemed so out of character, so out of context for whatever was starting between us.

We were on an actual, typical, regular date.

And despite the rocky start of Randy's presence at the taco place, I was enjoying my time with Parker.

"Fro-yo flavors can tell a lot about a person, so choose wisely," Parker said as he held the door open for me.

"Like what?"

"I'll tell you once you pick."

The place was empty, which was comforting after our run-in with Randy at dinner.

I inspected my selections. There were ten flavors, and I had it narrowed down to Double Dutch Chocolate and Red Velvet.

I decided on both.

"Interesting selection," he murmured with a smirk. He walked over to the Graham Cracker flavor and filled his bowl.

We headed to the toppings bar. Parker loaded his bowl with cookie dough, and I sprinkled on a few walnuts and gummy bears.

"Gummy bears?" he asked.

I nodded.

"Yet another fascinating choice." He doused his bowl with chocolate hot fudge, and I opted for a small squirt of marshmallow topping.

We set our desserts on the scale by the register, and Parker paid.

We settled into a table outside. He took a seat in the chair directly to my left even though he could have chosen to sit across from me. He put his feet up on the chair across from him, and I settled my feet next to him on the same chair. We were both relaxed, at ease with one another and with our desserts.

"So what does chocolate plus red velvet say about me?"

He shrugged, a little smile lighting up his face. "Who knows? I just thought it was fascinating watching you think so hard about what flavor you wanted."

I glared at him over the top of my bowl, punching him lightly in the arm. He held his arm in protest, a big smile plastered across his face. I couldn't help the delight that seared through my chest.

I wasn't used to lightheartedness in my life. I was used to the heavy, dark shit.

I liked this side of life a lot more.

I liked the things that Parker brought to the table, specifically the feelings he ignited inside of me.

"So the toppings don't mean anything, either?" I asked.

"Actually, the fact that you chose gummy bears does say something about you."

"What's that?"

"You're kind of disgusting."

I couldn't help the laughter that bubbled up from my chest. And when he laughed along with me, my heart fluttered in some strange, unfamiliar way.

I'd never felt that before.

Ever.

"It also tells me that you're a kid at heart. You don't let other people see that side of you. You hide it, but you can't hide it from me."

I felt the smile slide off of my lips as I considered his assessment of me.

No one had ever told me that I was a kid at heart. I'd been forced to grow up too fast when my best friend had been murdered. The only other time I'd allowed myself to connect with another person, he'd also left me.

My very first thought was that Parker's assessment of me was completely inaccurate.

But as I stared at him, his words prodding uncomfortably in my head, I realized that maybe he was right.

Maybe he already knew me better than I knew myself.

And that thought was pretty unsettling.

eleven

We finished our frozen yogurt and headed to our cars.

An odd presence seemed to follow us as we walked. The hairs on the back of my neck stood at attention. I had a strange feeling I couldn't identify. It had to be the fact that I'd run into Randy earlier that night. That had to be the strange feeling that stuck with me.

Our date was at its natural end, but it was clear that neither of us really wanted it to be over. I supposed I could invite him to my place. But I wasn't ready for everything that inviting a man to my place promised. I was still leery about starting something, let alone starting something potentially serious.

We stood outside my car. I was wondering if he was going to kiss me. I wanted him to.

He moved in close to me. Our eyes locked together. My back was pressed up against the driver's side door of my Porsche. It was reminiscent of when he moved in toward me when we'd left the store earlier that night, but this time I didn't stop him.

He was a whisper away from me. His eyes flicked from mine down to my lips, and then back up to my eyes.

He smelled fresh, like springtime in a grassy field after a heavy rain. I closed my eyes and took in a deep breath. It wasn't because of nerves. I wanted to memorize his scent. It was some sort of masculine cologne that fit him perfectly. He threw me off balance, but he had spent the entire night making me feel comfortable.

I waited for his lips to connect with mine, wanting it with every fiber inside of me.

And then I felt his lips on my neck, the scruff from his unshaven chin prickling against my sensitive, heated flesh.

A soft sigh escaped my lips as I leaned my head back to give him better access to my neck. I could stand there all day if it meant his lips were on my body. Anywhere.

I really fucking wanted him to kiss me. If I was being honest, I wanted much more than his kiss.

But the little sneaking suspicion I felt around every single person who came into my life told me that I had to play it smart. I couldn't let him take advantage of me because of who I was—or, rather, who my father was.

I had to make sure that he had the right intentions where I was concerned. My biggest fear was that he only wanted me because of who I was born to.

I'd seen what happened to Katie, and Chad hadn't even been a musician. He'd just been a guy who wanted more than life gave him.

Parker pushed his hips into me. Hard. The rocking snapped me out of my thoughts and brought me back to the present.

I could feel the heat from his body, the craving he had for me evident as his hard cock nearly burst through the zipper of his black jeans.

I gasped as he pushed toward me once more, his teeth biting softly into the flesh at the base of my neck.

"Fuck, Jimi," he muttered, and then he backed away from me, his eyes flashing. I couldn't tell if he was angry or horny, but his eyes held some combination of both.

We were in a standoff, his eyes locked on mine.

A cold chill crept its way through me. I turned away, opening my car door.

He pulled on my elbow. "When can I see you again?"

I shrugged. "I'll be around. You know where to find me."

I got into my car before he could stop me, before he could actually kiss me.

Because based on how it felt when his lips were on my neck, I knew his mouth on mine would kill me. End me.

Ruin me.

twelve

I picked at my muffin. The store was empty. Even the café seemed emptier than usual. We typically at least got a little rush at lunch time to break up the afternoon lull, but it was a little after noon and I sat alone on my lunch break.

I wasn't hungry. I couldn't stop thinking about the non-kiss outside my car the night before. I couldn't figure out why Parker hadn't tried a little harder to kiss me. His lips were on my neck. He'd only been a few inches away from my lips.

I was obsessing over it. It was stupid to feel rejected. Clearly he wanted me. Clearly he saw it going somewhere. He'd asked when he could see me again.

He still didn't have my number, I realized. And I was the one who got into my car, the one who decided to walk away before he really had the chance to give me what I wanted.

I didn't even know what that meant.

I had no idea what, exactly, I wanted from him.

I was monumentally confused.

I picked at another piece of muffin and set it on my plate next to the other crumbles I'd left behind.

A voice sounded next to my ear. "What the fuck did you do to that muffin?"

I nearly jumped out of my seat. I'd been so lost in my thoughts that I hadn't seen him walk in.

I turned with a glare in his direction. "Jesus, Parker. Do you always sneak up on people?"

He grinned before pulling out the chair across from me and sitting.

"Did I invite you to sit?" My voice was snide, and Parker certainly didn't deserve it. But I was irritable after a rough night and a morning of obsessing over the very man sitting across from me.

"Someone's crabby today. Blue bean?" A look of snarky concern crossed his features.

"What the fuck is a blue bean?"

"Like blue balls, but for girls."

My response was a glare. I had nothing. No witty response.

He laughed at my glare. "You're incredibly sexy when you give me that look." He lowered his voice and leaned in toward me, his eyes glued to mine. "I wonder what sorts of faces you make when you're getting fucked."

I gasped. He had some nerve talking to me like that. Fucking asshole.

But if I was being honest, I loved it.

"Like you'll ever find out," I finally said, picking up a chunk of my decimated muffin and shredding it some more.

Parker broke off a piece from the top, a good piece with nuts and berries, and popped it into his mouth. He earned himself another glare.

"What? It's not like you were eating it."

"What are you doing here?"

"Bothering you."

"Don't you have, like, band practice or something?"

"In a few hours." He pulled his cell phone out of his pocket and checked the screen. He powered off his phone and then set it on the table, facedown. "Can I take you out again tonight?"

"I don't know, Parker. I don't think you and me are a good idea."

"Give me three reasons why."

"You're demanding, you're irritating, and you're stubborn."

"I'm challenging, I'm handsome, and I'm persistent."

"Most of those were synonyms," I pointed out, taking a sip of my Coke.

"I'm a master at turning negatives into positives."

"Clearly." I set my Coke down, and he picked it up and took a sip. I threw up both hands at him. "What the fuck?"

"I was thirsty. So dinner?"

"I changed my mind. You're not irritating. You're infuriating."

"All I hear you saying is how handsome you think I am."

"And delusional."

"So you admit I'm handsome?"

"If I agree to go out with you, will you leave me alone?"

"Probably not."

"Your persistence leads me to believe you have an ulterior motive."

The smile fell from his lips, and he glanced away from me. "Such as?"

I shrugged.

He looked angry. "Don't act like it's nothing. Clearly you're thinking about something, and nothing will ever work between us if you don't tell me what it is."

"Why do you care?"

His eyes were warm and sincere as they stared into mine. "I like you, Jimi."

"But why?"

He looked away from me, squinting his eyes for a moment before answering. "Look, I don't chase women. I've never needed to."

"So I'm a challenge?"

He shook his head. "That's not it. It's this connection. I don't get it. I felt it the second I first saw you."

"When was that?"

He paused, his eyes glancing across the store. "You were folding shirts the night of our event here. The second I saw you, I was drawn to you. To your blue eyes. Eyes like ice. I want to warm them, to warm you. To your dark hair. Darker than night. And then that smile. Fuck, that smile lights up your whole beautiful face. The whole room. I can't help but want to make you smile just to see that light."

I felt his words. They warmed over me, pushing me away from my doubt and right toward Parker's arms.

I grabbed my Coke, chugging down what was left in the cup to ward off the emotions I was feeling. I wished I had something stronger than Coke.

"From that first night, Jimi, it was inexplicable. Still is, actually. You make me want to change. You make me want to stop doing the stupid shit I do. You make me want to explore what it means to be in a relationship. But I can't do any of that without you."

"Okay," I blurted out at the end of his spiel.

"Okay?" He looked surprised.

I nodded.

"What does 'okay' even mean?"

I shrugged. "I don't know what I want. But I believe that you're sincere."

"If you think I'm after you because you're some challenge, or because of who your dad is, or because of some other reason, you're dead wrong. I'm after you because I like you. You're sexy. You're smart. You're funny. You're interesting."

"Go on," I said, smiling.

"Oh fuck. And there's that smile." He readjusted in his seat, making a big show of it and causing my smile to widen even more.

I'd been called a lot of things in my life, but no one had ever pegged me as a person who lit up a room with my smile.

It was something I needed to hear. Parker seemed to know what I needed, and that told me that we had the potential to be great together.

I just had to figure out how to stop getting in my own way.

"What time do you get off tonight?"

"Eight again."

"I'll be here before eight."

"Are you sure about this?"

He nodded. "I'm sure. I spent six weeks on the road thinking about you. I'm not giving up now."

thirteen

"You've got two minutes." The voice came from behind me, and once again, I jumped.

I whirled around. "You really need to stop sneaking up on me."

Parker pulled me in for a quick hug, kissing my temple in the process. "But that look of fear on your face is priceless. And then I get to pull you into my arms to make you feel better."

"You get your kicks from scaring ladies?"

"Just you."

"Well stop. You keep this shit up, I'll have a heart attack before my thirtieth birthday."

"How old are you?"

"Twenty-two. You?"

"Twenty-eight."

"God, you're old."

He chuckled. "I've always been partial to the young ones."

I liked that he was older than me. Damien had been almost the same age as me, and while I had never felt unsafe with him, I felt a lot better when Parker was around. I thought back to the night when Vinnie had confronted me in the break room. Parker had swooped in to save the day, immediately earning a piece of my trust despite the fact that I still had a hard time trusting his intentions.

I finished straightening the rack of books I had been working on, and then I punched out. Parker walked me to my car.

He slammed me up against the driver's door, his body pressed against mine.

A tingle of fear ran through me, but after our conversation at the café earlier that day, I pushed that fear out of my mind. He cared about me. I believed his sincerity.

His lips found my neck again. I was dazed with need for him, crazy with lust. After our non-kiss the night before and his confessions during my lunch break earlier that day, I needed him. I needed him to kiss me. I needed him to fuck me.

"Where are we going?" he asked, his voice gruff and low against the sensitive flesh of my neck. "Because I need to get you the fuck alone. Now."

"My place," I said without thinking. It didn't matter if I was ready to bring him there. I wanted him, and he wanted me. This was going to happen, and my place meant it was on my terms. "Take the ten to Overland and follow me from the exit."

"Text me your address."

I pulled out my phone, and he grabbed it from me, programming in his number.

I sent the text, not even realizing in my lust that I was giving him my number.

After those six long weeks of resistance, I gave it up to him so easily. Too easily.

But it didn't matter. It wasn't like we were going to my house to play checkers.

It took about twenty-five minutes to get to my place from the store. I pulled onto my street into my usual spot. Parker pulled in behind me and was out of his car and beside my door before I'd even finished gathering my purse from the passenger seat.

He opened my door for me and held out a hand to help me out of the car. Gallant for a self-proclaimed asshole.

We walked in silence to the door of my building. I unlocked the front door, and then we took the stairs up to my second floor condo. I opened the door and flicked on the light, leading him in and closing the door behind him. I locked it while he looked around, surprise touching his dark features.

"I pictured a lot less white."

I shrugged, looking around. My walls were barren. I liked the clean white. I liked the fact that a person couldn't just walk into my home and define who I was based on what colors my walls were or what pictures I hung on them.

"I hate decorating."

"You just seem more… red than white. Maybe rust."

"Rust? Did you just say I seem like rust?"

"Do you know what that color means?"

"Colors mean nothing."

"That's not true. Colors are symbolic."

I tossed my keys on the counter and set my purse next to it before turning back in his direction, taking one step closer to him. "Symbolic like frozen yogurt flavors?"

He shot me a look.

"Okay, so what does black mean, then?"

He cast a glance in my direction. "It means a lot of things. Protection. Seduction. Authority. Secrets. Why do you ask?"

"Because I've only ever seen you wearing black."

He nodded once. "Rust means lust and corruption."

"You see me as lust and corruption?"

He took a step toward me. "I definitely see you as lust," he said, reaching out to run his fingertips down my cheek. I shivered at his touch, and he noticed. I backed up, bumping into the counter where I'd set my purse.

He moved in another step, trapping me.

I felt him consuming me, surrounding me the same way he'd consumed my thoughts since the first moment I'd met him. Each passing day only caused my obsession for him to grow, whether or not we were together. And having him here, in this space, in this place where I lived, where he'd be able to strip away the guard I kept around myself, was dangerous.

The last time I'd let down my guard, everything had been taken from me.

"And corruption?" I asked, my voice rushing out in a soft whisper.

"Oh, Jimi. You're definitely going to corrupt me. I think you already have. And I'm going to corrupt the shit out of you tonight."

All the breath squeezed out of my lungs at his carnal promise, and then he lowered his head as he moved in close to me.

My breath caught in my throat as the anticipation of his mouth on mine caught up with me. I'd waited for this moment, wanted it since that first night when I'd met him at Vintage.

And it was finally time.

His lips pressed against mine, firm and assured, and then his mouth opened, his tongue meeting mine confidently.

His kiss was full of arrogance, the same arrogance he walked around with every day. Normally I'd view a guy like him as a total douchebag, yet he just wasn't.

I felt the pressure of his hips coming toward me again. The edge of the counter was hard behind me, digging into my back, but I couldn't feel it with the tingling sensations exploding in my body.

His mouth didn't leave mine as one of his hands balanced on the counter beside me and the other hand came up to grab my breast. He was rough with me, his kiss demanding as his hips continued to assault my own.

Both of his hands came under my ass suddenly, lifting me onto the counter. I spread my legs as he stepped between them, his tongue still dancing erotically against mine.

I'd never kissed a man like him before.

I'd never felt so alive.

He was kissing me with this intensity, this passion, this force that proved to me that he was feeling the same things I was. His lips battered mine, yet his movements were sensual. He wasn't gentle, yet there was an obvious tenderness to his actions.

A fusion of emotions attacked me: desire, excitement, lust, apprehension, joy, fear.

My hands moved between us, cupping his cock through his jeans in my hands. He was rock hard for me, and I wanted him inside of me, moving in me, pushing me into an orgasm unlike any other I'd felt in my life.

He growled into me, a feral, sexual, masculine sound that lit my blood on fire. He reached between us and grabbed my hand, halting my progress and pulling away from me.

The kiss stopped.

Everything stopped.

My heart included.

"What's wrong?" I murmured.

His eyes studied my face for a moment. I felt flushed, my lips swollen from his kiss. I saw all sorts of emotions cross through his eyes, none of which I could name in the daze he'd sent me into with that kiss. "Jesus Christ, you're fucking gorgeous," he finally said.

He stepped away from me and walked into my family room, glancing around. I jumped from my perch on the counter, following him.

I had a sectional couch. I had a nice entertainment set-up that I hardly ever used, preferring silence to the television running constantly in the background. I had a couple of sitting chairs, one of which I tended to fall into after work most nights with a book.

He froze when he saw his hat sitting on my coffee table.

"I figured you got rid of that." His voice had a touch of disbelief to it.

"How could I get rid of the one thing I have that belongs to you?"

He muttered something under his breath, but I didn't quite catch it.

He reached under his shirt and unbuckled his belt, pulling it off slowly, meticulously.

"Come here," he demanded.

I complied.

"Hold out your hands." I did, and he pulled both of my arms, somehow swinging me around so my hands were together behind my back. He wrapped his belt around my wrists tightly, buckling the belt so my hands were bound together behind me.

"What are you doing?" I asked.

"Keeping your hands off of me."

"Why?"

"Because I have never been this hard before in my life, and if you fucking touch me, I'm not going to be able to corrupt the shit out of you like I promised."

I chuckled. "You could've just told me not to touch you."

He moved in close to me. "Don't talk back." His voice took on a hard edge, and suddenly I was a little more nervous that I'd been a few moments before.

I didn't know him. At all. And he was binding my hands behind my back in my own home.

Danger signaled in my head, but lust was much louder.

He stalked toward me, and I backed up, stumbling a bit until I felt the couch hit behind my knees. I sat, uncomfortable with my hands behind me, anxious about what was coming next, what he had planned for me.

Despite the fear stirring in my abdomen, I wanted this. I wanted him. The fear of the unknown only ignited that desire.

He knelt, nudging his way in between my knees. He shoved my shirt up so that the hem was above my chest. He eyed my breasts covered in a lacy black bra with greed. I wanted to touch him, to pull him into me, to kiss him like he'd kissed me with all of that fire back in the kitchen, but the switch had been flipped.

He eyed the ink that wrapped from my back around my torso with curiosity. He looked like he wanted to ask a question, like he wanted me to turn around so he could see the rest of it, but he let it go.

He leaned forward, his lips finding my chest as he placed open-mouthed kisses between my breasts, leaving a white hot trail of fire as the scruff on his chin scratched against my soft skin. He licked the ink that wrapped around my side before he continued his way down my body.

He moaned as he kissed my stomach, lowering himself to the top of my jeans. He unfastened the button and yanked down the zipper, and then he reached around me and pulled my jeans down with my panties, pushing them to my ankles. I was still wearing my shoes, I realized absently.

He was eye-level with my thighs, and he looked up at my face, his eyes meeting mine. He pressed my knees open wider so my pink flesh was exposed to him.

The danger he held in his eyes almost gave me my first orgasm of the night.

It had been awhile since I'd had sex, since I'd been pleasured by someone other than myself, since I'd had a man's attention focused on me.

Parker was most definitely the right choice to reintroduce me to this fantastic world.

His face charged toward my pussy without preamble. He pushed two fingers into me as he licked his way through me, sucking and biting as his fingers plunged punishingly into me.

I came apart. I lasted all of thirty seconds before I shattered under him, unable to pull him to me like I wanted to do since my hands were bound behind me.

I felt a tear fall from the corner of my eye once my legs stopped shaking, the force of the pleasure causing my eyes to water. Parker kissed his way back up my abdomen, kissing away the lone tear in a gentle display that was so at odds with what he'd just done. His eyes met mine briefly before his mouth pressed against mine once more. The tang of my own flavor bit at my taste buds as his tongue charged forcefully back into my mouth.

He pulled back. "You taste that?" he asked, his voice a whisper.

I nodded.

"So fucking sweet," he said, and then his mouth was back on mine.

He kissed me for minutes or hours, I'm not sure. I'd been with a few men before, but never any as rough or demanding as Parker.

"On your knees," he demanded, pulling his mouth from mine.

I complied, not sure what else I could do.

Not wanting to do anything else.

Not wanting to displease him.

He unzipped his black jeans and lowered them a few inches. He pulled his cock out from his boxers and stroked it a few times. If I'd pictured it a hundred different ways, none did justice to the real image in front of me.

His body was chiseled, and his cock was perfect.

My mouth watered in hot anticipation at the gorgeous sight before me.

I craved it. I craved Parker, and I wanted to please him the way he'd just done to me.

"Open your mouth," he said. I did. He ran his fingertips down my cheek again, from my temple down to my chin. It was one of his moves, I'd noticed, a way for him to show a softer side before he was about to do something rough.

And I liked rough with Parker.

He stepped toward me. My hands dangled behind me, still bound. I wasn't sure how to do this without my hands.

"You look fucking gorgeous like that," he said softly. I tried to imagine what I looked like from his point of view.

On my knees.

Hands bound behind me.

Mouth open, waiting.

Shirt pushed up to my chest, bra still on, pants around my ankles.

My long, straight, almost black hair messy, unable to brush it away from my face.

He gazed down at me for a few quiet seconds, a soft sigh releasing from his chest, and then he grabbed the back of my head with his hand as he pushed his cock into my waiting mouth. I wasn't expecting him to push in so quickly. I immediately closed my lips around him, trying to create friction between us. But he kept pushing in rather than pulling out. I opened my throat as I felt his length sliding down. I tried to move my head back, tried to get him to thrust back, but he wouldn't budge. I breathed noisily through my nose.

Fear started pounding in my brain, filtering down to my eyes, my ears, my chest. My heart palpitated. I felt my hands shaking behind me, my knees shaking beneath me.

"Relax," he growled, and I did, following yet another of his commands.

He finally pulled back, and I sucked in some air.

"Again." He pushed back into me, but this time I was prepared.

His hand found the back of my head as he slid down my throat again, a shudder quaking through him as he pulled back and I rounded my lips around him.

"Perfect. Exactly like that."

He thrust in and out of my mouth a few more times before he pulled out completely.

He walked behind me and pushed my shoulders so that I tipped forward. He gentled my fall, and I turned my head so my cheek met my carpet. He yanked hard on the hands bound behind me, and then he pulled my hips up so that my ass was perched in the air.

"Do you like being tied up? Do you like being at my mercy?"

"Yes," I whispered, shame filling me at my admission.

I fucking loved it.

I fucking loved the shudder that ran through him because of what I was doing to him with my mouth. I fucking loved the sounds he made as he growled with pleasure.

A dark, twisted part of me loved the panic he created in me, and then the utter relief when he destroyed that panic.

I felt him remove my shoes and then my pants. My shirt covered my back, and I was glad. I wasn't ready to show him my tattoos yet. It seemed somehow more intimate than the actual act of what we were doing. I heard some additional rustling, probably as he stepped out of his own clothes, and I heard the familiar tear of a foil wrapper.

He pulled on my hips, positioning me where he wanted me, and I was his ragdoll, his toy. I wanted to be whatever he wanted me to be. Somehow I already trusted him.

He thrust into me sharply, roughly, unexpectedly. I cried out from the pleasure of the pain, and a throaty, feral groan grumbled out of his chest at my scream.

"Your body was fucking made for mine," he growled, propelling violently into me. Skin slapped against skin as he pounded away at me.

I cried out over and over, moaning his name on the pleasure and screaming in the pain. I wasn't sure which feeling was most prominent.

It was agony mixed with heaven. I never wanted him to stop. He pulled on my hands, using them to force himself harder into me, pushing me to my limits. The carpet rubbed against my cheek, the friction stinging my skin.

He pushed harder and harder into me, to the point where I thought my body would break if he didn't stop, but I never wanted it to end.

The muscles in my body tightened around him, tensing before exploding into the most severe climax of my life.

He yelled out a string of curses as his body tightened over me momentarily before detonating into his own devastating release.

He collapsed over the top of me, my arms still bound behind me as I lay flat on the floor, his weight pressing my exhausted limbs into the ground.

He blew out a breath, and then he trailed kisses along the shirt still covering my back. He leaned up as he unbound my hands.

He leaned back against the foot of my couch. He pulled me into his arms, cradling me to him, kissing my forehead. "Jimi. You okay, baby?" he whispered to me softly.

The tender display almost brought tears to my eyes again.

I nodded. "Never better." My voice sounded raspy and foreign to my ears.

He ran his fingertips gently down my stinging cheek. "Fuck, I'm sorry."

"For what?" I asked, my voice lethargic.

"Rug burn. Does it hurt?"

I shrugged. It did, but pain was all relative. I'd never felt more alive than when Parker was driving into me and my face was planted against the floor.

I'd take the pain of Parker's pleasure over the pain of losing everyone I loved any day.

fourteen

I showed him to the hallway bathroom, and I headed to my own bedroom to freshen up. We met back in my family room. He was already sitting on my couch, his feet perched on my coffee table. The hat that had adorned my table for the past six weeks was now perched backward on Parker's head.

"Your statute of limitations is up," I said, nodding toward his hat. "That's my hat now."

He chuckled. "Don't think so, babe."

I walked over to him and pulled it off his head, putting it on my own. Facing forward.

"You a Sox fan?" he asked.

I shrugged. "I don't give a shit about baseball."

"At least you know which sport they play."

I sat on the couch beside him and mirrored him, stretching my legs out to reach the coffee table. "I'm smart like that."

"So you don't like baseball. What do you like?" He scooted closer to me, resting his arm on the back of the couch behind me as I leaned in a little closer to him. He was warm beside me.

I shrugged.

"You do that a lot," he said.

"Do what?"

"Shrug."

"It's my thing."

"Stop."

"Why?"

"It screams indifference, and I just don't see you as someone who doesn't care."

His assessment of me caused me to chuckle. "What do you see me as?"

"I think you are someone who cares a lot but who has gotten used to people using you or ignoring you because of your dad. Or maybe you've gotten used to being in the shadows. But that's not where you are with me."

I turned toward him. "Where, exactly, am I with you?"

"On my mind. Constantly." His answer was immediate, as if he'd anticipated the question before I'd even asked it.

I wasn't sure how he managed to do it, but Parker James constantly surprised me.

He kissed my temple. "Are you hungry?"

I nodded.

"What do you want?" he asked.

I shrugged. "I've got stuff to throw together a salad."

"Sounds perfect."

I stood up and stretched, and Parker followed me. He perched on one of the stools at my counter while I got to work in the kitchen.

I tossed some lettuce into a bowl in an attempt to put together our dinner. My movements were slow. I'd never been sore like this after sex before.

But, then, I'd never had a man slam into me with quite the flair Parker had.

He watched me, and after a while he stood and wandered quietly around my family room. I wasn't sure what he was looking for, but he was quiet for a few moments. I glanced at my wrists as I continued to shred the lettuce. Red welts lined my arms from the belt that burrowed into my skin as he pulled on it.

Long sleeves would definitely be in my future for the next few days.

I felt him move in behind me. We were both fully clothed again except for bare feet.

His heat pressed in behind me as he swept my hair off of my neck. I felt his scruff tickling the sensitive part of my neck, sending goose bumps down my arms. His tongue darted out, and then he suckled briefly on my flesh.

His voice was close to my ear, soft and raspy and musical. "Can I help you with anything?"

I shrugged as I ripped what little was left of the poor head of lettuce and tossed it into the bowl. I couldn't speak, not when he was so close to me. He weakened all of my defenses and backed me into a corner that I couldn't find my way out of—that I didn't want to find my way out of.

He spun me around to face him, gripping my wrists behind my back in his hands. His eyes stared into mine, dark and dangerous, and I realized once more that I really knew very little about this man.

He was an incredibly talented musician.

He fucked like an animal.

I wanted him.

Apart from that, he was a stranger I'd let into my home and into my body.

A flash of fear prickled through me, fear that I wasn't quick enough to erase from my eyes.

His lips curled up as he watched the fear play through my eyes.

"Are you scared, Jimi?"

"N—no," I stuttered.

"Don't lie to me." His voice was cold and sharp.

I took a breath. "I just don't know you."

"Only naughty girls let strangers into their homes for a quick fuck."

"Is that what this is?"

He shrugged.

Disappointment shot through my gut. I wanted him to defend what we had. I didn't like that he was minimizing the things I'd felt, that he was making it sound cheap when the emotions I'd been feeling were real and valuable.

"Your eyes give you away, Jimi." He let go of my hands and ran his fingertips up my arms. I shivered.

"Stop calling me that," I said, pushing his chest. He didn't budge; instead, he looked mildly annoyed that I'd tried to push him away.

"Why?" he challenged.

"Because you're just here for a quick fuck. Nicknames imply affection."

He grasped my chin in his fingertips, forcing my eyes to stay on his. "I never said I don't care about you."

"How do my eyes give me away?" I changed the subject.

He pressed a soft kiss to my lips, a kiss that was at odds with our conversation. "You looked so disappointed when I shrugged."

"I was."

"Why?"

I pulled my chin away from his grasp, desperate to look anywhere but at him.

"I'm not letting you get away with a non-answer."

"Because I like you, okay? And I'm scared of what that could mean for me, but I'm terrified of what that could mean for you."

"Why don't you let me handle myself?"

"Because there are some forces that you can't fight against."

"And you think you're strong enough to fight those forces for me?"

"No," I whispered. "And that's what terrifies me."

"Someone once told me that people only look strong because the others around them are weak."

"Are you saying I'm weak?"

"I'm saying being strong is an illusion. Sometimes it's okay to be weak. Vulnerable."

I didn't know what to say to that, because I knew he was right, but I couldn't allow myself to be vulnerable. I couldn't let him see that side of me. I had to at the very least put up the front that I could handle whatever this was, to pretend it wouldn't shred me into a million tiny pieces by the time we were done.

Because I knew that someday we'd be done. Something that came on this strong this fast didn't have the capability to make it long distance.

"Can you hand me the cucumber?" I finally asked, changing the subject.

"Talking to you is like playing verbal dodgeball."

"Yeah, well dealing with you is like playing emotional Russian roulette."

"Good one." He passed me the cucumber.

"So tell me more about your music," I said, trying anything to change the subject.

"It's my thing. Like yours is shrugging. Or is yours something else?"

"Mine's you," I answered. My words came out of my mouth unfiltered. But really, my craving was disturbing. Dangerous.

I caught him by surprise. "Me?"

"You're dangerous, Parker."

"I don't know about that," he whispered. "I'm more of a protector, Jimi."

I believed his words. I moved toward the refrigerator to grab the salad dressing. I heard him muttering softly behind me, so softly that I was sure he hadn't wanted me to hear him, but I did. "I shouldn't even be here with you, but I'm here breaking the rules because I can't stay the fuck away."

I briefly wondered what rules he was talking about, why he shouldn't be here with me, but I understood what he meant. It went without saying.

He was this playboy, this man on the road to stardom. He could have whoever he wanted. He should be in an alley behind some venue getting head from a random girl he'd never see again.

Instead he was here with me, at my home, watching me domestically make us a salad for dinner while he contemplated whatever the hell was starting between us.

It was completely wrong. We were all wrong for each other. But I had all these feelings, these emotions created by the gorgeous man standing in my kitchen, and I wasn't strong enough to push him away. I wasn't strong enough to protect him from the destruction I'd eventually cause in his life.

We were quiet as we ate salad and washed it down with scotch over ice. I didn't have any other liquor at my place. I hadn't entertained too many guests. Only one, in fact, since I'd moved in: my dad. He bought me the place and came over for a one-on-one housewarming party, giving me a bottle of aged scotch as a housewarming gift.

The scotch tasted disgusting. I liked wine. Beer. The occasional rum and Coke.

But I was getting drunk. Fast.

Our silence wasn't awkward; the exact opposite, in fact. We didn't have anything else to say after our revelations. I had about a million questions. I wanted to get to know him, to understand him, to appreciate him, to fall for him. But instead we sat in comfortable silence, sharing a meal. I'd read somewhere once that sharing a meal symbolized peace, and our moments were peaceful together despite the whirling of my mind and the dizzying sensation of the scotch.

It was hard to reconcile the peacefulness of our meal with the vicious sex we'd shared less than an hour earlier. It was difficult to look at this man sitting across from me and not want him to fuck me again with every fiber of my being.

And the more scotch I drank, the more I wanted his cock pulsing inside of me again.

I pushed my plate away, having eaten only half my salad. I wasn't hungry anymore. I couldn't focus on eating when I could only focus on Parker.

"What's wrong?" he asked, breaking the silence.

I shrugged.

"I really fucking hate it when you do that."

I giggled. Actually giggled. I couldn't remember the last time I'd sat with someone and giggled.

Come to think of it, I couldn't remember the last time I was drunk, either.

I felt weightless and happy like a child.

"What?" he asked, annoyed.

"You hate it when I shrug?"

"I hate your indifference. It's not you."

"You know that pretty much the only thing I allowed myself to feel for the last year was indifference until the day you stepped into Vintage?" The words rushed out of my mouth. I hadn't meant to say them, but the scotch was speaking for me.

Surprise lit his face.

I was starting to form a habit of surprising him. And I loved his reaction. It was the same every time. His eyebrows lifted slightly, and the dark edge in his eyes was momentarily replaced with a bright light. His lips quirked, and he tended to run his fingers through the scruff on his chin. Not always, but most of the time.

"Why?"

"Why what?" I asked, hoping he wasn't really going to ask me to explain.

"Why did you feel indifference? Why was I the one who made you feel again?"

I shrugged.

"Goddammit." He glared at me.

"Sorry," I murmured. "I forced emotions away for a long time after my ex left. I'm not sure what about you made me start to feel again."

"Probably my outrageously good looks."

A hint of a smile played at my lips. "Probably."

We were quiet again for a few comfortable moments.

"It was your voice, Parker. I put on the Flashing Light album when the line started forming in the store. It was the first time I'd heard your music, and I was drawn to you."

"To me?"

I nodded.

"Not to Fitz?"

I shook my head. "I like his sound. At first I couldn't figure out what kept replaying in my head. I was drawn to your music from the first note of the first song, but something beyond the lead's voice kept washing over me. I finally realized that it was you. I was drawn to your voice. To your words. And eventually to you."

"How do you know they're *my* words?"

"I read the booklet."

He smiled sheepishly.

"Did you write all those songs, Parker?"

He nodded. "I once heard that a song can make you forget or remember. I wanted to write the words that could make someone feel that. Forgetting. Remembering. Every other emotion. So for you to tell me that my words made you feel… Jesus, Jimi. It sounds cheesy, but you saying that means fucking everything to me."

Our eyes met over the table. I didn't know what to say to that, but our eyes said it for us.

"Anyway," he said, breaking the meaningful silence between us, "Fitz has a better voice, so he sings."

"I disagree with that assessment. But I'm no expert."

"Some would argue that you are an expert."

"Because of my dad?" I sighed dramatically. I hated the labels that came with a rock star daddy. "Hardly."

He shook his head. "Not because of your dad. Because of you. You listened as a fan. You can judge that record however you want. You can take every experience you've had in your life and bring it to the table every time you listen. So that makes you an expert." He took another bite of salad, not done eating.

I stared across the table at him, enjoying just looking at his face. Studying him, getting to know every line, every expression, every sentiment expressed in his eyes. "I love that."

"It's true of any art form. None of us are experts, and we're all allowed our own opinions. On anything."

"Well this expert likes Flashing Light's lead guitarist better than lead vocalist."

"Surprising given your father."

"Not really. Why would I go for vocals when that's my dad's role?"

"Touché. You done?" He nodded toward my salad.

"All yours."

He pulled my plate on top of his and proceeded to scarf down the rest of my salad.

"They don't feed you on tour?"

He shrugged. "Not homemade food."

"I could've made you a nicer meal than salad."

He shoveled in the last bite. "This is perfect, Jimi. As are you."

I lowered my eyes to the table. "Shut up."

"You don't know how to take a compliment."

"No arguments here." I picked up our empty plates and brought them to my kitchen sink. "I've spent my entire life assuming people only want to talk to me because of my dad." I rinsed the two plates, and I felt Parker move in behind me again. That was becoming his signature move.

His voice was low and close to my ear when he spoke. "But you assume I want something else?"

"I heard you defending me in the alley to Vinnie when you couldn't have had any idea I was listening."

I set the two plates and forks in the dishwasher, trying to move out of his orbit even though I was finding it more and more difficult to. I cleaned up the counters and put the salad fixings away. He leaned against the counter and watched me.

"I already told you about the first time I saw you. I couldn't let him talk shit when I'd already put you up on a pedestal."

"Don't be ridiculous."

He didn't answer. Instead, he stalked toward me and pressed my body back into the countertop. "I'm not being ridiculous. I'm being honest."

He leaned down and nuzzled my neck in that way he had. His scruff against my skin was outrageous. I was about to tear my clothes off for him when he pulled back suddenly. He glanced at the clock on my oven.

"Shit. I didn't realize how late it was. I have to go."

I glanced away from him so he wouldn't see the disappointment in my eyes. "Okay."

I expected something further, some sort of explanation after all we'd shared. I'd taken for granted that he'd spend the night with me. It was what I wanted, but we weren't dating. We weren't exclusive by any means. He had a life, a busy one at that, so I hid the disappointment I felt.

Disappointment.

Another emotion that I'd missed in the total absence of emotions I'd experienced over the past year.

"I'm sorry." He was sincere, but I had no response.

So, as usual, I shrugged.

"That fucking shrug."

A smile tipped my lips.

"When can I see you again?" he asked. I was about to shrug when he stopped me. "I swear to God, if you even shrug right now…"

"What?" I prodded, provoking the beast.

He stepped in front of me, his body flush against mine, and he grabbed my chin roughly. My eyes met his, and his were hot with desire.

"You'll be in big trouble. And then I'll fuck you. Hard."

"Fuck me hard before you go," I whispered, the ache for him overwhelming me.

"I can't," he said, stepping back as regret filtered through his dark eyes. Disappointment washed over me. "Are you working tomorrow?"

I nodded. "Until eight again."

He leaned forward to kiss me. It was one chaste kiss on my mouth.

"I've got practice all day tomorrow and a few other things to take care of. I'll meet you when you get off. Sound okay?"

I nodded.

"See you at seven fifty-seven."

I laughed, and he disappeared out my front door.

I locked it behind him, alone in my home with the myriad of emotions that he had caused exploding through my blood.

fifteen

A floorboard squeaked softly.

Footsteps.

Someone was in my condo.

I stilled in my bed.

The only person who had a key to my place was my dad, but he was in Seattle. Maybe. Somewhere in the upper Northwest, for sure.

I'd had copies of my keys made, but I'd never handed one out. Not to anyone. Not a single one.

I kept my breathing shallow, trying to be silent.

I heard the door to my bedroom open. I stilled in my bed. Fear pounded in my ears. I looked around me, desperate for a weapon. Anything. It was too goddamn dark. I couldn't see an inch in front of my eyes.

Fucking drapes didn't even let in the moonlight.

Terror crawled up my spine.

Someone was in my bedroom, and I didn't know what to do.

I didn't know if I should turn on the light, or if I should stay completely still.

I didn't know if I should start screaming.

I didn't know if someone was here to rob me, or to rape me, or to murder me.

All I knew was fear.

Adrenaline surged through me in a sudden moment of clarity. I reached over to my nightstand and grabbed the television remote as quietly as I could. If nothing else, I'd slam it against the intruder's head.

I'd kick him in the balls.

I'd fucking kill him to protect myself.

A brief vision of Katie flashed before my eyes in the darkness of my room.

Katie, my best friend.

She hadn't seen the danger until it was too late.

I wouldn't be so unfortunate. I was awake now, and despite my fear, I was lucid enough to fight.

And I'd fight for my life even if it meant fighting to the death.

I reached over and turned on my light, temporarily blinded.

The intruder froze by the door, shocked by the brilliant light. He was wearing a dark sweatshirt and dark pants, and before anything else registered, I flung the remote with all of my might at him. It hit him in the stomach.

"Fuck!" he yelled, doubling over in pain as I looked at my nightstand for something, anything else to use as a weapon.

I always looked at the idiots in scary movies, wondering how they could be so fucking dumb. Anything in my room could be considered a weapon. I'd already used my remote. I was seconds away from leaping from the bed and crashing my forty-two inch flat screen over his head when he yelled out again.

"Stop!"

The voice was familiar, but I couldn't place it. I was too groggy and the bright light was still temporarily blinding me.

"Damien?" I whispered.

It couldn't be.

He was gone, and he wasn't coming back.

I knew that, but a brief moment of nostalgia filtered into my veins.

I didn't want it to be Damien.

I didn't miss him anymore.

I didn't want him in my life anymore.

I couldn't miss him when he'd left me with indifference, and now that void was starting to be filled by a stranger.

"Jimi, stop! It's Parker!" My eyes finally focused in the bright light after complete darkness.

The stranger.

"P—P—Parker?" I stuttered. "Jesus! You scared the fucking shit out of me!"

"I'm sorry."

"What the fuck are you doing here? How did you get in?"

"You gave me your key earlier."

"I did?" I glanced at the clock. It was after four in the morning.

He nodded. "You don't remember?"

I shook my head. I thought I'd remembered the night in detail, but maybe I'd had more to drink than I had realized.

"I had some shit to take care of, but I told you I'd try to come back," he said. "So you gave me a key."

"I don't even know you. Why the fuck would I give you a key?"

"As I recall, I got to know you pretty well earlier this evening. If you need me to prove it, I would be happy to show you how well I know you. Now can we move past this so we can go to sleep? I'm really fucking tired." He kicked off his shoes and peeled off his socks. He unbuckled his belt, lowering his black jeans to the ground.

He stood in just his black t-shirt and his black boxer shorts. My heart started racing. And then he pulled his t-shirt over his head and threw it haphazardly on top of his jeans.

If my heart was beating wildly before, I wasn't sure what this was. I was seconds away from cardiac arrest or something.

He was tall and lean, but he hid some serious muscles beneath those clothes. Google hadn't done him justice. His abdomen was a perfect six pack of carved muscles, and his arms and chest looked strong without being bulky.

In a word, he was perfect.

He had ink on his smooth skin. From where I sat up in bed, I could make out a Tiger with some tribal designs on his bicep. A snake wound its way across his chest and onto his torso, and a series of words that I couldn't read from my position were written down his entire right side. There were other designs—flowers and words and artwork—but the ferocity of the tiger was what called out to me. His left arm was bare.

The art made him different. Beautiful. He stood apart from the rest because of the intricate designs he placed permanently on his body.

I itched to know the meaning behind every needle that had ever prodded his skin.

My mouth watered as I gazed at his perfect physique.

"You can stop staring any time," he said with a smirk.

"Don't have a body like that and take off your shirt if you don't want me to look."

He chuckled. "Sorry. Turn off the light."

I shook my head. If I turned off the light, the view would disappear. I wasn't ready for that.

He walked around and settled in on the empty side of my bed, sliding his feet under the blanket.

I watched his every move, studying him and learning him.

I was suddenly wide awake.

I had a man in my bed—a very sexy man, by the way—who wanted to just go to sleep?

It was late. He was tired. I'd had a few hours of sleep and I was somewhat lucid.

I sighed as I leaned over and turned out the light. He reached for me and pulled me toward him. My body fit perfectly against his, and even though I didn't want to go to sleep, I had to resist his temptation for the night.

sixteen

I woke up alone in bed the next morning.

Dreams are funny things. They could mean nothing. They could mean everything.

They can stay with you all day and make you feel warm and lighthearted.

They can stay with you all day and make you feel guilty and shameful.

Or they can fuck with your mind to the point where you aren't sure what the hell to believe anymore.

I glanced over at the clock. It was a little before nine. I had two hours before I needed to be at work.

The other side of my bed was virtually untouched. Smooth.

I checked my nightstand. The remote was in place where I'd left it. It wasn't on the floor where it had fallen after I'd thrown it at my intruder.

The fear from the night before had felt so real, but it had all been nothing more than a really vivid dream.

I really needed to stop taking my sleep medication.

I finally got up and fixed myself some breakfast, and then I took a shower. By the time I looked at the clock, I realized how late it was. I had to be at work in less than twenty minutes, and it was usually a solid twenty-five minute drive.

I let my hair air dry as I rushed to my car and sped the whole way to Vintage.

When I pulled onto the street where Vintage stood, I saw the flashing lights of police cars. As I slowly approached the store, I found that the lights were parked in front of my store.

I typically parked in back, but that day I was too scared to drive around to the back. I had to know what was going on. I pulled along the curb in front of the store. Police tape lined the sidewalk.

The store was closed, not that anyone would've been able to get near the entrance anyway with all of the police officers walking around. One of the front windows had been shattered. Glass was scattered along the sidewalk in front of the broken window.

I threw my car into park and rushed out as fear took hold of my chest. "What's going on?" I asked the first officer I saw.

"Move along, lady," he muttered.

"I work here," I said.

I rushed in front of the police tape. Another officer halted my progress. "Ma'am, you can't be here."

"It's okay," I heard Tim's voice beside me. "She works here."

"What the fuck is going on?"

"They're investigating. There was a fire in the store. Luckily Anna from next door happened to be driving by this morning and saw a small fire in the window. Without her quick thinking, we could've lost a lot more." We both glanced over at Anna Ureta, the beautiful soul who had saved Vintage. She stood in the entrance of her bookstore, Anna's Literary Antiques, watching the commotion.

"How bad is it?" I asked. Police were everywhere.

He shrugged just as Barry walked up to us. "Police said someone broke the window with a rock and then threw in a bottle filled with gasoline," Barry informed us. "They tossed in a match. It was a throw and go. A smash and dash. A toss and—"

"So it was deliberate?" Tim cut off his third rhyme, voicing the question in my head.

Barry nodded, and then an officer stole his attention from the scene.

"Go home, Rox," Tim said quietly. "We'll clean up the mess. You shouldn't be here."

I glared at Tim. "Why not?"

"The press will be here any minute. You don't need that shit."

He had a point. The press knew who I was, but, thankfully, they left me alone.

For the most part.

I always felt like someone was watching me, though. That feeling never went away, but it was the price I had to pay for growing up the daughter of a rock god.

An arm slipped around my waist. "What's going on?"

I was immediately comforted by Parker's presence. I didn't even question why he was there. The fact was that he'd come when I needed him, as if by some premonition. I didn't care how it happened. All I knew was that I felt better the second I felt him.

I turned into him and allowed him to hold me for a moment as the weight of what happened to my store pressed in on my chest.

Someone had tried to destroy Vintage.

The question was why someone would want to do that.

"Someone broke a window and lit up a bottle filled with gasoline."

He sucked in a sharp breath. "Jesus. Why would someone do that?"

"I have no idea."

"Are you okay?" he asked, pulling me in a little closer.

I shrugged in his arms.

"It's okay not to be, Jimi. It's okay to be scared." He was murmuring soothingly into my hair, an odd act considering the way he'd jammed his cock down my throat the night before.

"I know."

"Let's get out of here. I'll take you home."

"I don't want to leave," I finally said. "They might need my help."

"Can I at least get you away from here, then?"

I shook my head. "No. I want to stay."

"Why don't we go to that bar across the street? You can watch and be close if they need you."

"Why?"

"I just want to protect you. Media will be here any second."

I sighed. "Fine," I conceded. "Let me just go tell Tim."

"Who is Tim?"

"My manager."

He raised his eyebrows like he didn't believe me, like he thought there was something more. Frankly I didn't care. I didn't have to answer to him. He wasn't about to turn me into some weakling who needed him.

But I'd be lying if I said that he didn't comfort every worry, heal every wound, and soothe every ache when he held me in his arms.

I touched base with Tim. Parker stayed back, but his eyes watched my every move. Just to spite him, I gave Tim a hug. It was clearly a hug between friends. A hug between coworkers after our place of employment had nearly gone up in flames wasn't inappropriate.

The fact that I was using it to make Parker jealous may have been a little inappropriate, but that was a whole different issue.

Once we were seated in the bar across the street and our orders had been placed with a cute little waitress who looked at Parker with lust in her eyes, Parker started asking me questions.

"Why does Tim look at you like that?"

"Why do you care?" I countered. "You don't own me, so stop acting like you do."

He blinked and looked away from me. "Sorry," he muttered.

"What's with the jealousy?"

"I'm not jealous. I've just never been good at sharing."

"We never labeled this as exclusive," I said as the waitress set down our drinks—beer for Parker, a glass of red wine for me. "We've fucked a total of one time."

He glanced up at the waitress, and I did, too. So I may have said that last line just to piss her off. I smirked at her.

If she spit in my drink, at least the alcohol would kill the germs. I probably deserved it.

"I know, but it meant something to me." His eyes were fixed on a spot out the window.

I stared at him for a long moment, and then I turned my attention back to the store across the street without responding.

seventeen

Media came and went. Police came and went. Eventually, all that was left was Barry and Tim and a few melted records, scorched books, and broken dreams where Vintage still stood strong.

The window had been boarded up, duct tape running along the expanse where the glass used to be. It looked miserable, and I felt sad. But I knew Barry would have repairmen out that day—the next day at the latest. It was just how he operated his business.

I was three glasses of wine in. I realized as I looked at the clock on my phone we'd been sitting in the same spot for a couple of hours.

"I'm ready to leave," I announced. Parker and I hadn't said much in the hours we'd been sitting. He'd been nursing his beer while I stared in disbelief at the crime scene across the street. Ever since he'd confessed that banging me had meant something to him and I hadn't responded, he'd withdrawn from the conversation.

He was waiting for me to admit that it had meant something to me, too. It had, but I wasn't ready to confess that just to appease him.

I wasn't used to talking about my feelings. I thought back to my relationship with Damien. I thought I had loved him, but the I Love Yous had never been part of our vocabulary. Maybe it was because we hadn't really loved each other. We'd depended on each other. We'd needed each other.

But I wasn't entirely convinced that love was part of the equation for us.

I wasn't sure why I was thinking about Damien. I wanted to be in the moment with Parker, to feel the way he'd made me feel the night before.

Despite feeling scared when he'd shoved his cock down my throat, being with him was comforting.

He made me feel different. Special. Unlike anything I'd experienced before.

I wanted more of it. I just had one thing standing in my way.

It was me. I was standing in the way, and I wasn't sure how to move myself enough to get out of my own way.

Parker signaled to the waitress. "I'll take you home."

I shook my head.

Parker sighed dramatically. "No?" he asked.

"No. I want to go to the store."

"Babe, media is probably still swarming. Let's just get you home." His voice was gentle and soothing, but I wasn't about to budge. "Let Tim clean the mess."

I shook my head. "I've worked there for four years. A piece of me is in that store, and I need to make sure that we're going to be okay."

"Fine," he said, his voice flat. "I'm coming with you."

He paid our bill without question, and I found that exceedingly chivalrous. I had enough money to buy the bar we were sitting in, yet he treated me to my wine and the nearly untouched spinach and artichoke dip I just had to order.

The gentlemanly action completely contradicted his attitude. He was essentially a caveman. He only wanted to come with me to keep an eye on me while I was with Tim. Part of me didn't care, though. Extra hands could certainly help with the mess over at the store.

We walked across the street. Parker clutched my hand to his as he inspected the streets for anyone who might bother me. I knew I was safe with him.

The excitement had died down, and the media had cleared out.

"Sorry, we're closed," Barry called out from his position in one of the aisles when the chimes above the door jingled at our entrance. He must've been crouching on the floor, because I couldn't see him.

"It's just me," I yelled back.

"Roxy?" he asked, standing.

"You need some help?" I asked. Parker hung back behind me, but he hadn't let go of my hand.

"Tim got most of it. I told him to head home, so you should, too. I've got a window guy lined up for later. Alarm and cameras are lined up, too."

"Can I help pay for anything?" I asked. I needed to do something.

He shook his head. "Thanks for asking. You're a good kid."

"Are you okay, Barry?" I asked.

I saw some emotion cloud his eyes, and then he nodded. "Yeah, kid. I'll be all right. Now clear out of here. Be here on time tomorrow."

He turned back to whatever task he was doing, and I followed his orders.

Parker and I walked toward my car, and I stumbled on a crack in the sidewalk. He caught me, steadying me. "You're not okay to drive. I'll take you home." His phone made a noise, but he ignored it, his arm slipping around me as we walked toward the parking lot.

"I'm fine." It was an automatic answer, although truthfully my ability to drive was probably a little iffy. I just hated the idea of being without my car. I didn't want to have to figure out how to get back to work the next day.

"I'll take care of it," he said, as if reading my mind. "I'll get you home, and then tomorrow I'll get you back to work."

"Fine." I'd started to notice that arguing with him was pretty much futile. "Let's just go."

He helped me into his car. One of my dad's songs was blaring through the speakers. He turned it down but left the volume on low in the background. I glanced at the stereo and saw that he had the radio on. It made me feel a little better that my dad's band happened to be on the radio. He hadn't been listening to Black Shadow.

If it would have been a CD playing the music, it would have been a completely different story. I was still scared that he was only into me because of who my dad was, but he'd made me feel like that wasn't the case at all.

I glanced over at Parker's handsome profile. "I have a question for you."

He turned around to back out of his space, pausing for just a second to look at me. "What?"

"How did you know to be here today?"

He finished backing out and put the car into drive before answering my question. "What do you mean?"

"I mean how did you know to come to the store today? How did you know that there would be a fire and I'd need you?"

"I didn't. I just missed you, so I came to visit. I'd actually planned to grab a coffee at the café, but a few afternoon drinks worked better."

I felt my phone buzz with a text. I pulled my phone out of my pocket and checked the screen. It was my dad. *Are you alone right now?*

I sighed. My dad tended to worry about me, but this was out of left field even for him. *No. I'm with this guy I'm seeing. Everything okay?*

Fine. Just had a weird feeling. Always worried about you. Be safe.

It struck me as interesting that he had a weird feeling about me hours after someone had tried to burn down my store. *Always. You, too. Miss you.*

Miss you CC.

Parker's eyes narrowed in my direction. Apparently he wanted my undivided attention.

"What?" I asked.

He looked pointedly at my phone. "Everyone's eyes are always glued to their screens."

I didn't have a reply, so we drove in silence back to my place.

I thought he was going to walk me in once we got there, but he didn't. Instead, he sat in the driver's seat, staring out the windshield with the car running as he waited for me to get out.

"What's wrong?"

Parker let out a heavy sigh. He didn't take his eyes from the windshield.

"I've been wrestling with telling you this all day."

My heart leapt up into my throat in one of those weird moments that showed me how much he already meant to me.

He was quiet again.

I'd been too wrapped up in the drama that day. I'd chalked up his peace to comforting me, to not knowing what to say to me when my heart had been broken by the fire.

But clearly something was eating him, and he was about to reveal it.

"You're scaring me." My voice came out in a whisper.

He turned toward me. He took my hand in his, and I glanced up to meet his eyes while he played absently with my fingers. "Don't be scared." His eyes were warm, and it made me a little less scared.

"We're writing."

"Flashing Light?"

He nodded. "We're working on new material." He leaned forward to kiss me softly. "I'm not going to be around much the next few weeks."

I nodded. "I understand." If anyone got it, I did.

Just because I understood it didn't mean I had to like it.

I already knew I didn't like the idea of being with a musician.

But sometimes the heart makes decisions without consulting the brain.

eighteen

Nearly a month later, Parker and I were still together. He made me feel safe and protected. He made me feel cherished.

Loved?

I wasn't exactly sure what being loved entailed. All I knew was that I felt different when I was around Parker.

My relationships for my entire life had been a series of interdependence. With Parker, I could be myself. I could be an individual. I had to be. He had things to do. He had a life—a busy life that included playing lead guitar for a band gaining in popularity. He'd even admitted their manager was negotiating another tour, but he didn't want to jinx it by talking about it.

His career was taking off, and mine remained stagnant. I'd started to feel some aspirations to look beyond my retail career at Vintage when I'd first met Parker. For the first time in my life, I wondered what else I could be doing after he'd asked me why I was working there. But then someone had tried to burn the place down, and suddenly I felt connected to it like I'd never felt before.

After the fire, I'd spent a lot of time at Vintage.

Truthfully I didn't know that much more about Parker than I had gotten to know in those first few days after he'd returned from his six weeks on tour with Flashing Light. He was good at dodging questions, and I was good at pretending like I didn't have them.

So we plodded along, getting to know a little here and a little there when I wasn't working and he wasn't doing whatever it was he did with the band.

And he was almost always with the band.

Writing a new album meant Parker had essentially locked himself in the house he shared with the three other men in his band, escaping for only an hour or two at a time here and there. Long enough to sit at the café and eat dinner while I was working. Sometimes long enough for a phone call of apology that he wouldn't be able to see me on whatever given night, but not always.

I understood all too well. Having grown up around it, I was well aware that every band had a different process. I could never be the one to stand in the way of Parker's success.

It was unfortunate, but it was our relationship for the time being.

We hadn't been alone in weeks—not even long enough to have sex. We hadn't fucked since the first night at my house. Part of me wondered if he was avoiding me, but the other part of me knew I had to put faith in what we had. I was learning to trust him, even though I hardly saw him.

Four weeks later, I was nearly desperate for his touch. It was times like these that I hated emotions the most. I longed for the days when I hadn't felt anything, because it was better than the ache between my legs that my own fingers did little to alleviate.

What we had was too new to categorize as something beyond lust, so I tried to look at it as a growing period. The time we spent away from each other only enhanced what I was feeling for him. Our stolen phone calls at ridiculous hours of the night when we were both beyond exhausted were enough to keep my interest—and his—and I looked ahead to the days when we'd have more time together.

He confessed to me that he was writing some of the best material of his life, that the desperation he felt in missing me, in longing for one woman, was pushing him to new heights, to words and creations that he'd never expected.

Maybe I wouldn't have been so bothered by the time away from him if not for all of the strange things that kept happening to me.

I'd told my dad about the weirdness. He was the only one I'd told, in fact. I would have told Parker, but I hadn't spent enough time with him to fill him in, and I didn't want to ruin what little time we did share.

One day when I got home from work, I could have sworn that someone had been in my condo.

I was meticulous about where things were placed. I was fairly minimalist. I had only one picture on display, and it was of my dad and me.

That picture had been moved. I knew I hadn't moved it, yet it was just slightly out of place. Slightly turned to the left when I'd specifically placed it to face me when I was sitting in my favorite reading chair.

Part of me wondered if I was going crazy. Maybe Parker had picked it up and set it down and I just hadn't noticed.

But the other part of me was certain someone had been in my condo.

I decided to chalk it up to the same feeling that someone had been watching me my entire life.

It came with the territory of being a rock star's daughter. At least that's what I told myself.

Because the alternative was much too terrifying to even consider.

It was four weeks to the day after the first time Parker had fucked me when he walked into my store with a smile on his face thirty minutes before my shift ended.

"What's with the smile?" I asked, finding it contagious.

He walked behind the cashier counter where I was ringing up a customer and grabbed me around the waist, pulling me into his arms and kissing me roughly.

"Parker!" I protested. I was working, for God's sake.

"Sorry," he muttered to the customer. I finished ringing him up, and then I turned my attention to the man who couldn't seem to stop smiling.

"What's going on?"

He paused for dramatic effect. "We finished writing."

"You did?"

He nodded. "And I'm taking my girl out to celebrate tonight. When do you get off?"

My girl.

I hadn't been someone's *girl* for a long time.

It felt pretty damn good.

I glanced over at the clock, trying not to blush at his comment. "Half hour," I said. "How's the new material? When do I get to hear it?"

"It's fucking amazing. I really think this is going to mean huge things for Flashing Light."

I was happy for him. Ecstatic.

Really, I was.

But a little thought nagged the back of my mind.

If he got big, if his band did, would he still want anything to do with me?

I was just the daughter of Gideon Price. If I'd been born to anyone else, there wouldn't have been anything special about me. I was average without make-up, pretty with it. I was average height and scrawny. I didn't have many talents and I didn't have many ambitions.

So what was it about me that Parker was drawn to?

He sat in the café sipping coffee while I finished my shift. I went in back to clock out.

"Tim, I'm heading out," I yelled. He was sitting in the office, staring at some paperwork.

"Can you come in here for a minute?" he called back.

I walked over to the doorway of the office. "What's up?"

"Rox, I hate to do this to you. I don't even know how to tell you."

"Tell me what?" I asked, my heart suddenly beating a little faster with concern.

"I'm looking at these bills for the installation of the alarm system and the new window and the video cameras. They don't jive with the budget. I'm going to have to cut everyone's hours."

"I'd rather have you cut my pay than my hours."

Tim looked up at me. "What?"

"Cut my pay. I don't need the money, but I do need this job."

"I know you do. So do I. So does Virginia. But we're not making enough to justify the number of people on staff. I'm going to talk to Barry. We might even need to cut back the store hours."

"Fine," I snapped. "I get it."

Tim sighed. "I'm sorry, Rox."

I walked away from him because I had nothing further to say.

"Ready?" I asked Parker. He was still sitting in the café sipping his coffee.

He nodded and stood, pushing in his chair and tossing his empty cup in the garbage can. We walked together toward our cars. "Where to?" I asked.

He leaned over and kissed my cheek. "How about we go to your place and get changed and I'll take you to dinner?"

I nodded, a shiver rushing through my system at his simple, sweet kiss on my cheek. It held the promise of so much more.

We arrived at my place, and he grabbed some clothes out of his backseat before following me up.

He headed to my hallway bathroom while I went to my bedroom to get changed. I felt sudden nerves course through my veins. This was only our second real date even though we'd known each other for nearly three months.

I pulled my favorite black dress out of my closet and paired it with black heels. I ran a brush through my hair and touched up my make-up, and I was good to go in fifteen short minutes.

I found Parker standing in my living room, staring at the picture that I'd found misplaced only a week earlier.

"Where was this taken?" he asked without turning to look at me.

"London. I worked as my dad's assistant on tour in Europe a couple of years ago. I fell in love with London."

"I've never been there," he said, finally turning around. He let out a low whistle. "Damn, Jimi. You clean up nice."

I sucked in a sharp breath. I'd never seen Parker in anything but black jeans paired with a black t-shirt. He was wearing a black button-down shirt and black dress pants. The colors hadn't changed, but he looked classy and handsome in dressier clothes.

"As do you."

He took a step toward me. "How hungry are you?" he asked.

"I ate lunch about eight hours ago, so I'd say pretty hungry."

"Dammit."

I gave him a look of curiosity.

"If you weren't that hungry, I was going to offer a quick fuck before we left."

I laughed. "I sort of feel the need to be wined and dined before all that. Seeing as how it's been a month since last time."

"Don't remind me," he groaned, readjusting himself. "I'm desperate."

I took a step toward him.

"You better not come any closer," he said. "I can't guarantee I'll act like a gentleman when you look like that."

I closed the final gap between us. "Who said I'm looking for a gentleman?" My voice was raspy as I leaned in toward his ear and took his lobe between my teeth.

A low growl emitted from deep in his chest. He hauled my body against his, and his lips were on mine—back where they belonged—before I knew what hit me.

His kiss was swift but packed some heat. He pushed back from me, turning away and heaving in a breath. "Let's go," he said, his voice hoarse.

I smiled despite wanting to rip off his clothes and followed him out my front door.

We pulled into the lot of South Steakhouse. It wasn't far from Vintage. I'd been there a few times before with my dad, but I'd never had a date bring me there.

He guided me with his hand on the small of my back as I followed the hostess to our table. He pulled out the chair for me and then sat across from me, and I couldn't help but drink him in for a moment before opening my menu.

A text came through on my phone just as I was deciding between the New York strip steak and the salmon.

Normally I wouldn't have checked it on a date, but I'd forgotten to turn off my volume.

If I didn't check it, the damn thing would keep alerting me until I did. I pulled my phone out of my purse to silence it when the message on the screen caught my attention.

It was from my dad.

Scheduled to be home late tonight. Free for breakfast?

I glanced up at Parker, who was studying his menu. I shot off a quick reply to my dad. *I work at noon. I'll be at your house by ten.*

I silenced my phone and figured I'd check his reply later. He tended to worry about his little girl, so I always tried to reply right away. But I was on a date with Parker. My date deserved my full attention.

"What was that about?" he asked, not looking up from his menu.

"Sorry," I apologized guiltily. "It was my dad. No more interruptions."

He raised an eyebrow but kept studying his menu. That was the end of our conversation. His silence struck me as a douchebag move, but I let it go. Maybe I was the douchebag. I had, after all, opened a text while we were on a date.

I thought back to his words about how everyone's eyes were always glued to their screens and supposed that cell phones were sort of his pet peeve. I stored that in my mental file of things to remember about Parker.

The waiter took our orders. I sipped wine and watched as Parker tossed back his beer before calling the waiter over to order a quick second.

"So tell me about this new album," I said.

I was curious about what he'd written. I wondered if it would give me some insight into who he was, this man who'd occupied my thoughts for the better part of the past three months.

He smiled sheepishly. "I wrote a lot of it while we were on the road. Some before I met you. But I have to be honest with you." The waiter interrupted his thought by delivering his beer. Parker nodded to him before he chugged half of it down, and then he continued talking.

"Roxanna Cecilia Jimi Price, you're my lucky charm."

I paused with my wine glass halfway to my lips. "Excuse me?"

He grinned. "Ever since I met you, my material has been top notch. I don't know what it is, but the more I thought about you, the better my lyrics became. And when we set my words to our music... Jesus, Jimi. It's special. It lights up Flashing Light in a brand new way, and I have you to thank for it."

"Parker, we hardly know each other."

"Exactly. That's what it's about." He finished the other half of his beer. "It's about finding a connection with someone you don't even know. It's about doing things you should with people you shouldn't. Breaking the rules. Exploring shit you'd written off." He paused, and his eyes connected with mine. His voice lowered to a sexy rasp. "Most of all, it's about you."

My heart warmed at his sentiment, but my brain was stuck on his words. "You mentioned once before that you shouldn't be with me. Why shouldn't you be with me?"

A flash of guilt crossed his eyes, but it disappeared as quickly as it had come. "It's just, you know, this is all new. I shouldn't want the things I want with you."

"And what is that, exactly?" My heart pounded in my chest as I considered his potential responses.

A server came to drop off bread at our table, breaking the moment between us.

Parker grabbed a roll and tore off a chunk. He shoved it in his mouth and chewed it, and I wasn't sure how to get back to the conversation we'd been in the middle of.

Eventually our dinner came, and topics changed. He asked me about Vintage, and I filled him in on my earlier conversation with Tim. We chatted about nothing important, and disappointment lanced through me at the loss of what we could have said.

I didn't bring up my dad's offer. I decided to keep that to myself for now.

I wanted to know so much about this enigma sitting across from me, and instead our conversation moved back to safe topics.

I just wanted to know when I'd ever really get to know who Parker James was.

nineteen

We arrived back at my place after dinner. We stopped at a liquor store so Parker could pick up a case of beer. He bought me a bottle of wine, too, and when we walked into my place, he opened a beer and I poured myself a glass of wine. We went out to my balcony, and we sat on the outdoor sofa facing the direction of the ocean even though we couldn't see it from Beverly Hills.

We propped our feet up on the rail, and Parker pulled me toward him, his arm around me as I cuddled into his comfortable nook. We fit together like puzzle pieces.

It was one of those perfect June California nights, warm with a light breeze. We sat in silence, sipping our beverages and enjoying the quiet.

"You asked me something before, and I never answered," he finally said, his voice soft and gentle in the quiet of the night.

I froze, not sure if he was finally going to answer what I was desperate to know.

"You asked me what I want with you."

"And?" I prompted.

"And it's complicated."

My heart raced. Complicated? That could mean any number of things. "I've got time."

He sighed. I glanced up at him, and he looked far away. His eyes were squinted toward the blackness in front of us. From my quick glance, I had a feeling he was going to leave something out when he spoke.

"All I know is that I like you. I like taking you out to dinner. I like chilling on your balcony. I like sitting in the café drinking coffee while you slurp your Coke. And I really, really liked that time I fucked the shit out of you. I want to do it again."

Somehow he had the ability to make me blush in the darkness. No man had ever made me blush before.

"Then do it," I whispered.

My question didn't really get an answer, but I was happy with this solution.

Parker took my wine glass from my hand and set it next to his beer on the table beside him.

His arm that wasn't around me came across his body and his hand cupped my cheek. It was a sweet and gentle contrast to the first time we'd been together.

The only time we'd been together.

He leaned down and brushed his lips softly to mine, and a little piece of my soul broke off and latched onto his. It was a gentle kiss, tender and sensual. It was far from sweet, though. A level of heat was always present between us, but as he kissed me on my balcony, the heat intensified.

He pulled on my torso, guiding me onto his lap so I was straddling him. He laced his arms around me and pushed his very hard cock up toward me, and I grunted softly into him. He answered with a soft sigh, breaking our kiss as his neck stretched back. "Christ," he muttered, the veins in his neck corded.

I leaned forward to kiss the skin on his neck. I licked it, nipped it, and sucked it. He tasted delicious.

His arms tightened around my waist. He flexed his hips up into me again, driving me wild with need.

I'd dreamed so many nights of Parker's cock entering my body that I couldn't take the anticipation any longer. I moved back and unbuckled his belt. I lowered the zipper slowly, my eyes concentrating on my task in the dark. I reached into his boxers and grasped his cock. He hissed in appreciation, and then I pulled it out.

I glanced up at him, and his eyes met mine. His were heavy with lust, dark and glinting in the moonlight. He'd never looked so dangerous and so sexy at the same time.

I moved forward again, balancing on my knees. I held his cock in one hand and used my other hand to move my panties to the side. I moved to lower myself over him.

"Hang on," he muttered, reaching into his pocket. He tore a wrapper and rolled on a condom, and then I resumed my work, grasping him in my hands. I looked up at him. His head was leaned back, his eyes closed.

I lowered myself over him, gasping as he entered me.

He filled me completely. I sat down as low as I could, taking in every last inch of him. His hands found my shoulders, and he pushed me down, somehow managing to inch his way in even more.

I lifted my body up slowly, until he was almost all the way out of me, before slamming back down. He pressed down on my shoulders, holding us both still for a moment. The feel of his body inside of me, neither of us moving, was emotional and sensual.

We were both quiet, but I wasn't sure how long I'd be able to do this quietly. He felt so good, so perfect. While my balcony was private, that didn't mean that my neighbors wouldn't hear us.

He let go of my shoulders and we resumed movement. Our eyes were locked in the darkness.

He leaned his head back as I slowly rode his perfect cock on my balcony.

My body started tensing for release when a noise sounded below us. A door sliding, and then voices. My downstairs neighbors were on their patio, too.

He opened his eyes and picked his head up, his face inches from my own. His eyes were almost black in the darkness, in our stolen moment of exhibitionism on my balcony.

I could feel his cock pulsing inside of me. I resisted the force of his hands on my shoulders, pulling upward just slightly, wanting the friction. He pushed my shoulders back down, his eyes still locked on mine in the dark, and my body took in every inch of him again. He eased the pressure on my shoulders, and I moved upward slowly. It was the leisurely movements that drove me wildly toward the cliff.

The voices continued. I had no idea what they were saying because I could only focus on the fact that Parker's dick was inside of me and he felt so good and I needed to keep my mouth shut because I was about to scream from the pure pleasure of him.

He looked around for a second and handed me a small throw pillow I kept outside. "Bite it," he whispered.

He knew I was about to come. He could somehow tell from the way my body reacted to his.

We'd only been together one other time, but it had been enough for him to learn my body, my sighs and moans, the way I contracted around him.

It was perfect timing. I grasped the pillow between my teeth just as I shattered into an intense and very silent orgasm. He thrust up into me a few more times, moving as quietly as he could. He leaned his head back once again, his eyes closed as he pushed up hard into me in his own climax.

I tossed the pillow back on the couch and relaxed forward onto him. He wrapped his arms around me, his cock still inside of me.

We stayed there together until the voices downstairs moved back inside. I may have fallen asleep for a few brief minutes. Parker gently shook me awake, kissing my forehead and lifting me to pull out of me.

I had no idea how much time had passed until we finally moved inside, his beer and my wine long gone. I checked the clock. It was well after one in the morning.

I was exhausted. The wine made me tired, but the sex wore me out.

"I better get going," he said softly when I turned to walk down the hall to my bedroom.

I sighed, hoping he'd stay. Leaving after sex was becoming his habit, and I wondered why.

But I didn't ask.

The fact that I was wondering was my own damn fault. I had ample opportunity to ask, but I didn't. I wasn't sure we were in that place yet. We'd had sex twice now, but that didn't mean we were exclusive.

He'd written an album of songs, some of which I inspired. But that didn't mean we were exclusive.

For all I knew, he was using me for his inspiration. He fucked me when he needed to, and then he had to leave. And maybe he had to leave for some other woman.

Or maybe he just had things to do.

There had to be some reason, but I was weak. Part of me was scared to learn the truth, while the other part of me yearned for it.

So I let the weaker part win. For tonight. I was too damn tired for the conversation, anyway.

I walked him out. He pressed his lips softly to mine once more at the door, and then he was gone.

I headed straight for my bathroom, washed my face, took my sleeping pill, and went to bed.

twenty

"CC, just come with me."

My dad was very convincing. I was grateful for a few minutes of alone time with him. His blushing bride was off doing her make-up or spending his money somewhere, so it was just the two of us. We'd just finished a breakfast of homemade waffles with strawberries and scrambled eggs prepared by my dad's live-in chef. It was my favorite, and my dad knew that.

He was buttering me up.

I just wasn't exactly sure *why* he was buttering me up.

We were drinking coffee by his pool, a modern affair with a swim up bar and tons of palm trees and beautiful landscaping. One thing I loved about my dad's mansion was his backyard. It was a paradise oasis.

I sipped my coffee.

"Is Jadyn going?" I knew what newlyweds did. I knew what rock stars did. I refused to think of my dad as either of those. It really helped me maintain my sanity, especially considering the woman was only a few years older than me.

"Of course she is."

I sighed, thinking back to the conversation I'd overheard at his wedding. I was just about to open my mouth to inform my dad when he spoke again.

"I don't want to hear anything bad about her. You're just going to have to deal with the fact that she's my wife now. But I need you to come with me. I need to protect you."

To *protect* me? I didn't know I was in danger. "Why do I need protection?"

"There are things you don't know."

"That's a non-answer."

My dad flashed me the grin that told me that I wasn't getting anything else out of him. I was sort of used to his over-protection, so I didn't read too much into it.

"You'll be busy, Dad. I don't want to interrupt your tour just so you can protect me." I threw some finger quotes up in the air around the word "protect."

"Stop it, CC. You're my top priority. I'll cancel the rest of this fucking tour if it'll keep you safe. You know that."

"I get it. Don't cancel anything. I'm perfectly fine here."

"It'll just be the last leg of the U.S. tour. Four weeks. We've got three openers, including some up-and-comers. They're young like you and they're one hell of a good time."

I shrugged. "You know if I come it's not because I'm interested in having a good time with your openers."

"I need you anyway."

"For what?"

"Remember Europe?"

I remembered Europe. I loved every second of Europe.

As much as I hated the fame associated with my dad's lifestyle, he'd invited me to work as his personal assistant for the two months his band toured Europe. Traveling Europe as an eighteen-year-old fresh out of high school was an offer I couldn't refuse, even though it thrust me into the very world I expended so much energy resenting.

I'd kept track of his schedule, made sure he arrived at his appointments on time, and did pretty much everything else he asked me to do. As much as I hated the lifestyle, being behind the scenes hadn't been so bad.

"You've got people for that, Dad. You don't need me. Don't fire someone just to give me something to do."

"I wouldn't do that. Rebecca's getting married, so I need someone to keep me on schedule when she's out."

"You want me to be your assistant?"

He nodded. "If you can't do it or don't want to, I'll find someone."

"Let me figure things out with Vintage. I'll get back to you."

He sighed. He wasn't used to people telling him he had to wait for anything, and I loved the little bit of power it gave me. Not many people could reduce Gideon Price to a sigh, but I had a special talent.

"Two things. First, I want you to know that I'll pay you handsomely. Double what I paid you in Europe. And second, once you agree to come with me, I have something to tell you."

That statement caused a sigh out of *me*. My dad was as good at dishing it as I was.

"You're the worst," I whined.

"I know."

"What's it about?"

He took a sip of his coffee and glanced around the yard for a few seconds before answering. "It's complicated." He stared off into space.

"Fine, I'll go. Tell me."

He chuckled as his eyes returned to me. "You've got your mother's patience."

It wasn't often he mentioned my mother. It always struck me as odd. I didn't like being compared to her.

"Oh, and you're a paragon of patience," I said with a healthy dose of sarcasm.

"Your mother's patience and your father's wit."

I rolled my eyes.

"You're serious? You'll come with me?"

I nodded. When my dad wanted something, he always got it. It was easier just to give in, anyway. Particularly when he was dangling information in front of me.

"Fine. I'm just not sure how to tell you."

"Did you knock up the lovely Jadyn Snow?"

"Right. You do know her former profession, don't you?"

"Adult movie stars can't have kids?"

"She had her tubes tied when she was twenty. She wants nothing to do with kids."

"No little brother or sister for me, Daddy?"

He chuckled. "I've got my hands full with one kid."

"The road's not a great place to raise them, anyway," I muttered.

"You turned out fine," he shot back.

I shrugged. "So what is it, then?"

He took a deep breath and looked around, as if checking to see if anyone was listening. He expelled his breath slowly, and then he lowered his voice to a whisper. "It's about Damien."

I felt a punch to my gut at the mention of his name. It wasn't even a mention, really. It was more like my dad mouthed his name in my direction.

Emotions raced tumultuously through me.

I wondered for one brief second if I would've felt it so hard if I had never met Parker. He'd caused me to feel again after so much time in darkness, and I wasn't sure how to balance this new information with everything else I was feeling.

I sucked in a breath and waited for him to continue.

"He's safe, CC," he said, his voice still soft as his eyes locked on mine. "That's the main thing. And I need you with me so I can keep you safe, too."

I thought he'd meant he just wanted to keep me close to him, the way a father protects his daughter. I wasn't aware that my safety was an actual issue. "What do you mean?"

An icy chill gripped my heart as I recalled the strange series of events that had occurred over the past couple of weeks. Or was it months? Time bled together in my mind.

Things moved in my house. That feeling of being watched, the same feeling I'd felt my entire life. Cars following too closely. The fire at Vintage.

Oh fuck... the fire.

Had the fire somehow been related to the other things that had been happening to me?

I had brushed every damn thing off, but the second my dad mentioned Damien and the fact that he was safe, suddenly I was questioning everything. And to my father, my safety became a priority.

Was I in danger?

My dad's voice remained quiet. "There's a lot you don't know."

"Then fill me in."

"I can't."

"Why not?"

"Because if I do, I risk his safety. But worse, I risk yours." I knew who he was talking about. He didn't need to say his name again.

"What the fuck are you two into? How do you know where he is?" My voice was rising to a hysterical level.

The lovely Jadyn Snow appeared at the patio doors, looking camera-ready. She sauntered toward us.

My dad glanced over at his blushing bride and back at me. "Later," he said, effectively ending our conversation and leaving me with far too many unanswered questions. He stood and walked over to Jadyn, taking her in his arms. I stared at the water swaying gently in the pool in front of me, wondering when I'd ever get the answers I was suddenly desperate for.

twenty-one

I left my dad's without any real information but with tons of questions. I had to get to work even though I wanted to stay and hear what he had to say about Damien.

My thoughts wandered to what we'd had as I drove.

We had never been good for each other, but neither one of us had the option of opting out of what we had until one of us *had* to get out.

I still wasn't exactly sure what happened.

It seemed like my dad knew a hell of a lot more than he was letting on, but I was fairly certain he wasn't going to tell me.

All I knew was that I had been completely dependent on Damien, and when he left, I had to change the way I lived my life. I had wanted to get away from my mother the second I turned eighteen. Damien's parents had bought him a house. He had room for me, so I'd moved in with him.

I had loads of my own money courtesy of my rock star father, but he took care of me. He gave me a place to live. He cooked my meals. He cleaned our house. He bought me clothes and make-up and toothpaste and groceries and anything I needed. He was my best friend. We both dated other people and didn't look at each other in any other way than friendship until one day we did. I'd been dating a boy—a musician, naturally—who had only been using me to get to my dad, and I came home heartbroken. Damien had worked to mend my heart, and that was when we became much more than friends.

And eventually, more than friends morphed into a dangerous addiction to one another.

I was addicted to the way he took care of me.

He'd been addicted to the sex.

He never demanded payment from me for living with him. He had his own money.

I didn't get involved in his business. He owned a restaurant, or rather his parents had owned a chain of restaurants and gifted one to him on his eighteenth birthday. He wasn't planning to run it full time until he was out of college. Because of school and the restaurant, he worked odd hours. But he was always there for me when I needed him, and that was all that had mattered to me.

And then one night he had come home from work with a bloody nose. A wound above his left eye was fresh and red. His lip dripped blood down onto his shirt. He limped in, clearly sore and unable to move.

He wouldn't tell me what happened, even as I held his head in my lap while I cleaned his face and dressed his wounds.

I cried as I held him, and tears leaked from his closed eyes. I wasn't sure if he was in physical pain or emotional pain, but looking back, I knew it was both.

I never asked him what happened. I stupidly waited for him to tell me things that I needed to know. The problem was that I had faith in what we had. I had expectations that he'd talk to me.

He must've had broken ribs, maybe other broken bones, but he refused to seek medical treatment. He stayed home for a week, until he was able to move on his own again.

I'd taken my sleeping pills like I did every night, and when I woke up, there was a note on the pillow next to me. Damien and everything he held dear to him—except for me—was gone.

I read the note that he'd left for me. It gave me enough of the truth to simultaneously answer the questions I had while a thousand more formed in my head.

I'm in trouble, Roxy. You're better off without me. I won't be back, but I will think of you every single second of every single day. Stay in this house if you want. If I stay, I put you at risk. If I tell you more, I put you at risk. This is a forever kind of goodbye. Please don't hate me. I couldn't take it.

That was all it said.

Damien wasn't into drama. If whatever he was into was bad enough to leave a note like that for me, then I trusted that the note held the truth.

I had no choice except to learn how to live without him. I had to learn how to be self-sufficient, or as self-sufficient as the daughter of a rock star with a healthy bank account needed to be.

Part of it was just learning to live on my own. That was something I'd never had to do before, and it wasn't something that I could throw money at. It was something I had to learn by immersing myself in the experience.

So I moved out of Damien's house and into the condo my dad generously bought me. I got rid of nearly everything that reminded me of him, including simple things like pictures and mementos and more complicated things—like my emotions.

It hurt that he was gone, but the sinister thought that he hadn't broken my heart by leaving me was what attacked my conscience and left me feeling guilty.

Part of me was broken by the loss, but the other part of me wondered if I'd been given the gift of freedom.

I hated my mind for that traitorous thought, and it was that thought that pushed me into the numbness that had clouded over me from the time Damien had left to the time I'd first heard Flashing Light in the store.

I could easily block everything out. I'd read somewhere about how actions become habits after two weeks of consistently doing them. So I blocked my emotions for two weeks. When I felt sadness, I trained my mind to focus elsewhere.

And it worked.

It worked so well that once I'd blocked it all out, it was just gone. I had no way of getting it back, and most of the time that was fine.

It just took meeting the right person to help me dig out of the fog and recall everything that I'd been missing.

I kept Damien's note in the back of a drawer in my bathroom with a picture of the two of us. I kept his Nirvana CD because it had been his favorite. And that was all I had left of him. A note, a photo, and a compact disc.

The note and photo were stored together under a pile of make-up that had been bought with Damien's money. The CD was mixed in with my others.

I'd finally moved forward after a year. I'd finally found someone who made me feel things, who made me happy and angry and who made me laugh and who made me excited to look toward the future.

I felt things with Parker intensely—maybe *too* intensely, sometimes. I supposed that's what came from shutting off emotions for almost a year.

I loved the way Parker made me feel, though. What Damien and I had shared in the past had nothing on the intensity that came with my feelings for Parker. I was powerless to stop the speed at which I was developing feelings for him.

The guy in front of me slamming on his brakes brought me back to the present. "Fuck!" My voice was loud in the silence of my car. I was alone—truly alone in my car and in my life.

I told myself that I had Parker, that I had my dad.

But beyond that, I had nothing else.

I didn't even really know Parker. We had some connection that I couldn't explain, but it wasn't sustainable. Nothing in life was.

My car stopped mere inches from the one in front of me. A second's hesitation and I'd have been exchanging insurance information with the man in the car ahead of mine.

As we started accelerating again, I looked ahead and saw no one in front of him.

Why had he slammed on his brakes?

I brushed off the question. He was probably looking for an address. People were dumb and dangerous behind the wheel.

I pulled safely around him, and once I was parked in my usual space in back of Vintage, I checked my cell phone.

One new text from my dad. *Dinner tonight. Just you and me. You free?*

I wrote back immediately. *Yes.*

I'll pick you up from work. What time?

Eight.

He didn't reply, but that was his style. I knew he'd wait for me in the parking lot, parked as close to my car as he could. He'd take me wherever he wanted to go, and we'd talk then. He'd fill me in.

He had to, because now that the answers to questions I'd had for a year were within my grasp, I had to know the truth.

Time moved so slowly at work that it was nearly moving backward.

It was lunchtime when Parker walked into the store. He ordered a coffee and then sat in the seat he always sat in, waiting for me to take my break. He knew my schedule better than I did.

"Hey." I pulled out the chair and sat across from him.

"Hey." He looked tired. He still looked good—always good—but I noticed dark circles under his eyes. His hair was a little more disheveled than usual.

"What's up with you?" I pointed toward his hair.

He shrugged and didn't say anything.

"The shrugs must be contagious."

"Must be." He sighed and looked away from me.

Something was definitely wrong with him, but it didn't appear that he was going to let me in on his issues.

"Look, I only have ten minutes to chat right now. Are you going to tell me what's wrong? Because if you're not, I'd rather go out back for a smoke break than sit here trying to solve the puzzle."

"You don't smoke." His eyes were drifting off somewhere to my left.

"You don't know that."

"I've never seen you smoke."

"For one thing, we haven't been together that long. You don't know me." It wasn't really true. I'd started to let him in. He knew me better than Tim. Better than Virginia. But I'd been over-analyzing things between us for a few days, and it was easy to take my shit out on him when he was being a cranky ass. "And for another thing, I smoke when I'm stressed." I grabbed his coffee and took a sip. I was disappointed to find it was tea.

"I only smoke before and after performances." His eyes finally landed back on me. "Why are you stressed?"

It was my turn to look away. "Don't pretend to care."

He reached across the table and took my chin between his fingertips. "It's not pretending." His eyes locked on mine. All

I saw was sincerity. "I wouldn't be here right now if I didn't care, Jimi. What's got you stressed?"

I didn't want to tell him what my dad had told me. I wasn't ready to reveal anything about Damien to him, especially not when things were just starting between us. I needed time to sort my feelings. I needed time to find out what was going on with Damien.

And maybe I needed some time away from Parker while I sorted through all of it.

The thought made my heart and my head hurt, but maybe it would be for the best.

He let go of my chin when I didn't answer, and he sighed again. This time it was in frustration.

"We need to work on our communication," he muttered.

"If we need to work on stuff this early on, maybe what we're doing isn't right."

His eyes flashed with anger. "Is that what you think?"

I rolled my eyes. "Don't be such a drama queen. I said 'if we need to work on stuff.' You're the one who said we're not communicating."

"Can I take you out after work? I have some things I need to talk to you about."

I shook my head. "Sorry. I've got plans."

"Break them."

"Can't."

"What are your plans?" He played with the rim of his cup as my eyes followed his hands. God, his hands and the magic he could make with them.

"None of your business."

"Jesus Christ, you're frustrating."

"Thank you. I need to get back to work."

"When can I see you?"

"I've got dinner plans. Maybe after that."

"How long will you be?"

I stood up. "I have no idea, Parker. If you want to talk to me so bad, you'll be available when I'm done."

I wasn't sure why I was so goddamn crabby with him. It wasn't his fault that my dad had come and dropped a bomb on me that left me feeling like my world was about to implode.

But Parker didn't have to be a jerk, either. I was allowed to be emotional. I was allowed a crabby day.

And even as I thought it, I realized that he was just as entitled to those things. Just because he was a boy didn't mean that he couldn't have a bad day, too.

Nine out of ten of the boys I knew tended to be moodier than the girls I knew, anyway.

As he stalked angrily out of my store without so much as a goodbye or a hug or a kiss, I realized that we were both just having bad days. We were both tense, and it wasn't fair to take that out on each other.

And apparently neither of us wanted to talk about the sources of the tension that was coming between us.

It couldn't be good that we were both hiding things from one another, but in his defense, he had told me that he needed to talk to me about some things.

Maybe later that night I'd find out more than I had bargained for.

My fight with Parker threw me off for the rest of the day. I was short with Tim, who certainly deserved better, but worse, I had to give him some warning about my upcoming plans.

During the afternoon lull, just before two o'clock, I met Tim up by the registers. He was looking through the binder where he kept information he needed. I wasn't sure exactly what was in there. Schedules, maybe. Pricing. Probably semi-important shit I'd never bothered to look at.

He was looking at a page with a pencil poised in the air. Occasionally he would mark something. Occasionally he would underline.

I knew he still nursed a crush on me, but it was something that would never be returned. We were the only two in the store. Virginia was scheduled to come in at four.

I grabbed a pile of t-shirts because I needed something to focus on while we talked. I hated awkward conversations.

"I've got something to talk to you about."

"Hmm?"

"I think it might help with the staffing issue." I kept folding the shirts. Anything to keep my hands busy, anything not to have to look him in the eyes.

He stopped underlining things in pencil in his book and looked over at me. "What's going on, Rox?"

"My dad asked me to go on the last leg of his tour."

"How long?"

"Four weeks."

"Starting when?"

"About a week."

He nodded. "Whatever you want to do. That's fine. We'll work it out."

"Thanks, Tim. You treat me better than I deserve."

I felt a warm hand on my arm. I looked down and saw Tim's pasty whiteness. "You deserve the world. You're so much better than you ever give yourself credit for. I think it's one of the things I like most about you."

I glanced up and saw his eyes on mine. Tim was a wonderful person. He just wasn't the right person for me.

twenty-two

My interminable day finally ended, and as predicted, my dad was waiting for me outside of the store next to my car.

Or, rather, my dad's driver and head of security, George, was waiting there. I opened the door to the back of the black Tahoe with black windows, SHADOW loudly declaring the owner of the car via the license plate. My dad was sitting in the backseat, cell phone glued to his ear.

"I have to go." He ended the call and stuck his phone in his pocket. I was pleased he got off the phone for me, but I felt bad for whoever was on the other end of that conversation.

I got in and sat beside him. "Where to?" he asked.

I shrugged and looked out the window. I didn't care where he took me to dinner. I cared about our conversation.

I cared about the things he had to tell me.

"How was work?"

I shrugged again.

"You gonna talk tonight?"

"Seems to me like you're the one who has something to say."

He sighed and shook his head, a smirk forming on his lips. "You know that you're the only person in the world who gets away with talking to me like that, don't you?"

"Not even Jadyn Snow?"

"Not even Jadyn Price."

I pressed my lips together. "Good thing you love me."

"That I do. I know we have things to talk about, but it has to wait just a little longer."

"Why?" I asked.

He pulled his phone out of his pocket and pointed to it, like I was supposed to discern some meaning from that.

I shot him a look that clearly said I had no idea what the fuck he was talking about.

He mouthed some words at me. "Someone might be listening."

After a year of wondering, I supposed I could wait a little longer.

Parker flashed through my mind. I still felt unsettled about our fight. I tried to look at the positives. It was good for us to fight, to allow each other to see our emotions. It was bad to take our shit out on each other. And that was exactly what we'd done.

George pulled the Tahoe in front of South Steakhouse.

I thought about telling my dad that I had literally just been there for dinner the night before, that I wasn't dressed for a steakhouse, but I didn't want to wait longer for answers to questions I'd pushed to the back of my mind for longer than I should have.

I made a bargain with myself. A dangerous one.

I told myself that no matter what my dad was about to tell me, I had to filter it through my Parker lens. I liked him. I was developing these intense feelings for him that certainly transcended lust. In my quest to protect him by first staying away and later by holding him close, he'd become important to me.

"This okay?" my dad asked. We were waiting for George to get our table situated. My dad never just walked into a restaurant and asked for a table. Too many people would recognize him. Part of George's duties were to get my dad's tables. He was an invaluable asset to the Price estate.

"It's fine." It wasn't, really. I didn't want to eat at the same place again. But I did cherish time with my dad. He was the

one person on earth who understood me better than anybody
else.

We were more alike than I cared to admit, but I saw it
every time we were together.

"Leave your phone," he said quietly. I pulled it out of my
purse and followed his directions. He set his phone next to
mine.

My dad never—and I mean *never*—went anywhere without
his phone.

George ushered us in, and my dad and I settled into a
table in a quiet back corner. My dad took the seat beside me
rather than across from me.

He ordered a Newcastle, his beer of choice, and I started
with a glass of red wine.

Our waitress eyed my dad with unconcealed lust, and I
almost threw up on the table.

She stepped away to get our drinks, and my dad started
talking. His voice was low and he moved in toward me to
ensure I was the only one who could hear the conversation.

"We had to leave our phones in case either of them are
bugged. Mine was swept last night, but call it paranoia. I don't
trust anyone anymore."

My heart rate sped up as I considered the implications of
his words. "What's going on?"

"Look, Damien's fine. He's not coming back. He told me
about the letter he left you. I'm sorry he left that way. I'm
sorry he broke your heart."

"Why are you apologizing?"

"Part of it's my fault for introducing him to them."

"To who?"

"It's a long story."

The waitress dropped off our drinks, and my dad stopped
talking. "You two ready to order?" she asked. We both shook

our heads. Neither of us had cracked open our menus, and I had a feeling this was going to be a long meal. "I'll give you a few minutes to decide."

I waited until she was out of earshot to speak. "I've got time, Dad."

"I know, but I don't. Not much."

"I'm confused. Why did you take me here to tell me these things?"

"I can't talk at home. I never know who might be listening."

"Your wife included?"

"Anybody. There is only one person I trust in this world after everything I've been through."

"Who?"

"I'm looking at her."

I felt unfamiliar tears prick my eyes. I'd spent so much of my life resenting the spotlight placed on me because of my dad that I never really considered things from his perspective. It couldn't be easy being the man everyone wanted a piece of. I placed my hand over my dad's. "I love you, Dad."

"I love you, too, CC. Can I give you the short version?"

I nodded.

"Damien got caught up in some debts with Randy."

Randy.

His name at our table was like dropping a bomb on a quiet town when the residents were sleeping.

"I paid them off, but it wasn't enough. Damien needed protection, and I needed him away from you. I had to take care of you, CC. I need you to understand that."

"He left because of you?"

He sighed heavily. "In part, yes. D met Randy at my house a few years ago. He prospered at first, so his bets increased. And then he started losing. He was fine for a while, but when he kept betting big to win back the losses, he got into a hole he couldn't get out of."

"This was all gambling debts?"

"Sports. Mostly football, but D would bet on anything. He lost a bundle on fucking bowling one time."

My eyes were wide. I was shocked that I'd lived with a man who essentially lived a double life I knew nothing about.

"Why would Randy give a fuck about Damien if you paid off his debts?"

"Randy holds grudges. Against me, specifically." He paused and took a breath, as if drawing in strength to say what he was going to say next. "And he knew that he'd hurt me most by hurting you. I'm so sorry, CC. I'm sorry that I took D away from you."

His voice was earnest. I could hear the sincerity. I could hear the grief he'd held back.

"Where is Damien now?"

"I helped him start over." My dad's eyes darted around us, and his voice lowered more. "He's in Connecticut. He's doing well, CC. He's not dating anyone. He's working for a local newspaper, picking up freelance photography work."

"And I'm not safe anymore? That's why you want me to come with you?"

"Randy's a twisted motherfucker. He made some threats, and I'd just feel better having you close."

"Why is he threatening you?"

"It's complicated, but the moral of the story is that former porn stars prefer rock stars to bookies."

"Jadyn?"

He nodded, and then he grinned. He looked young when he grinned. Boyish. I could see why women loved him, even though he was my dad. He was charming, but more than that, he was talented. And he was richer than God.

"Can I be honest with you?" I took a sip of my red wine.

The waitress came back over. "Ready to order yet?"

"We'll both take the New York Strip medium with a baked potato," he said to her. "That okay?" he asked me.

I shrugged. It was fine if I wanted to eat the same damn thing from the same damn restaurant two damn nights in a row.

I wasn't hungry after our conversation, anyway.

She strutted away, and our conversation resumed.

"You were going to be honest with me," my dad reminded me.

"I've blamed myself this entire time. I thought something was wrong with me. First Katie died, then Damien left. I've been scared to get close to somebody."

"It's not you. Life happens. You can't blame yourself."

"I've met someone. Someone I really like."

"When can I meet him?"

I laughed. That was my dad. I could sit there all night and talk up Parker. He wouldn't like him until he met him for himself.

"I'm not sure."

"Why? You embarrassed of your old man?"

"Hardly. He's a musician."

"Ah." He nodded in understanding. "And you're afraid of what that might mean?"

I nodded. "I've been terrified this whole time that he only wants to be with me because of you."

It was hard to admit that to my dad, but given the honesty of our night together, he deserved the truth. He deserved to know that I didn't blame him for what happened with Damien. I would need some time to process everything my dad had confessed to me that night, but the only person I blamed was Damien. I was suddenly furious with him that our entire relationship had been a lie. That's how it felt, anyway.

"Oh, CC. I wish I would have spent more time when you were growing up telling you what a precious star you are. You have never given yourself the credit you deserve. You're a beautiful woman. You care too much. You're kind and selfless. You deserve someone who will treat you the way you deserve. And that's why I need to meet this kid. What's his name?" My dad's eyes moved to something on the other side of the restaurant. He was quietly scanning during our conversation, probably checking to see if anyone around us could possibly be listening.

"Parker."

His eyes moved smoothly back to mine, but they were unreadable. "What's the name of his band?"

"It's called Flashing Light. They just moved to LA from Chicago."

My dad was quiet for a minute, as if contemplating that information. Our food arrived, interrupting our moment. While we ate, I filled my dad in on the latest events of my life.

I'd already told him about the feeling of being followed home, of the strange items misplaced in my condo, of the fire at Vintage. We reviewed each occurrence, and he listened quietly as I spoke, as if he was taking it all in and committing it to memory while calculating the possibilities in his mind.

"Could it all be Randy?" I asked suddenly.

"You're going to be opposed to this, but I'm going to get George to put someone on you." He hadn't respond to my question, yet he answered it anyway.

"Like to watch me?"

"More like to protect you. Just until we leave."

"You're right. I'm opposed to that idea."

"Too damn bad."

I sighed. Part of me wished I hadn't told him, but the other part of me felt a little relieved that I'd have someone with me.

"When do we leave?"

"A week from tomorrow. Have you talked to the people at Vintage?"

I nodded. "I did it tonight."

Our waitress brought our bill over, and my dad paid with a wad of cash. "Ready?"

I nodded, and just like that, our meal was over.

I had the answers I'd been looking for, I supposed, but it didn't really make me feel any better. If anything, it left me feeling like the relationship I'd shared with Damien had been a complete and utter lie.

But it was in the past. It didn't matter anymore. I'd moved on, and now I was trying to move forward. Parker was my present, and I wanted to focus on that.

But I was going away for the next month. We'd already been away from each other for six weeks when he'd gone on tour. Then we were essentially apart from each other while he worked on his album for another month.

And now we'd be apart again.

If we were ever going to grow closer, to get past this "getting to know you" stage, we needed to actually find time to spend together.

When we got back in the Tahoe and started on the road back toward the store, I checked my phone. My dad checked his, too. He sighed at the same time I did when we each saw the number of messages we'd missed.

I had a few texts from Parker.

The most important one had apologized for our fight and requested that I let him know when I was available to talk. He'd told me to name the time and place, and he'd be there.

I tapped out a quick text. *My place. One hour. I'm ready to talk.*

I set my phone down and looked over at my dad. His brows were knit together as he concentrated on whatever was on his phone. My dad had always been busy, but I missed those days before cell phones took everyone's attention away from the present. Parker had a good point about eyes being glued to screens, and ever since he'd said it, I'd started to notice it more and more.

I knew if I reached out, if I spoke, if I indicated for even a second that I wanted his attention, my dad would focus on me.

But I didn't want to have to do that.

I wanted the attention without having to ask for it.

So I stared out the window, lost in thought about everything my dad had revealed to me.

It was odd how little I felt. Maybe the door to feelings had been closed where Damien was concerned.

Maybe I was okay with that.

I'd already mourned the loss of Damien.

I wanted to feel angry, and a part of me felt betrayed. But it was hard to drum up feelings of anger over the pain that was a year old. If I'd never met Parker, surely I'd feel differently. But I had met Parker, and I was fine.

It was *because* of Parker that I was fine.

It was a strange feeling to rely so much on someone I knew so little about, but there it was.

George pulled into the Vintage lot.

"You okay?" My dad set his phone down long enough to say goodbye.

I nodded. "I'll be fine. Can we meet sometime in the next couple of days to go over the schedule?"

"Of course. I'll have Rebecca email you everything you need."

"Thanks, Pops."

He grinned. He hated it when I called him that—said it made him feel like an old man—so of course I did it even more often just to be spiteful.

"George and I are going to follow you home just to make sure you're safe. Okay?"

I shrugged. "Do I have a choice?"

"Nope."

"See you at my place, then."

I got out of the Tahoe and into my Porsche. As much as I would never admit it to my dad, I really did feel safer knowing he was behind me, making sure I got home safely. It felt good to know that the car following me was my dad's instead of someone unknown.

When I pulled into my usual spot, I saw Parker's old Jimmy a few spaces over. He was sitting in the driver's seat, his face lit by his cell phone.

Oh God. This was awkward.

I wasn't ready to introduce my dad and Parker just yet, but it looked like I didn't have much of a choice.

I got out of my car. The Tahoe was double parked in the middle of the street. My dad opened his back door and stepped out to give me a hug.

"Thanks for telling me the truth," I said, clinging to him. His arms were always warm comfort. No matter what. While he sometimes did things that pissed me off, and while he'd kept the truth from me about Damien, he was my dad and I loved him.

"Love you, CC," he said. He got in the Tahoe and waited for me to approach my building, but instead I headed toward the Jimmy and knocked on Parker's window.

He jumped a little in surprise at my knock. When he saw me, he tossed his phone on the passenger seat and smiled.

He opened his door. "Hey, Jimi." He stepped out and pulled me into his arms, planting a kiss on my lips. Clearly he hadn't noticed the Tahoe. "I'm sorry about earlier." He leaned his forehead to mine, and I pulled back from him.

"You want to meet my dad?"

"Sure, babe. Whenever you're ready. We can go to dinner or something."

"How 'bout now?"

His eyebrows shot up. "Now?"

I nodded toward the Tahoe.

"Oh. Now's fine, then. I guess."

I giggled. Parker James was flustered. If there was one thing I didn't expect, it was to see him flustered over something as simple as meeting my dad.

But, then, my dad tended to be an imposing guy. He was a rock star, for God's sake. He was intimidating just because of who he was, not to mention the fact that he was my father.

Meeting parents was never easy, but if Parker stood any chance of being a permanent fixture in my life, he'd have to meet my dad at some point.

My mother, too, I supposed, but I couldn't even remember the last time I'd seen her.

We walked over to the Tahoe. My dad rolled down his window.

I wasn't prepared for this in any way.

"This is Parker," I said to my dad. "Parker, this is my dad."

My dad nodded. "Gideon Price. You can call me Mr. Price."

I laughed nervously.

"Don't fuck around with her, kid," my dad said. He had a hard edge to his voice that served as a warning, and I didn't doubt that he'd fuck shit up if he got wind that Parker mistreated me in any way.

He rolled up the window and the Tahoe pulled away.

Parker looked mildly surprised, but not shocked. I, on the other hand, was a little shocked and more than a little embarrassed. I understood that my dad wanted to protect me, but he was straight up rude to Parker.

"I'm sorry," I muttered, pulling my key out of my purse as I walked toward the front door to my complex.

Parker was quiet behind me. There wasn't really much to say. That had gone far worse than I'd expected in the twelve seconds I'd had to process the fact that Parker was going to meet my father.

We walked through the front doors of my building. "He's usually not quite that big of an asshole." I pulled open the door to the stairs, opting for the exercise. Besides, the elevator would have been torture after that encounter. Enclosed in a tiny space? It would have been beyond awkward trying to avoid eye contact.

We walked in silence.

I unlocked my door and pulled it open, locking it behind us once we were inside.

"Want a drink?" I asked.

Parker headed toward the kitchen and helped himself while I stepped out of my shoes. Apparently we were at the stage where he was comfortable enough to dig through my fridge. He pulled out a beer I'd stocked especially for him. "What would you like?"

"I've got an open bottle of wine. I'll get it."

Parker settled into my couch, kicking off his shoes and setting his feet on my coffee table. I joined him with my glass of wine a minute later.

"Talk." My voice was firm. I didn't want to deal with the awkwardness that had fallen between us earlier. I wanted to move forward, and he said he wanted to talk.

He sighed. "I don't know where to start."

"How about why you look like you haven't slept in three weeks?"

"I haven't." He chugged down half his beer.

"Why not?"

"Between writing, missing you, and working with our manager to set up a last minute tour, I feel like I haven't had a minute to breathe."

"You're here with me, Parker. Take a breath."

"But even here I'm out of my element, Jimi. I hate talking. I hate feelings. I hate being away from you. I'm not used to this shit."

"What shit?"

He chugged down the other half of his beer and stood up, heading to the kitchen for another one before answering. "Caring about someone other than myself."

"Sorry for fucking up your life." I did my best to keep the sarcasm out of my tone, but I failed miserably.

"Stop. It's not like that, and you know it. I'm not being fair to you. We've hardly seen each other, hardly even given this a chance. Tell me if I'm wrong, but I think we both want to give this a chance. Yes?"

I nodded.

"Nods are good. Better than shrugs."

I smiled. "This is new for both of us, Parker. But I have some things I need to talk to you about, too."

He looked at me curiously. "So who talks first?"

I shrugged.

"And there's the girl I know."

"Shut up."

"You first, then."

"I'm going out of town for a few weeks."

He raised an eyebrow in my direction. "I am, too."

"So let's sort this out when we both get back. Let's just have some fun tonight and stop with all the serious talk. I get it, Parker. You're stressed. You've got a shitload on your plate. You're a musician. I know what that entails, and I'm not going to sit here and hold you back from your dreams. So maybe we need to just put this on hold for a minute and resume when we both get back."

I really wasn't sure where that speech had come from. I didn't want to put things on hold with Parker, but I'd found out an overwhelming amount of information that night that I wasn't prepared to deal with. The words had spilled out of me unfiltered.

I needed some time, and going with my dad would give me that. It would allow me to push everything out of my mind for a while. It would give me time to put Damien truly in my past so that I could look ahead to my future— hopefully a future that included the man fidgeting on the couch next to me.

"You want a break? From us?"

"No, I don't." I couldn't meet his eyes. It was hard to tell the person who you wanted to spend all of your time with that maybe we were better off without each other for a while. "But it might be healthy for us, Parker. It'll give us time to figure out what this is. I don't know about you, but my feelings for you are intense. Strong. Undeniable. Scary as fuck. And then my dad filled me in on some shit tonight that I need to deal with."

"Jimi," he said softly, his fingers lacing through mine, "I don't want a break."

"I don't, either, but our lives are going to pull us away from each other for a little bit, and maybe we need to just let it happen. When you're back, when I'm back, we can reevaluate."

"I guarantee I'll be in the exact same place where I am now."

I finally glanced over at him, and our eyes locked. His eyes flashed with a hundred different emotions.

"I will be, too." I sighed. "So it's not an official break. It's a temporary pause. We'll find our way back."

He leaned over to me, his lips finding my neck. "Maybe I can find a way to convince you that it's not even a pause."

The scruff on his chin scratched my sensitive flesh. His lips trailed from my neck up my throat, up my chin, and landed on my lips.

Our mouths opened to each other, his tongue darting against mine with aggression and intensity. I felt everything inside of me tighten with desire. Tingles zipped up my spine. Butterflies soared in my belly and up into my chest. His kiss held intensity and passion.

His hand danced slowly up my torso, landing on my breast. A quiet groan emanated up from his chest when my hand advanced toward the rock solid erection confined in his jeans.

He leaned up over me and shifted us so that I was positioned beneath him. The two other times we'd had sex hadn't been quite so intimate. Kissing him while I was under him gave me a completely different feeling from kissing him any other way.

I felt cherished beneath him. I felt like he cared for me, like he wanted more with me than a good time. I knew he did, but his actions spoke volumes. And when he kissed me that way, as his body thrust toward mine even though we were both fully clothed, that was when I felt the honesty in what we were doing.

This was more than a good time. This was more than a couple of nights. This was more than feeling good.

This was real emotions, intense and powerful and undeniable.

He backed off of me and pushed off his pants. He tore his shirt over his head. I shimmied out of my own clothes from my position on the couch, and when I looked up and saw Parker James standing in front of me, fastening on a condom, I realized that it was the first time I'd seen his naked body in the flesh in front of me.

I'd dreamt about it, though. And he looked exactly as delicious as I'd imagined in my wildest fantasies that attacked my subconscious in the middle of the night.

He was gorgeous. He was perfect in every way.

And, at least for the time being, he was mine.

He made his way over to me. My eyes were glued to the snake that wound its way around his torso. It struck me that we had the same image tattooed on our bodies. The only difference was that his was on his front, and mine was on my back. The symbolism wasn't lost on me.

Snakes were symbolic for many things. In many cultures, they represented healing. Rebirth. Life.

Snakes also meant evil. Many religions saw the serpent as a representation of the devil.

I wondered which symbol Parker was going for.

I read the words that he'd permanently etched onto his skin. I didn't have much time because he pounced on top of me, but I'd read enough to make out the lyrics in the chorus of Flashing Light's "Trial and Error."

It was one of the songs that had made me feel again after a year of numbness when Damien had left me.

I'd selfishly only considered myself for so long that as Parker pushed into me, I couldn't help but think about what he'd gone through that had prompted him to write such an intense song that clearly held meaning to him.

I can't keep trying
You're killing me slowly
I can't keep dying
But I'm dying for you
You told me I'm a sucker
Just a crazy motherfucker
I'm done with this life
You're handing me the knife
We tried, we tried, we tried
But all we got was an error

The song played in my head as Parker pumped in and out of me.

I wanted to think about how little I actually knew about this man who I was falling for. I wanted to think about how dangerous he was. I wanted to consider how dangerous I was for him, too.

But his hands were everywhere. His mouth dragged down my neck as we made love on my couch.

My mind was lost, focused on the pleasure and the feelings he was driving into me.

All of that combined with his powerful thrusts pushed me into an oblivion that was more intense than anything I'd ever experienced before.

twenty-three

"Can I see?" he asked softly, kissing the ink that wrapped around from my back to my torso. His head had come to a rest just below my breasts as we both regained composure for a few moments full of panting.

In my ridiculous lust for him, I hadn't thought to cover up. I'd ripped my shirt over my head and tossed it on the floor. I'd pulled off my bra while he'd procured a condom from some pocket in his pants.

I wasn't really ready to explain everything that my tattoos symbolized, but I was ready to let him see that part of me. It was a part of me that so few people ever got to see, but I wanted to let him in. I wanted him to know the real me.

I nodded.

Parker stood. "Be right back," he said, heading toward the bathroom.

He returned, and I hadn't moved.

He eyed me as he pulled on his jeans.

"Tell me about yours, first." I tried to keep the pleading out of my voice, but if I was going to let him in on the most intimate part of who I was, I wanted to know something equally intimate about him first.

He pointed to the tiger on his bicep. "This tiger was my first. I took Mandarin in high school, and we learned about the Chinese symbolism of tigers. I loved the idea of etching power and protection onto my skin."

"So you have someone protecting you all the time?"

He shrugged. "You could say that. Now you go."

I stood up and turned around.

I hated people who got tattoos just to show them off. Mine were intensely private.

The butterflies on my upper arm were for Katie. She'd loved butterflies. She'd been obsessed with them, actually. She had promised me that someday she would get a butterfly tattoo, and she'd even drawn one that represented her and one that represented me.

Her life had been cut short before she'd had the chance to get her tattoo.

At her funeral, every person who attended released a butterfly into the air. Putting her butterfly on my skin was my tribute, my way to keep my best friend with me forever. And I added the second butterfly—the one she'd drawn to represent me—to symbolize our friendship. It only seemed appropriate to etch both of the butterflies she had designed on my skin.

Some people put family permanently on their bodies. Others burned skulls into their skin. On my back, I put myself on my skin. My initials: RCP. I'd learned a long time ago I was the only one I could really count on in life, but the letters symbolized many things to me. Resiliency, Courage, Perseverance. They were reminders of what I needed most.

Eventually I added an arabesque design that morphed into a snake surrounded by roses. The design twined around my initials.

Parker was silent behind me. I wished I could see his eyes, see his reaction.

"Your initials?"

I nodded. "It's not narcissistic, I swear. It means many different things to me."

"You don't have to defend it, Jimi. It's gorgeous. You're gorgeous."

I let out a breath. I hadn't realized how nervous I had been for his reaction.

I felt his lips on my neck, his breath near my ear.

"What does your snake mean?" He backed up and traced the snake with his fingertips, sending a shiver though my body.

"Healing. Rebirth."

"When did you get it?"

"About eight months ago. What does your snake mean?"

"Another symbol of protection for the Chinese, but also the idea of mended fragments."

I was quiet, processing his words. Questions formed in my mind, but I didn't want to ruin the moment by asking them. But mended fragments was the same idea as healing.

Again I realized how little I knew about him. What had he gone through?

In time, I'd learn more, just as he would about me.

But just as I wasn't ready to talk to him about my past, he had a past he was entitled to keep to himself.

He ran his fingertip across my back again.

"I could stare at this forever, Jimi. I want to lick every inch of your back."

As nice as that sounded, I was suddenly exhausted.

He smacked my ass, a sharp crack in the quiet room. I jumped, but otherwise I didn't react. I liked when he was rough with me, but the gentler side of him that had emerged that night was nice, too.

"Maybe tomorrow," I said, turning around and wrapping my arms around his neck. His jeans were rough against my naked front side.

"Not likely. We have studio time booked tomorrow."

"Already?"

He nodded.

"That's fast."

"We have a pretty solid investor in our corner that's helping push things through."

I yawned. "That helps." I moved to pick up my clothes, but he batted my hand away.

"Are you ready to sleep?" His sudden change of the subject was strange, but I was too tired to care.

I nodded. "You staying?"

"If you've got room."

I smiled. "Plenty of room."

I double checked the lock on my front door, but knowing he was staying was actually a huge relief. My dad had said he'd send someone to keep an eye on me, but I liked the protection of Parker. Maybe his tiger and his snake could protect both of us.

twenty-four

I awoke tangled in Parker James. As my eyes fluttered open to the new day, I couldn't help the smile the formed on my lips.

He was still asleep. He slept in nothing. I slept in only a shirt.

My first thought was that I'd forgotten to take my sleeping medication the night before. I'd slept through the night. That never happened. Ever.

It was one of those great sleeps where I awoke feeling refreshed instead of groggy. I didn't remember any dreams, and I preferred waking up that way. It didn't leave me with a feeling of shame or fear or horror. Instead, I just felt happy that Parker was sleeping next to me.

I studied the snake that wound across his torso, protecting him. I studied the words in his song. It was the words "I'm dying for you" that stood out most to me.

There was significance there. I felt the sudden urge to know what that significance was. We were moving slowly, spending small bits of time together when our schedules allowed, and the pace was starting to become maddening.

I wanted to move forward with him. I just wasn't sure how to do that without knowing more about him.

Fuck, I wasn't even sure what "moving forward" entailed, exactly.

We were in a stagnant state where we were unable to move in any direction, particularly since we were both going out of town for a while. When we were both back home, maybe we'd finally find the time.

Parker's eyes opened slowly, dark and heavy in the morning light. Sleepy Parker was perfection. His hair was a mess, sticking up everywhere. I ran my fingers through it, a gesture that came out far more intimate than I'd intended.

Parker smiled at me, a slow smile that morphed into a grin.

"Take your shirt off and get on." Those were his first words of the day, spoken in a rasp that had the effect of immediately turning me on.

I followed his directions, pulling my shirt off and tossing it beside us. I climbed over him, and he positioned the head of his cock toward my entrance. He swiped it along my clit, sending a tingle of need through my torso.

"Fuck. Do you have a condom?" he asked.

I nodded and reached over him toward the drawer in my nightstand. He moaned as my breasts brushed against his chest.

I had no idea how old those condoms were, but it was habit to keep condoms in my nightstand. A girl just never knew when she'd need one.

I handed one over to him, and he fastened it on quickly as I took my position back over him. He poised his cock in the air, and I lowered myself down over him.

"Fuck yes," he moaned, that morning rasp turning into a growl as I lifted myself up and pushed back down. His hips met my thrusts.

I lowered down as far as I could, taking in every last centimeter that he was offering me.

This was definitely my preferred way to start the day.

He grabbed my hips and thrust. He somehow took control from the bottom, setting our pace as he lifted me up and down over him, creating the friction that drove us both toward climax.

It was another moment of perfection between us as I collapsed over the top of him.

He ran his fingertips softly through my hair, a sweet gesture that contrasted with his rougher side, and I felt myself fall just a little more for him.

When we'd first started whatever this was together, I was certain that one of us or both of us would get hurt in the end.

But the more time I spent with him, the less I saw an actual end for us.

We lay together for a long time. I may have fallen back asleep, or he may have, and then my alarm was beeping and waking us up to let us know that I had to get in the shower to get ready for work.

"When will I see you again?" I asked as he pulled on his shoes.

"Studio today and tomorrow. And then I leave."

"So this is goodbye?"

"I think so," he said sadly. "For now. Not for good."

As he turned toward the door, I felt the urge to tell him I was inexplicably falling in love with him.

But I didn't have the nerve to admit it to the one person who probably needed to hear it.

He looked a little lost as he gazed at me. Something was up with him, but I already knew him well enough to predict that he wouldn't divulge whatever it was. He wasn't used to feeling so strongly for one person, and I wasn't going to push him. I trusted that he'd wait for me, and that was enough.

"I promise to text or call you every day. You promise, too." His voice was nearly desperate.

I wanted to ask him where he was going. I wanted to tell him where I was going.

But I didn't. He'd tell me when he was ready.

"I promise."

He grabbed me around my waist and hauled me against him. His lips rested on mine for a moment. "I hate that I have to be away from you." He leaned his forehead against mine.

"Do it for your career. I'll be here when you get back."

He nodded, smiled, kissed me one last time, and headed out the door.

I sighed as I shut the door behind him.

I had no way of knowing when I'd see him again. I had no way of knowing what would change between us, if anything, or whether I'd still feel the same way about him—or if he would still feel the same way about me.

I wanted to believe that nothing would change, that we'd pick up right where we left off.

But something told me it wasn't going to work out that way.

Life almost never worked out the way I expected it to. Why would this be any different?

twenty-five

My dad's tour resumed with a concert in Philadelphia on Wednesday night, and we were set to leave the morning before. The first stop after a tour resumed always required a bit of rechecking and reworking, and the band was going to switch up the playlist for the last leg of their tour.

My schedule at Vintage only took me through Saturday, and Tim left me off the schedule when the week ended. Parker hadn't lied; he'd texted or called me every day, but we'd only chatted for a few minutes at a time. Either I was at work or he had to get back to work, so time was tight. When he wasn't in the studio, he and the rest of the members of Flashing Light were busy revising, reworking, and practicing.

He would send me random texts throughout the days to let me know he was thinking about me.

He never left my mind for a second.

As much as I was excited to spend the next few weeks with my dad, I couldn't help but feel the loss of time spent away from Parker. He gave me things I had been missing for a long time, but more than that, he gave me things I hadn't even known I needed.

Safety, for one.

I wasn't sure what was going on between my dad and Randy. When my mind called on the memory of the night Randy had hit on me, a twisted fear wrenched through me.

Having Parker close helped me with that fear.

I supposed Bruno—the ex-cop George recommended to follow me until I left for the tour—also made me feel protected, but I hated having someone watching me everywhere I went.

Parker was different, though. He managed to make me feel safe without hovering the way Bruno did.

I figured I'd be fine while I was on the road with my dad, but I had no idea what I'd be coming home to.

All of those thoughts ran through my head as I packed on Monday night.

My thoughts had been filled with everything I needed to do to get ready for this last leg of the tour. Rebecca, my dad's assistant, had been hugely helpful. I wished her well in her upcoming wedding, she filled me in on the basics, and I memorized the schedule and searched for restaurants and attractions in each city that might interest my dad.

It was easier for Rebecca, who knew all of that shit in her head. That wasn't something she could just relay to me.

So I called her often, texted her even more often, checked in with my dad, and checked the itinerary Rebecca had made for the next four weeks. I ran everything by Rebecca once more and finalized every last detail, comparing the bus schedule to the tour schedule. I confirmed hotel and restaurant reservations, just two of the luxuries my dad depended on when he was on tour.

I'd be riding on the crew bus. Each band member had his own bus—my dad often said that was what kept them together for so many years—and my dad and his new bride would be riding alone.

Rebecca typically rode with the crew. The crew had been with the band for years and years. They were like a family to me, a group of people I'd grown up around, including Keith, the band's manager, and his wife, Vanessa, who had become a friend over the years. She was kind and took care of the crew, ensuring everyone had everything they needed.

Stepping in last minute as my dad's assistant had given me a lot to think about, which allowed me to stop obsessing over

Parker for a few minutes. It gave me something interesting to focus on, a project that I had limited time to complete. I threw myself into it, but he never left my mind for very long.

I was still curious about where he was going, what he was doing. If he'd be thinking about me.

If he'd find some other girl while we were apart.

We'd never labeled whatever was starting between us as exclusive. I'd never put so much trust into someone before, but then again, I'd never experienced a true adult relationship.

With Parker, though, there was a balance. We were both adults living our lives, adults who had met by chance and who had more in common than I thought possible after the first time we'd met in the break room of Vintage.

After I'd finished packing and was about to take my sleeping pills to head off to bed, my phone buzzed with a text. It was Parker.

What are you doing?

Getting ready for sleep. You?

Thinking about you.

What about me? I settled into bed with my phone.

About how blue your eyes are. About your hair and how it flies around you when I'm fucking you. About sex.

I thought about that one. He was a guy. Guys thought about sex. So I needed some clarification on that point. *Sex with me?*

My phone rang a few minutes after I sent the text.

"Hi." My voice was soft.

"Only you, Jimi. Just you."

"I miss you." My voice was raw with emotions. This wasn't me.

I'd grown a lot in the past year. I'd learned to rely on myself, because in the end, I was the only one who would always be there for me. And now I was finding myself dependent on Parker. He made me smile. He made me *feel*.

Hanging my hopes on a relationship with a musician was stupid. It was suicidal. It was the worst possible idea for me after everything I'd been through.

But the heart has a goddamn mind of its own.

If I could choose who I fell for, I never would've chosen Parker. For one, he was too much like me, but worse, he was a musician who would always put his career first. And I'd never expect anything less than that. He had to put his career first. Musicians didn't have any other choice if they wanted to taste true success, to reach a level like Black Shadow.

But I did have a choice. I could choose to let his career ruin us before we even gave us a chance, or I could choose to accept what he did for a living.

In the interest of my heart, I chose the latter. As it turned out, I didn't really have a choice at all.

"I miss you, too. God, I miss you so fucking much. It's like I left a piece of myself at your place when I left the other morning."

"I'll keep it safe, Parker."

He sighed. "It's been almost a week."

"I know. You know what I miss most?"

"What?"

"Your arms. I've never felt warmer or safer than when I'm in your arms."

"I've never felt more complete than when I hold you in my arms."

"Where are you right now?"

"At a gas station."

"With the band?"

"Yeah. We're somewhere between Albuquerque and Texas, I think. I waited to call you until we stopped. I just needed a minute away from them, you know?"

"I get it." I laughed. It was such a boy thing, not wanting to talk in front of the guys. Not wanting to show emotion.

"We're stopping at a hotel tomorrow night. I'll call you then and we can talk longer."

"I'll be on the road by then, but I'm not embarrassed to talk in front of other people." My voice held amusement.

"I'm not embarrassed, Jimi. Far from it, actually."

"Do they know about us?"

"Yes." His answer was immediate. That made me trust that he was being truthful. "They wanted to know what was inspiring my lyrics. Plus I never stop talking about you."

"I want to see you onstage."

"We've got some local gigs set up when we get back."

"I'll come to every one of them. I'll stand up front and wear a low cut shirt so you can see down it from up there."

"You'll distract me. I'll forget the words."

I giggled, and then I heard some voices in the background.

"I have to go." His voice was apologetic.

"Be safe, Parker. I'll talk to you tomorrow."

"Bye, Jimi," he whispered.

We hung up, and I drifted off to sleep with Parker on my mind.

twenty-six

"What are you doing here?" I whispered in the dark.

"I had to see you."

"I thought you were somewhere between Albuquerque and Texas. Which is a city and a state, by the way."

He chuckled. "I was. I came back for you." Parker's lips dragged across my skin, leaving tingles in their wake. It was dark, but I could smell him in my room. He smelled like sunshine, a bright contrast to the pitch blackness of my bedroom.

"How did you get in here?"

"That key you gave me." His voice was lost in the skin of my abdomen.

Giving him a key to my condo was the same thing as giving him a key to my heart. A key to my condo—my most private place, the place I called home—held the same meaning as letting him into the private confines of my soul. I didn't remember giving him a key.

"Flip over," he said. "Grab the headboard with your hands." I followed his directions. He pushed my shirt up, exposing my back.

It was too dark for him to see my tattoos, but it didn't stop him. "I told you I wanted to lick every inch of your back." Kisses trailed down my back. I felt a dart of a tongue followed by a hot breath of air. More tongue and the scratch of his scruff along my skin.

He ripped my shorts with my panties down my legs. I kicked them off. I was useless lying on my stomach. My arms were stretched above me, and he took full control of my body.

His mouth moved across the planes of my back. His fingertips trailed down the curves of my back, over my ass, and down into my pussy. He pushed a finger in and held it there for a few seconds before backing it out. He continued to kiss every part of my back while he fingered me, my body grinding down to meet the thrust of his fingers. The angle was perfect, offering me a dizzying pleasure as I gripped the headboard in my hands and pushed down onto his strong fingers. I unraveled beneath him, my body bursting into an intense orgasm that drove all coherent thought from my mind.

I released the headboard from my grip, flexing my fingers to get the blood flowing back into them. I flipped over, ready to return the favor, but as my eyes focused in on the room around me, I realized it was empty.

And it was light.

Another dream, this one even more vivid than the last.

Every part of me wished that Parker was beside me in my bed instead of on a bus somewhere in the middle of the United States.

My body ached. I flexed my fingers and realized that they ached, too. I must have been gripping something just as I'd been gripping the headboard in my dream.

I ran my fingertips under my shirt, brushing against one of my nipples. It hardened. I gasped with the pleasure of my own touch.

I had to alleviate the ache between my legs. As much as I wanted Parker in my bed with me, this was going to be a long four weeks without him.

Hell, it was going to be a long four weeks surrounded by *people*. I didn't know when I'd get enough time alone to do this again.

So I settled back into my bed, dipped my fingertips into my panties, and took care of the writhing ache that being apart from Parker left in me.

My fucking alarm clock interrupted me just as I was about to hit my release. I hit it harder than I should've and finished taking care of myself. A glance at the clock when I finished let me know that I didn't have much time to kill—just enough to shower and head over to my dad's house, where my car would be parked for the next month.

I hauled my suitcase down to my car, spotting Bruno sitting across the street. I was told to ignore him, to continue with my life like he wasn't watching, but I gave a small wave in his direction. It was hard to see his expression through his blacked out windows.

I threw my suitcase and a few other odds and ends in the backseat of my car, and then I started it up and headed toward Santa Monica Boulevard, my normal route toward Hollywood Hills where my dad lived. Traffic was light, but as soon as I turned onto the main road, a car got right on my ass.

I slowed down, hoping the asshole would go around me, but he didn't. He stayed on my ass. I wasn't as scared as I'd been the last time I was followed. This time, at least I knew that Bruno was somewhere behind me.

But being followed like that still filled me with anxiety, especially after my dad had filled me in on some of the puzzle pieces of Damien's past with Randy.

My cell phone rang, its jarring jingle startling me.

I grabbed it off the seat next to me, checking the screen. It was an unknown number. I slid the screen over to answer it, tossing it back on the seat and talking through my Bluetooth. "Hello?"

"Ms. Price, it's Bruno. Keep going straight and don't hang up. Change lanes for me, please."

I didn't know jack shit about Bruno, but my dad had hired him, so I had to trust him. I did as I was told, signaling my intention ahead of time. The car behind me didn't signal, but it did follow me into the other lane.

"Motherfucker," I heard Bruno mumble.

"Is everything okay?" I asked, my voice small.

"Yes, ma'am. Just keep driving."

"Where do I go?"

"Ms. Price, head back into the right lane. Just follow my directions, and don't worry. I'm right behind him."

I took in a calming, cleansing breath, glad that my dad had stuck Bruno on me despite my weak protesting.

"Just keep heading toward your father's house for now. I'm running his plates."

It was an easy drive. There was hardly any traffic on a midweek late morning, and it would have been peaceful to drive in the serenity of the outskirts of Los Angeles at this time of day if I hadn't had someone following me.

"Ma'am, take a left on Fairfax."

I followed his directions. It was the street I normally took toward my dad's, anyway.

"I'm going to take care of him. You keep going toward Mr. Price's house. Drive cautiously. Watch behind you. Call your dad immediately if you think someone else is following you."

He cut off the call, and I kept driving toward my dad's. I took a right on Hollywood Boulevard, and I looked behind me. There was no one back there anymore.

I wasn't sure what Bruno meant by taking care of him, but he'd been good on his word.

I took another cleansing breath, but this one was a hell of a lot shakier than the first one I'd taken on that ride. Parker flashed through my mind, and it felt like the only thing that would make me feel better were his arms wrapped tightly around my torso.

I missed him.

I missed him more than I thought I would.

He'd become a fairly permanent fixture in my thoughts despite the limited time we had together. Knowing that we'd be apart from each other for the next month was daunting.

But I had plenty ahead of me to focus on. Time on the road would certainly become long. Missing Parker would get even harder, but hopefully getting away from California would help me escape the anxiety-filled drives and strange occurrences that I'd chalked up to Randy.

I hoped that a month was long enough for Randy to deal with the fact that my dad had married Jadyn. I hoped maybe he'd just build a bridge and get over it.

Hopes were funny things, though.

Much like dreams, it was easy to build up hopes in my mind. But most of the time, reality tended to turn out a different way.

twenty-seven

I pulled into my dad's expansive driveway. He was waiting there, motioning for me to pull into an empty space in his six-car garage.

Once I cut the engine, he clicked a button and shut the door.

My dad pulled me in for a hug when I got out of the car. "You okay, CC?"

"I'm alright."

"You're shaking."

"It was scary."

"Having Bruno watch you doesn't seem like overkill now, does it?"

I shook my head, fighting back the tears that I felt burning behind my eyes. I couldn't start my month long stint as my dad's personal assistant by crying.

I pulled back, because if I let my dad hug me any longer, the dam would burst. Between missing Parker, fear for my safety, and relegating my history with Damien to the past, I was on emotional overload.

"It's fine. I'm fine. I'm ready for this tour. I'm ready to be the best PA you ever had."

"Rebecca's got some pretty big shoes to fill."

"I've got this," I said, forcing a smile that I didn't really feel.

Jadyn Snow and her four suitcases waited by the door.

"Hi Mommy," I said. She rolled her heavily made-up eyes.

"You okay, Roxanna?" she asked with barely concealed false concern. I hoped my dad caught on, but he was busy talking to George.

"I'll be fine. Rough start, but it should all be behind us now. Did you pack enough?" I motioned toward her suitcases.

"A girl's got to have some choices."

"Or an entire wardrobe," I muttered. Traveling with Jadyn Snow was *not* going to be the highlight of the next four weeks.

George hauled our bags into the Tahoe. Another of George's security contacts drove us to the airport so he could take the Tahoe back to my dad's place since George was going with us. The five of us headed toward the airport.

"Any news on who was following me?" I asked my dad. He made some non-committal grunt, and that was the end of it. He may have known something, or maybe he hadn't, but either way, I wasn't getting anything else out of him.

Sometimes I hated that I gave in so easily, but I'd learned long ago that putting up a fight just wasn't worth it.

I pulled out my phone to text Parker. I didn't want to worry him, but I did want to hear from him. I just needed that one brief moment of connection, even if it came in the form of a text. I needed to know that he was thinking about me.

On my way to the airport and missing you.

I was all the way through security and sitting in the first class lounge before a reply came. I was sitting by myself in a chair in the corner. I had my earbuds in. Flashing Light was the only album I'd downloaded to my playlist. It was all I wanted to hear.

My dad never sat at the gates; he preferred the stuck-up first class lounges where he was able to obtain a few moments of peace before his flights. When he sat at the gate, too many people recognized him.

I hated first class lounges. Maybe I was the more pretentious of the two of us for feeling that way, but I didn't like sitting with the rich and famous, eating free apples and drinking free glasses of wine when the people in there had bundles of money to pay for that shit.

I smiled as I read his text. *I miss you, too. On the bus. Just woke up.*

It's after noon. #Lazy

Not much else to do on a bus but sleep or watch TV. #Bored

I supposed that was true enough. My phone buzzed with another text, but I was listening to the voice that came over the loudspeaker informing us that our flight was on time. Boarding would begin in a few minutes. First class would board first, which meant of course that we would get on the plane first. But my dad always waited until the very last minute possible to make his appearance. I guess it gave him some privacy. I headed to the restroom quickly—I hated the tiny ones on planes—and when I returned to where my dad, Jadyn, and George sat, I finally checked the last text Parker had sent me.

And text my girlfriend, of course.

Girlfriend? He'd called me his *girlfriend?* And that was the text I'd waited to check?

A little tingle stuttered in my chest.

I wasn't sure how to respond to that.

Another text came through while I debated how to reply.

Okay, just ignore that last text. No reply for a full ten minutes can't be good.

I grinned at my phone. He clearly felt as out of place in this relationship as I did. Maybe that's what made us so good together.

Not ignoring. I wouldn't do that to my boyfriend.

My phone rang a second later.

"Aren't you on the bus?" I answered.

"I don't give a fuck. I needed to hear your voice." Parker was quiet, and I hadn't realized how much I had needed to hear his voice, too. I stood and wandered over to the window, and then I told him that.

"You okay?"

"I'm okay." I watched a plane gain speed and then take off. Planes always sort of amazed me. How did they stay in the air with all of those people, the luggage, the drink carts? Fascinating.

"You sound like you're not okay."

"Just some stuff this morning."

"Tell me."

"Someone was following me on my way to my dad's." It slipped out in the interest of honesty. Parker was easier to talk to when his intense eyes weren't staring holes through me.

"Following you?"

"Like right on my ass. My dad had a security guy watching me, and he took care of it."

"What does that mean?"

I watched the next plane in line get ready to pick up speed. I sighed. "I don't know."

"The verbal equivalent of a shrug." He said it lightly, and I chuckled.

"My dad wouldn't tell me. I don't even know if he knows. But I made it safely, and I'm about to board my plane."

My dad snuck up behind me and tapped my shoulder. "You ready?" he mouthed when he saw that I was on the phone.

I nodded.

"I have to go. My flight's leaving soon."

"I miss you."

"Miss you, too."

We hung up, and I felt warm all over. He'd called me his girlfriend. He was off doing his musical thing, but girlfriend spelled commitment. It meant that he saw me the same way I saw him. He saw more than a few fun nights together. He saw a future.

I floated toward the plane, glad that at least something was going right in my life.

Our flight was about five and a half hours long. My dad and Jadyn sat behind me. I sat alone, the first class seat next to mine empty. It was nice because it gave me some time to just sit and think by myself.

I pulled out my journal, and I scribbled a few lines about Parker.

Happiness. Love without the words. His eyes, his hair. His tattoos. God, those tattoos. Protection. The way he cares, the way he fucks. Together we are strong. Powerful. Intense. Unbreakable. Forever?

I didn't use his name. Writing in my journal had become both necessary and therapeutic. I stared down at my words, feeling everything that I'd written on that page.

How was I to know that all I was doing by writing those words was completely jinxing myself?

But worse, how could I have known that one of the words I'd written would turn out to be a complete and utter lie?

twenty-eight

The plane touched down. I was officially in Philadelphia, the land of cheesesteak and soft pretzels.

I glanced through the schedule for the next four weeks. We were winding our way down the east coast, down south, into the Midwest, and ending in New Orleans on the Fourth of July. Then we'd be heading home. The first leg of the tour had covered the western half of the United States.

We had twenty tour stops over thirty-one days. It would be a hectic and fast-paced four weeks, but it was what my dad lived for. He'd once told me that touring was his favorite part of being a musician, and the worst part of touring was being away from me. So he got to have both this time around.

We deplaned first and headed to the first class lounge while George sorted out our transportation to the hotel. It would be a few nights before we would have the comfort of sleeping in a hotel again. Rebecca had booked Four Seasons hotels for our entire trip when it was possible. They were my dad's favorites, and I didn't mind staying there, either.

I texted Parker to let him know that my flight had landed safely. I still didn't know where he was, and he still didn't know where I was. The mystery was one part endearing and one part irritating.

My dad arranged dinner in his suite for everyone involved in the tour who was staying at the hotel. That meant my dad and Jadyn, me, the rest of the band, Keith, and Vanessa.

I didn't hang out long after dinner. I headed to my room for an early night, opting to watch television in silence while I had the chance.

I slept like a baby in the comforts of the Four Seasons, waking from a dead sleep when my alarm jingled. I took my time in the shower, knowing it might be a few days before I'd have this luxury again.

I met my dad and his wife in their suite for breakfast, and then George arranged transportation to Wells Fargo Center a little before noon.

I saw the buses lined up behind the venue. Trucks and trucks of equipment ranging from the stage to the speakers to the instruments were lined up near the garages where the limo dropped us. I remembered my dad telling me once that they used thirty-two trucks for their last tour. I wasn't sure how many they had this time, but I knew the stage was bigger and better. Everything was always bigger and better than the time before.

In addition to Black Shadow's trucks, there were also trucks holding equipment for the opening bands. I realized that I'd never looked at the itinerary to see who the opening bands were, but I didn't really care. I just needed to know where my dad had to be and when. That was my job. I figured there were one or two openers before Black Shadow would take the stage. I thought my dad had told me that they'd added another band to the lineup for this last leg.

I had three things to do when we arrived at any venue. First, I had to check that my dad's dressing room backstage was stocked with his usual requests. The venue provided what the band asked for, and my dad always required a case of Newcastle for himself, two bottles of Pinot Noir for Jadyn, two packs of Marlboro Golds, a Zippo lighter, an iPhone six compatible docking station with speakers to listen to his pre-game music, and hot tea and honey. If anything was missing, I had to figure out how to get it there. Second, I had to make sure that my dad's pre-show playlist was queued into the docking station. Finally, I had to touch base with Keith to make sure everything was on schedule. Then I had to report back to my dad with accurate times for sound checks, fan meet and greets, and any other special pre-show arrangements that had been made—usually things like interviews for local radio or television.

I'd completed steps one and two. I was walking around backstage looking for Keith. He'd texted me to let me know that he was out by the trucks, so I started heading in that direction.

As I passed by the catering table, my eyes were focused straight ahead so that I could complete my mission.

And then I heard a familiar laugh. It was loud and sharp and grated on my ears.

The laugh was followed by a question.

Even the question was familiar.

"Did you see that blonde with the luscious tits back by Harper's door?"

It was a voice I would recognize anywhere even though I'd only heard it one other time.

Vinnie Williams, the drummer for Flashing Light.

I knew it without even looking.

My heart sank down to my stomach as my head moved slowly in his direction.

My eyes landed on Vinnie, who tossed his head to the side. The fringe across his forehead fell into yet another perfect sweep to the side. My eyes landed on the sandy-haired Fitz next. He stood across the table from Vinnie, and to his right was Garrett.

And then my eyes moved in slow motion to Vinnie's left. Directly next to Vinnie stood Parker James.

"I didn't notice." Parker was mumbling, looking down at the slices of sub sandwich in front of him.

"Price's daughter still got you distracted?"

Parker shrugged. "Don't fucking talk to me about Price's—"

I didn't hear the rest of his sentence, because I ran out the door.

Flashing Light was opening for Black Shadow?

How did I not see this coming?

It was so goddamn predictable.

How could Parker lie to me?

He had to have known I'd be coming here. He had to have.

I felt my heart splintering.

Deep inside, I supposed I'd always known. He'd only been interested in me so that he could get close to my dad.

The fact that Flashing Light was getting their big break by opening for Black Shadow was confirmation of my biggest fear.

This was exactly why I never dated musicians.

twenty-nine

I had said I didn't want to start this tour in tears, yet as I stood behind Wells Fargo Center in Philadelphia, Pennsylvania, that was exactly how it was starting.

I sat on the ground, my knees pulled into my chest and my head resting on them. Hot tears streamed down my face, but I wouldn't let anybody see. I hid my face just like I'd spent so much time hiding my emotions. I leaned against the cinderblock wall that separated the trucks hauling equipment from the fans itching to get a glance at their favorite rock stars.

I hadn't even felt this betrayed when I had found out that Damien had lied to me during the entire course of our relationship.

Seeing Parker on this tour was a knife twisting into my back. Everything we'd built together had all been a lie.

His words to me no longer meant anything. The fact that he looked as miserable as he did while he stared down at the catering table did nothing to comfort me.

Maybe he really did miss me. Maybe he had real feelings for me.

But he was touring with my dad's band. I'd let him in on my vulnerable side. I'd allowed him to see my tattoos. We'd shared hundreds of serious conversations and private smiles. He was well aware of my insecurities that people were only interested in me to get to my dad.

My dad held considerable influence in the very world that Parker was desperate to be part of. I'd been hesitant at first because I'd been terrified that it was the only reason Parker wanted anything to do with me.

And now he was actually touring with my dad.

Come to think of it, my *dad* should have told me about this. He knew I was dating Parker.

Fuck, I'd introduced the two of them just a few nights earlier. Certainly they'd have met when Flashing Light was first scheduled to go on tour with Black Shadow.

But they'd both acted like it was the first time.

Betrayal hit me from all sides, and a nagging poison in my gut told me that this wasn't the last of it.

I took a steadying breath in, held it for five seconds, and let it out slowly.

As hurt and angry as I was, I had to perform my assistant duties. I'd find a way to avoid Parker. I had to because I couldn't face him. Not like this, especially.

I lifted my head from my arms and squinted in the sunlight.

A shadow fell across my face, blocking the blinding rays of sunshine from my eyes.

The first time I'd ever seen Parker, I viewed him as a light in my dark world. And now that he stood in front of me, a silhouette against the bright afternoon sunshine, all I saw was darkness.

He held out his hand to help me up from my spot on the ground. I refused his help, standing up on my own and brushing off the back of my dusty jeans.

"Hey," he said softly.

I didn't respond. I was too angry to form words. I started walking back toward the building.

He followed me, a lost puppy dog. I ignored him, because I knew if I turned around and looked at him, I'd start crying.

I didn't want him to see how upset I was.

I focused on the tasks ahead of me, but I couldn't stop thinking about the betrayal. Why hadn't he told me? Did he think it would somehow work out better to leave out this huge bit of information?

He was a fucking idiot.

"I was going to tell you a million times. I just couldn't figure out how to say it without hurting you, so I kept putting it off. And then we had the studio time and I didn't get my chance and I knew I had to do it in person. I thought I'd surprise you, but you saw me before I had the chance to." He was pleading with me.

I didn't reply. His feeble excuses meant nothing. I kept walking, but he grabbed my arm.

"And waiting ended up hurting you, too. I'm sorry, Jimi. I don't know what else to say."

He whirled me around and pulled me in against him.

It had only been a few days since I'd last seen him, but those arms around me called on the deep emotional connection we'd made.

His hard chest and strong arms were good, too good, but it hurt too much. I couldn't be with someone who only wanted to be with me because of who I knew.

I felt in my core from the very beginning that this would never work between us. I should've followed my instinct instead of the fucked-up justifications I made in my head that holding him close would keep us both safe.

I finally found my voice. "I hate you." I ripped myself away from his arms and stormed inside, away from him and away from the gut-wrenching pain I felt just in looking at him.

I found Keith just inside the doors. "Everything okay, Rox?" He looked alarmed.

I took a deep breath and put on my game face. "Fine. What time do you need Gideon for sound check?"

Keith glanced at his cell phone clock. "Forty-seven minutes by the green elevators. You know where I'm talking about?"

I nodded. "He'll be there."

I headed toward my dad's dressing room. I rapped three times on the door, and I heard some shuffling and then, "Come in."

I entered. Jadyn looked disheveled, but my dad looked no worse for the wear.

I didn't even care that I was clearly interrupting whatever it was they had been doing.

All I knew was that it was stupid of me to let Parker get close to me. I should've known better. I should've been realistic with myself. But I hadn't done any of that, and now I was paying the price.

"You okay, CC?" My dad's voice was full of concern, and it was one more thing that I just didn't want to deal with. He'd been part of this sick betrayal, too.

"Fine. Keith said you've got about forty-five minutes until sound check. He'll go with you because I need a break. You need anything?"

He shook his head, his eyes wide as he stared at me.

"I'm going to my bus. You need anything, text me. You've got a meet and greet after the sound check. You'll have about twenty people who won their way into the check. I'll be back before your set."

He nodded, and I practically ran back to where I'd seen the buses parked earlier. I found Keith on my way, and he kindly directed me toward the bus that I'd be traveling on for the tour.

The driver, Hank, waited outside. I showed him my credentials, and he smiled at me, punched in a code on the door, and waved me onto the bus.

I looked at what would be home for the next month. I sighed. My dad was so goddamn over the top sometimes, but I was grateful that this was how I'd be traveling.

I stood next to the driver's seat and looked ahead. It looked more like a luxury apartment than a tour bus.

The living area consisted of two flat-screen televisions (For what? So we could fight over the sound?), two leather recliners, and a built in leather couch. There was a wet bar, a microwave, a refrigerator, and a counter with cabinets. Beyond that was a doorway and four bunks, and behind that was a bedroom that featured an actual bed, a dresser, and a full bathroom, complete with a shower. The water on tour buses usually wasn't the cleanest, so most of the band and crew would wait for a real shower in a hotel and would use the shower for storage. But it was nice to know we had a shower if we needed it. I figured Keith and Vanessa would sleep in the bed together—they usually did, but they had always been accommodating enough if someone wanted to trade places.

I located my suitcase, which was stored away with the other luggage in the bedroom at the back of the bus. I opened it, pulling out the one thing I needed.

I claimed a top bunk, climbed into bed, and closed the little curtain that would be my barrier of privacy for the next four weeks. My bunk was even top-notch, featuring my very own smaller flat-screen television, a light, a counter to store my personal effects, and an outlet to charge my phone.

I held my journal close to my heart, knowing the words that I'd written less than twenty-four hours earlier were in there, taunting me.

It was ridiculous to me that I'd never seen this coming. I'd turned a blind eye to the truth because I wanted to believe so badly that what Parker and I had was genuine.

I wished for the briefest of moments that I'd never met him.

But then the good stuff would've been gone, too. And I wasn't ready to part with the good stuff just yet.

I'd told him I hated him, and it was true.

I hated everything about him.

I hated how he smelled like sunshine. I hated how he looked, that scruff that scratched my skin and those eyes that could pin me to the wall and that hair that was always messy and begged for my fingers. I hated his words and his text messages and his music that made me feel things.

But most of all, I hated that he was perfect for me and that he had shattered me so easily.

I hated myself for letting him in and for allowing him to hurt me.

I opened the journal and reread the words I'd written just the day before.

Unbreakable.

That one word stared me in the face, mocking me and laughing at me.

I was past the point of tears. I was beyond the point of pain.

I'd always known whoever I got close to would be the third casualty in my life. First Katie, then Damien. I'd stayed away from love for a year because I'd been afraid that it would be my fault when I lost another person who I loved.

But instead, it was me who lost.

I was the third casualty.

Because the way things felt inside, I was certain that I'd been broken in a way that was beyond repair.

I was positive that I'd never recover from Parker's betrayal.

thirty

I'd been staring at the ceiling mere feet from my head, lost in thought for an indeterminate amount of time, when the jarring of my cell phone pulled me back to the present.

I glanced at the screen. "Parker" flashed at me.

I denied the call and sent it straight to voicemail.

It rang again. I ignored it again.

I glanced at the clock. Flashing Light would be taking the stage soon, and instead of preparing for the first night of a huge tour with his band, a tour that could literally make his career, Parker was calling me.

I needed to get back to my dad, anyway. I needed to make sure he was ready to go. As much as I wanted to, I couldn't wallow. I had a job to do.

So I swept the thoughts swirling through my mind away, feigning enthusiasm for the first night of this leg of the tour. Philadelphia deserved that from me, the assistant to the lead singer of the headlining band. I could fake my way through the next few hours, and then I'd go back to my cocoon made up of a bunk bed set too close to the ceiling of a bus and continue wallowing in my misery until morning.

Morning would greet us in New York City. We had a night off and then two nights at Madison Square Garden to prepare for.

I wondered where Parker would fit into all of that. Sometimes bands on tour together hung out, and sometimes they kept to themselves. My dad was a known life of the party, and he tended to be the one who brought everyone together on tours. He allowed everyone into his Black Shadow family. But he was married now, and I had a feeling that this tour would be a lot less wild and a lot more family-oriented.

I wasn't sure how my dad would feel once he knew Parker and I were over. And beyond that, I wasn't sure what he thought about Parker in the first place. When they'd met, my dad had been an asshole to Parker. Maybe it had all been an act, and I wanted to pick my dad's brain about it, but a few hours before the show wasn't the best choice in time on my part. My dad was a little busy, you know, being a rock star and everything.

I climbed out of my bunk and fixed my make-up. I ran a brush through my hair and sprayed some perfume on my wrists.

It was dark outside, which I couldn't have discerned from my bunk cocoon with the curtains against the windows drawn.

I found Vanessa waiting in the hallway outside my dad's room. She wore a simple black dress and bright red lipstick that made her skin look pale and like porcelain. She had nearly black hair cut in a blunt bob and equally dark eyes.

"Pre-game?" I asked.

Vanessa nodded.

"You on guard?"

She shrugged. "They always kick out the ladies during pre-game." I wondered briefly where my new mommy had gone. "You okay?" she asked, her dark eyes alarmed.

I shrugged.

I'd relied on myself for far too long, and maybe I just needed some girl talk. Maybe I needed some perspective. The loneliness was eating at me, and maybe Vanessa could help.

I was stubborn enough to know that she could offer all the advice in the world and I wouldn't take it—I'd still ultimately make my own decisions—but it couldn't hurt to talk to someone.

Vanessa's husband Keith had been Black Shadow's manager for as far back as I could remember. Keith and Vanessa had gotten married seven or eight years earlier, and I'd always looked at her as sisterly. Someone I could trust.

"Boy trouble?"

I nodded.

"Talk to me. I'm expert level on boys."

I laughed. She'd married a good guy, and I had no doubt that she had some experience in the man department.

"It's a long story."

She glanced around the empty hallway. A loud noise sounded from inside my dad's dressing room, and we both chuckled. "I've got time."

"Four weeks, right?" She nodded, and I sighed. "Fine. I met this guy and I really liked him. I fell for him, actually. The first guy I've fallen for since my ex left. And he fucked it all up."

"You know that's not nearly enough detail, right? Of course he fucked it up. He's a guy. It's what they do."

"He's a musician. He knew from the start that I was hesitant to get involved with a musician."

"Because of Gideon?"

I nodded. "It's hard figuring out who wants to be in my life because of me versus because of my dad."

She gave me a look of sympathy. Or maybe it was pity. I chose to believe it was the former, because I didn't want anyone's pity.

"Who's the boy?"

I sighed and leaned against the wall next to the door. "Parker James."

"From Flashing Light?"

I nodded. "You know him?"

"Yeah. I got the impression he was in a relationship."

"He was. With me. Until a few hours ago."

Her hand found my forearm and squeezed. "What happened, Roxy?"

"He didn't tell me that he was touring with my dad. It sounds so stupid when I say it out loud. I should've figured it out."

"Why did he keep it from you?"

"He said he wasn't sure how to tell me without hurting me."

"But he hurt you anyway."

I nodded in confirmation.

"And now you're stuck with him for four weeks."

"Essentially."

A loud noise sounded from above us, and I recognized it as a bass guitar.

"Sounds like they're on stage now. Want to go watch?"

I shrugged. Part of me wanted to go watch more than anything. I wanted to see him. I'd always been curious about Parker James on stage. But the other part of me never wanted to see him again.

I was in this confusing place where I was completely in love with him and completely in hate with him at the exact same time.

She grabbed my elbow and directed me toward the elevators. "Come on."

We made our way to the side of the stage where Parker stood, both of us flashing credentials at the security guards backstage. I saw his profile from where I was. Intensity radiated off of him in waves. He was in his element for sure, but I could also see an anger inside of him. It was vying for his attention when he was trying to focus on his music.

I'd put that anger there.

I'd hurt him as much as he had hurt me.

I stared at his profile. The strong jaw that worked magic against my body. His eyes were cast downward as his fingers moved nimbly across the strings of his guitar. He was concentrating on the music. He was lost in some element that I'd never seen him in, and it was fascinating to watch the transformation as his eyes lifted up and out toward the audience. His lips moved as he sang the bridge of the song behind Fitz. I'd never actually talked to Fitz before, but I knew who he was from the night the band had come into Vintage for a signing.

The night I'd met Parker.

The night my life had changed.

If I could go back to that night, I wondered what I could change so that I wouldn't have ended up in this very place at this very moment.

I believed in fate. I believed that things happened for a reason.

I knew that Parker and I would've crossed paths at some point in our lives, and I couldn't help but think that it would have been so much easier to have met him on this tour than the night I did meet him. If we were just starting now, I could be certain that he liked me for me. I could be certain that he wasn't interested in me simply to make it onto the music scene.

An evil part of me wanted to tell my dad that I didn't want him around. I knew what my dad would do. He'd kick Flashing Light off of their tour. Typically record labels put tours together, but my dad was the equivalent of a god in his line of work. If Gideon Price said jump, people jumped.

So if Gideon Price said he wanted Flashing Light off the tour, they'd be off the tour.

As much as I hated Parker, I couldn't do that to him. I couldn't do that to his career.

Besides, I knew that it would never happen. Not only would it be horrible press, it would be unprofessional on every level.

Staring at Parker as he performed, I could see how much talent he had. He was incredible, and he deserved success.

It was a shame that he had felt it necessary to go through me to get to my dad, but it was reality.

So I'd deal with him for the next four weeks. It should be easy enough to avoid him. I'd hang by my dad's side when he needed me, and I'd spend the rest of the time on the bus or with Vanessa. I didn't have to spend time with Parker James.

His head turned in my direction, as if I somehow held a magnet that pulled him toward me.

He watched me watching him for a few seconds, and I couldn't look away. A faint smile erased the anger I'd seen emanating off of him only seconds before. He still held the same intensity, but as he turned away from me and back to the crowd, I saw a subtle change in him. His movements were more fluid, his voice turned to warm honey, and those fingers shredded that guitar with the most masculine grace I'd ever seen.

thirty-one

I managed to avoid the after party. The first night was always a little crazy, but I didn't feel any inclination to participate. There would be other nights, nights when I'd be in a better place to celebrate than I was that night. So I called it an early night and headed back toward my bus.

My chat with Vanessa had been enlightening, but the few seconds when Parker's gaze had locked onto mine had told me so much more.

I tried falling asleep, but I couldn't. I was waiting to hear voices. There would be four other people traveling on this bus with me. They must all have still been at the after party, wherever that was. The bus remained still, so we weren't traveling to our next destination yet.

I couldn't get that look in his eyes out of my head, the one when he'd glanced over at me on the side of the stage. It had been laced with hunger, with need, and most of all, with love.

I knew I saw it there.

I started second-guessing myself. Had I been hasty in my decision?

He'd betrayed me.

But I hadn't stopped to listen to him.

I hadn't given him the time to explain his side of it. And if I had learned anything from my favorite book in the world, Atticus Finch taught me in *To Kill a Mockingbird* that I needed to stand in Parker's shoes and walk around in them.

I tried seeing things from his perspective.

I didn't know when the tour was arranged. All I knew was that it was very last-minute. I supposed it was even possible that he'd never met my dad. Maybe he deserved a chance to explain.

I wasn't sure why a few minutes to myself so strongly revolutionized my perspective, but when it came down to it, I didn't want to be mad at Parker.

I didn't want to be apart from him.

I was hurt, and I was weak. I was only human.

And that was the driving force behind me wanting to give him a chance to explain.

I'd already realized that this was my first real, adult relationship. And maybe this was my first real, adult choice to hang onto what we had.

A part of me hated him, hated what he did, but hate was a feeling. It was strong. And it wasn't the opposite of love. I'd learned that the opposite of love was indifference. Damien had brought out that side of me, but Parker ignited my passionate side. A very fine line existed between love and hate, and I was precariously teetering between the two. It wouldn't take much to sway me toward one side.

I climbed down from my bunk, desperate for some water. I opened the door that separated the sleeping quarters from the living area, and there sat Parker James on the leather couch, his eyes downcast. There was a melancholy air about him even from where I stood. He glanced up when he heard me.

Dark circles shadowed his eyes. His eyes were always dark, but the shadows were a little unusual. He looked beat down. His hair was covered with a backwards baseball cap. He wore a black hoodie and black jeans, his typical uniform. Black Nikes adorned his feet.

I wanted to run to him, to cuddle into his lap, to rest my cheek over his heart and listen to its steadying beat.

Instead I moved as if I didn't see him there.

I was too damn stubborn to make the first move.

I pulled a cold bottle of water out of the refrigerator and took a few sips.

"Can we talk?" he asked, his voice hoarse. I wasn't sure if it was from emotion or from singing.

I shrugged. I glanced at the clock at the front of the bus. It was a little after one in the morning, which meant everyone would be coming back soon.

I heard him mutter, "Goddammit." It was the shrug. I knew it would piss him off. That was why I had done it, if I was being completely truthful.

I sat in the recliner across from him.

He ran a hand over his face. He was clearly exhausted emotionally, mentally, and physically.

I couldn't help but think it was his own fault.

If he'd have been honest with me from the start, we wouldn't be in this place.

Or would we?

I thought about Atticus Finch's words again, and I tried to see it from Parker's perspective. We were just starting something. He was just gaining my trust. Would telling me before he left have softened the blow?

It was ridiculous to think I wouldn't find out, but Parker knew I didn't really follow my dad's career. I wondered whether seeing me there had been as big of a surprise to him as seeing him had been to me.

Unfortunately, though, that didn't excuse the lie.

I drew my knees up to my chest and wrapped my arms around them. I felt his eyes on me, powerful and intense as always. I couldn't meet his gaze. I was afraid of what it would do to me.

"I'm sorry, Jimi." His voice was just louder than a whisper, and it was resigned. He was clearly out of his comfort zone.

So was I.

The door opened, and Hank took his place at the driver's seat. He started up the bus, and then we started moving. We were backing up.

I looked with alarm at the front of the bus. Hank wouldn't hear anything going on behind him because he was trained not to.

I'd been played.

Again.

Motherfucker.

"What did you do?" I demanded, finally meeting Parker's gaze.

He looked at me unapologetically. "I knew you wouldn't listen unless you had to. I'm lucky you slept as long as you did."

"You hijacked my bus?"

"That's a little dramatic. I just made some arrangements for your travel companions."

"Fucking Vanessa," I muttered, focusing on the bottle of water I held in my hands. I unscrewed the cap slowly, deliberately, and took a sip. I refused to meet the inquisitive eyes I felt on me.

"She's worried about you."

"So much that she stuck me with you until we get to our next destination?"

"It's a two hour drive to New York City. Two hours for me to tell you why I waited to let you know my travel plans."

"Two hours to tell me why you lied to me."

"I never lied, Jimi."

"A lie of omission is still a lie."

He sighed in frustration. He stood and paced the small area in front of us. He ran his hand down his face again. Then he leaned against the counter, arms folded across his chest and one ankle crossed over the other.

He looked irritated and angry, but he held an air of cool and casual confidence about him. It seriously pissed me off that he was able to look so sexy when I just wanted to be angry. "Let me ask you a question."

Like I had a choice. I didn't acknowledge his statement.

"Would it have been any different if I had told you from the start? Would you have believed that I was interested in you and not your dad?"

He had a point. I shook my head. "No matter how you slice it, I see this for what it is now."

"That's just my point. There's so goddamn much that you know nothing about. And now that this is out there and you already hate me, I might as well tell you everything."

The catch in his voice caught my attention.

"More lies?"

He walked over and stood in front of me. His eyes were hard as he looked down at me. In the short space of time we'd gotten to know one another, I'd never seen him look so angry. The anger was cold and captivating. I couldn't look away.

His voice was sharp when he spoke. "I said this once already, and I won't say it again. I never fucking lied to you."

"So then what don't I know?"

"I've known your dad for a long time."

I should have been surprised. I should have felt sucker punched at what I considered yet another lie, what Parker considered another omission.

But somehow everything was falling into place.

I wasn't shocked.

The worst part was that I had to just sit there and take it. I had nowhere to run. I could run to my bunk, my protective cocoon, but I had only a curtain separating me from Parker. I could run back to the bathroom or to the bedroom and close the door, but he'd be right on the other side waiting for me.

So I was stuck in place, forced to talk to the one person I didn't want to see.

"We first met… God, maybe ten years ago in Chicago. I was in a different band at the time. There was a local battle of the bands to open for Black Shadow, and my band won. That was the first time we met. Your dad told me that I had real talent, but he could see that I was in the wrong place. That stuck with me. He told me he wanted to see me succeed, that he saw something in me. He gave me his cell number and told me to use it. So I did. I knew I had to take my chance if I wanted to make it in music."

He paused. I could see the passion in him as he talked about music and my dad. He headed to the refrigerator and pulled out a can of Coors Light. He opened it and chugged down half the can in his signature move.

I remained silent, watching him like a hawk. One part of me was relieved to finally be learning about who Parker James actually was while the other part of me was terrified what it all meant.

He continued talking. "Your dad became a mentor to me. He was like a father to me in ways my own dad never was. He believed in me, in my music. He saw that I was with the wrong people, and because of his advice, I left the band. I worked security for a few years as a way to make ends meet. I met Fitz backstage at a different show, and they were looking for a new guitarist. We formed Flashing Light shortly after."

He stopped to drink down the other half of his beer, and then he tossed the can in the trash. He grabbed a second, and I had to wonder how many he'd already had. "Want one?" he asked. I nodded, and he opened one and handed it to me.

I needed some alcohol to filter this story.

"So how did you end up on this tour with Black Shadow?" I couldn't help my question as it spilled out of my mouth. I wanted to remain neutral, to just listen as he spoke, but I had to know.

He resumed his pacing. "That's where things get a little complicated." He ran a hand down his face. He was nervous. "Your dad told me he'd gotten into some trouble with an old friend. He knew I'd worked security for a while, and he told me that if I moved my band out to LA and kept an eye on his daughter, he'd repay me in opportunities for my band."

My eyes grew wide at his admission.

My heart raced.

Anger boiled over.

Not only had I been betrayed by Parker, but I'd been betrayed by my dad.

The one and only person in the entire world I trusted completely.

"So you knew I'd be here all along." My voice was flat. It wasn't a question. It was a statement.

He nodded slowly.

"So you're on this tour because you watched out for me? Basically you're getting paid to fuck me?"

A look of horror like I had slapped him crossed his face. "God, no. Jimi, that happened because I couldn't stay away from you."

"Bullshit." I stood up, enraged by his words. He was a fucking liar. This entire time he'd completely played me. He led me to believe that we'd met by chance when he'd known exactly who I was. I'd truly been his ticket to stardom all along.

"You know I said multiple times that I shouldn't be with you. But once I met you, I couldn't stay away."

"It'll pass." I stepped around him and stormed to the bunks, throwing open my curtain and climbing into my bed.

I pulled my curtain closed, praying for privacy. It was futile, though. I couldn't escape him in this tiny space.

He ripped open my curtain as quickly as I'd closed it.

"It won't pass. It hasn't passed since the second I laid eyes on you."

I turned over to look at him, to spew some more venom at him because in that moment, I fucking hated him. I stared daggers at him.

But then he said the words that changed everything.

"I don't know what to do," he said, his eyes filling with unshed emotion, his voice laced with an edge of desperation. "I can't stop what I feel. I can't control it. I didn't mean to, but I fucking fell in love with you."

I wanted to feel the force of his beautiful words, but I was too angry. "You know something, Parker? There's a fine line between love and hate. And right at this moment, I hate everything about you."

I held his gaze until he turned away in defeat. I turned back toward the wall.

I don't know where he went, and frankly, I didn't care. He couldn't have gotten far. We were enclosed together in a little under four hundred square feet for the next two hours.

I closed my eyes and took a deep breath, and that was what broke the dam.

Tears rushed down my cheeks, thick and hot and fast.

I'd been betrayed by literally everyone I trusted.

Parker and my dad were in it together. Somehow they'd both managed to break my heart at the same time.

The pain I felt from this betrayal proved to me that I hadn't really been in love with Damien, at least not in a real, adult way. When he left, he broke me, but his absence had also taught me to live independently. I'd learned how to rely on myself.

I'd taught myself that blocking out emotions was the way to live.

The sharp and splintering pain caused by the betrayal of the only two people in existence I trusted made me value the indifference I'd forced on myself.

I wished I'd never started feeling again.

I wished I'd never heard Flashing Light's song.

But most of all, I wished I had never met Parker James.

thirty-two

I felt warmth along the length of my back as I sobbed quietly into my pillow. Or, I thought I was sobbing quietly into my pillow.

Apparently I wasn't.

"Shh, baby. Please don't cry." He finger-combed my hair away from my face tenderly for a few beats. I hated how peaceful it felt to have his body against mine, his fingers smoothing back my hair.

He wrapped his arm around my torso. "What can I do?" An edge of anxiety shaded his voice.

I couldn't pull myself together enough to respond, and having him so close to me was fucking with everything. We were crammed into a bed smaller than a twin mere feet away from the ceiling. I couldn't move over to get away from him because there was literally nowhere for me to go.

That sunshine smell, those strong arms, that feeling of comfort. All of it added up to this person who had not only used me to get to my dad, but to this person who had lied about it. I was stuck on the lie, especially after he knew how vulnerable I was where my dad was concerned. I didn't know how to get past that. I didn't know if I'd ever be able to get past it.

I let him hold me, let him soothe me and whisper to me. But I didn't say anything back. A few nice words and admission of love weren't going to change anything.

I must have eventually cried myself to sleep, because when I opened my eyes, Parker was asleep and the bus wasn't moving.

I wasn't sure how to detangle myself from him without waking him, but then I realized that I didn't care.

I checked my phone. It was a little after five in the morning. I rubbed at my eyes. They felt swollen and puffy from crying, and as I thought about the duplicity of my father and the man lying beside me, I felt a fresh wave of anger hit me.

The tears were gone for now.

The anger I felt overpowered the sadness.

I elbowed Parker in the ribs. His eyes flew open.

"Get out," I said, my voice hoarse.

His eyes were pained, and it wasn't from my elbow. "Don't make me go. Please." His eyes were pleading with me. I wanted him to stay. I wanted to forgive him. But the cut was too deep, too fresh, too painful.

I shook my head. "You've said what you came to say. We're in New York now. You can go. I'm officially releasing you from your bodyguard duties."

Parker sat up, hitting his head on the ceiling. "Fuck," he muttered.

I almost giggled. It was comical seeing him half-asleep and forgetting that he was in an upper bunk on a tour bus. But the anger simmered, dousing any possible humor I found in the situation.

He looked over at me. I saw nothing in his eyes but love. I'd seen it there before, but I'd been too afraid to identify it. And now it sickened me. He'd never want me for anything other than my father. He'd made that pretty fucking clear.

"Just go."

He sighed deeply, as if a weight pressed down on him, and then he climbed down from my bunk. I closed the curtain and turned over to go back to sleep.

But before I did, I had a text to fire off to my dad.

Truth's out. You can tell Parker I don't need a bodyguard anymore. Remember the other night when you told me that I'm the one person in the world you trust? Feeling's not mutual.

I didn't want his reply to wake me, so I shut off my phone, closed my eyes, and drifted back into a restless sleep.

It was the rough shaking of my shoulder that woke me up. I flipped over with a glare for Parker, but instead I met my dad's extremely angry eyes. And it was clear that it was directed at me.

It was like looking into my own eyes. My dad's eyes were icy blue. They looked even bluer set against his dark hair, the stubble along his chin, his tan skin. Fury stormed his expression. I'd seen that look in my dad's eyes before, just never directed at me.

"Don't turn off your fucking phone, Roxanna."

His voice was fueled with rage. He *never* called me Roxanna. Ever.

I sat up, careful not to make the same mistake Parker did. I turned my phone back on. "There," I said, waving my phone toward my dad's face.

He swatted my hand away. "This isn't some joke. I get that you're upset about PJ, but I—"

"PJ?"

"Parker." He looked at me like I had grown two heads. "Parker James," he clarified. "PJ."

"You're close enough that you gave him a nickname, but you didn't bother to tell me that you had him watching me?"

He shook his head. "I couldn't risk it. I had no way of knowing how close you two would get."

I rolled my eyes and climbed down from my bed. I walked past my dad toward the front of the bus. "That's an understatement."

"Look, CC, he feels awful. Hear him out, would you?"

I shook my head. "You're lucky I don't just abandon you, too. Let you figure out your own damn schedule."

"Don't be a brat. And keep your fucking phone on. There's a lot going on that you don't know about."

"That seems to be the theme of the tour thus far," I said, stretching my torso before collapsing on the couch in the living area.

My dad took a seat across from me in the recliner. He leaned forward, hands clasped together and elbows resting on his knees. He still looked furious, but I also saw the concern in his eyes.

"Care to inform me?" I asked.

"The fewer people who know, the better."

I rolled my eyes. "Including me, apparently."

He nodded. "Correct."

"Fine. Phone's on. But Parker, PJ, whatever the hell you want to call him, he's out. I don't want anything to do with him."

"Too bad. I call the shots around here, and I need you safe. That's why I invited you along."

"Is Rebecca even really getting married? Or is that a lie, too?"

The slightest look of guilt crossed into his eyes. "She's getting married. Just not this month."

"Goddammit, Dad! You didn't have to lie to me about everything."

"I didn't lie. I just left a few things out."

"Lies of omission are still lies!" I yelled. God, these two were frustrating.

"You know not a damn thing would have changed if I handled this any other way." He was right. I played with a fraying corner of the pillow my head rested on. "You've got my stubborn streak. It's one of the things I love most about you."

"What the hell do you think is going to happen with all these people around? I'm good. I don't need a bodyguard."

"I disagree. And I'm not only your father, but I'm your boss for the next four weeks. Parker stays."

He stood up and walked toward the front of the bus. "And CC?" he said, turning around in my direction again.

I glanced up at him. He had to have seen the defiance in my eyes, the fury in my face. But he said it anyway.

"Give PJ a chance. You're allowed to be angry at both of us, but he cares about you. A lot. Trust me on this. It's not about me, and it hasn't been from the moment he first saw you."

And just like that, my dad was out the door off to who knew where while I sat alone on a tour bus meant for eight people.

I was exhausted after a shitty night's sleep, and I had no idea where in the world I actually was. I knew we were in New York City, but I was alone on a tour bus. Everyone had to be somewhere nearby, but I sort of liked the solitude of an empty bus. Knowing my official PA duties didn't start for a few more hours, I headed toward the bedroom at the back of the bus, stretched out on the queen-size mattress, and drifted back to sleep.

"You really gonna sleep through New York City?" The voice pulled me out of my dead sleep. Constant interruption to my sleep was the one thing I didn't miss about being on the road.

Vanessa sat down on the bed next to me. "Did you forgive him yet?"

I shook my head.

"Why not?"

"Long story," I said, rubbing my sleepy eyes awake. "Suffice it to say chances of forgiveness are slim."

"You want to talk about it?"

"I really, really don't. But thanks for asking."

"Hey, we all need girlfriends. Consider me your bestie on the road."

"Noted, Vanessa. Thanks."

Parker's head appeared in the doorway. "Can I talk to her? Alone?"

Vanessa looked over at me. "You okay with that?" she asked.

I shrugged, which caused Parker to chuckle.

Vanessa stood and left, closing the door behind her. Parker gazed at me for a minute, his eyes full of this intense heat. I'd always seen his intensity, and in the moments when I knew he wanted to fuck me, I'd seen the heat. But this was some sensual combination of everything.

"What do you want?" I asked bluntly.

"Just a few minutes of your time. I'll keep it brief."

I didn't bother acknowledging his sentence. He was going to talk, and I was going to sit and listen. Why? Because I didn't have a goddamn choice. Daddy's orders.

I snuggled back down under the blankets. Parker sat on the edge of the bed, keeping his gaze on me.

"Gideon said that this doesn't change things. I've been thinking about this all night, and I can't come up with any conceivable way of making both you and your dad happy."

"So he wins. As usual."

"There aren't any winners in this, Jimi."

"Don't call me that." My voice was sharp. Sharper than I'd intended.

"Here's the problem. Every time I get close to you, I can't help but want to feel your body against mine. I can't help but

236

want to hold you, to kiss you, to make love to you. I hate myself for it. I hate myself as much as you hate me. But I was asked to protect you, and I plan to hold up my end of the deal."

He paused. It was like he was waiting for some reaction from me. I didn't give him one.

"We can do this one of two ways," he continued. "We can do this the fun way, or we can do this the hard way."

"Fun for who?"

"For both of us, Rox. We can see the eastern half of the states together. We can enjoy this tour together. We can sightsee. We can find Mexican restaurants where I can order a cheeseburger. We can get frozen yogurt and judge each other's toppings. We've had fun together from the beginning. Let's not let that stop now. I get if you don't want to be with me right now, but you're stuck with me. Why can't we try being friends? Why can't we try being civil?"

"You have got to be kidding." It was instinctual to say that, even though every little thing he'd just said to me sounded perfect.

Except the "friends" part.

Despite the lies, despite the betrayal, a teeny, tiny thought niggled in my mind.

As much as he had hurt me, I still wanted Parker James.

"Come on, baby. Let's get out and see New York City."

There was no show that night, which meant we were in New York City and free to do whatever we wanted.

Rebecca had booked a room for my dad and another for myself at the Four Seasons in New York City. I wanted to go check into my hotel, run a hot bath, and soak for the rest of the night with a good book. But definitely not with the man sitting in front of me.

At least that's what I told myself.

thirty-three

I lay in my king-size bed in a bathrobe by myself later that night feeling very alone. The television spoke softly to me, but that was my only company.

Parker couldn't be far. He was still assigned to watch over me, so if I was staying in, he would be, too. For all I knew, he was sitting outside my door.

I thought about checking the peephole, but I didn't have the energy to get out of bed.

I was lethargic. I glanced over at the clock. It was about dinnertime, but I had no motivation to put on clothes. Times Square was literally a mile away from my window. I glanced over at the city outside.

I should be out there, fighting my way through the crowds, my hand warm in Parker's. Instead, I was punishing us both.

I'd been to New York City before, and the energy always invigorated me. But it had little chance of invigorating me if I didn't leave my hotel room.

We had three more nights in New York after this one. We had concerts scheduled the next two nights at Madison Square Garden, but the last night was another free night. I'd feel better then. I'd go out then.

At least that's what I told myself. Who knew if I'd feel any better by then?

A soft knock at my door forced me to get up. I looked through the peephole. "What do you want, Parker?" I spoke through the door. I heard a soft thud from the other side.

"I'm going to dinner. Do you want to come with me?"

I tightened the belt on my robe, unlocked the deadbolt, and opened the door.

Parker let out a growl. "Christ Jesus, Jimi. Tell me you're wearing something under that."

I shook my head. "I'm not."

"Fuck my life," he muttered.

I turned around so he wouldn't see my tiny smile. As much as I didn't feel like smiling, he still managed to prompt one.

I walked back into the room and curled into the chair that faced the window, drawing my legs up under me.

Parker cleared his throat. "So, uh, dinner?"

"Not hungry," I lied.

"Then come keep me company. Please?"

His tone made me change my mind. It was some mix of frustration and hurt and pain. It forced me to realize that he actually was suffering through this.

If he didn't care about me, he wouldn't be here asking me to go with him. He'd gotten what he wanted. He was on tour with Black Shadow. He could've just ordered room service and avoided me.

And he was here protecting me or loving me or wanting me, but I was too hurt to let him in.

"Can I ask you a question?" I finally asked.

He nodded.

"If I say no, am I stuck with you tonight anyway?"

"You always have a choice, Jimi. But choices inevitably come with consequences. I'm not going anywhere. I'll sit outside your door all night if I have to, but it might be a little more fun for both of us to get out of here for a little while."

"I'll go to dinner because I need nutrition to survive, not because I want to spend time with you."

His eyebrows shot up. He was shocked that I'd agreed to go.

"Let me just get dressed."

"Don't do that on my account," he said, a sexy grin spreading across his face.

Fuck him and his hot face.

I grabbed some clean underwear, a t-shirt, and jeans from my suitcase and changed in the bathroom. I touched up my make-up and ran a brush through my hair, ultimately deciding to pull it back into a messy ponytail. I neatly hung my robe on the back of my door.

I met Parker back in the main area of my suite. He was flipping through the television channels mindlessly as he leaned back against the headboard, his legs stretched out in front of him and crossed at the ankles. I studied him for a moment before moving fully into the room.

He had the whole brooding bad boy thing going on. His dark hair was wavy and messy. A little bit of scruff outlined his jaw. His dark eyes were focused ahead on the television, but I could tell he had something on his mind.

I wondered if it was me.

I tore my eyes away from the drink that did nothing to quench my thirst for him and walked past him to my suitcase. I pulled out a pair of Toms and stuck them on my feet, zipped up my suitcase, and shut the curtains on the windows. I was ready to go.

"Pizza okay?" he asked, turning off the television and standing when he saw that I was ready.

I nodded. "Fine with me."

"I know a place near Times Square. You up for it?"

I shrugged, and he laughed.

I stuck my hotel room keycard in my wristlet with my wallet, my cell phone, some lip balm, and a pack of gum.

We walked toward the elevators, and Parker hit the call button.

The doors slid open, and we walked on alone.

I felt his eyes on me, but I stared at the numbers on the electronic dial. Anything not to acknowledge that we were in a tiny space together that was obviously filled with sexual tension.

We finally arrived at the lobby and Parker held the door open for me. "Cab or walk?"

"How far?" I asked.

"About a mile."

"Walk." I wanted to stretch my legs. A little exercise always helped refresh me, and just the smell of New York City gave me a little energy back.

The sidewalks were crowded with tourists and locals making their way to their destinations. Parker and I weaved in and out of them, always side by side but never touching.

The walk was brisk and had enough of a crowd to prevent conversation as we made our way to the restaurant. It was one of those places where patrons placed orders at the counter and the servers dished it right up. After Parker paid our tab, we grabbed some sodas and found an empty booth.

I took a bite of the steaming hot square of pepperoni pizza in front of me and moaned in ecstasy. It was possibly the best slice of pizza I'd ever tasted.

Parker visibly shifted in his seat, staring at me as I enjoyed my food. He muttered something under his breath that I missed.

"Excuse me?" I asked between bites, taking a sip of Coke.

"You definitely know how to torture a man."

I smirked at him and turned my attention to my food, doing my best to ignore him for the rest of my meal.

It was when we were walking back to the hotel that I felt a strange sensation that made the hair on the back of my neck stand at attention.

I glanced around, trying to pinpoint the source of the sensation. I was certain someone was watching me.

Maybe it was just paparazzi. People knew Black Shadow was in town. People knew who I was, even though they generally left me alone.

But this felt different. It was darker. Scarier.

Parker looked over at me and saw the panic written in my eyes. I saw a flash of fear in his eyes, too. That look told me he felt it, too. He looked around us, and I instinctively moved in a little closer to him. He wrapped his arm around my shoulder.

I froze, not because of the strange feeling that I was being watched.

It was because Parker's arm was around me and I wasn't prepared to deal with what that could mean. I was still trying to stitch the gaping hole he'd left when he'd cut through my heart. Even if I wanted to forgive and forget, the wound was too fresh.

The pain that lanced through my chest when his arm was around me was too much. I stepped away from him, out of his grasp. He gave me a look that clearly told me to get the fuck back into his arms, but I couldn't.

I knew from the beginning that Parker and I would be dangerous for one another, and I was right. It was silly to think that this could have turned out any other way, but the moment Parker and I moved beyond friendship, this moment of suffering was inevitable.

He couldn't have lied to me forever. Eventually I would have learned the truth about why he'd crashed into my life. Eventually I would have felt this betrayal. And if he'd have been up front with me, I'd never have given him the time of day, let alone the kind of access to my body, my thoughts, and my heart that I'd handed over on a silver platter.

I stalked on ahead of him, our moment on the street together gone.

He followed me through the front doors of the Four Seasons and toward the elevator. I seethed with anger.

"Can I just walk you up to your room and check it before you kick me out?" he asked once the elevator doors shut us in.

I folded my arms across my chest, refusing to look at him.

Because I knew that it would only take one look from him, and I'd break. I wanted him to wrap me in his arms, to kiss me, to run his tongue along every crevice of my body, to fuck me.

I wanted his protection again.

But I hated him. I hated what he'd done. I hated that he'd conspired behind my back, that he'd known things about me that not even I did.

I pulled my key out of my wristlet and practically ran down the hallway to my room once the elevator doors opened.

I stuck the card in the slot and opened the door after I got the green light. I didn't bother to hold the door for Parker, but he still made it in behind me.

I glanced around my room. Something was off, but I wasn't sure what it was. Parker stared at the windows.

"Motherfucker," he said, pulling his cell phone out of his pocket and shooting off a text.

"What?" I asked.

I gazed out the windows, trying to figure out what his deal was.

And that's when I realized that my curtains were open.

I specifically remembered shutting them before I left.

I looked for more clues. I heard Parker's phone ding with text as I glanced around my room.

The lid of my suitcase was askew, as if I'd left in a bit of a rush.

I had zipped it shut before I left.

Someone had been in my room.

It had to have been the maid. They had to have come in for turndown service. But even as I thought it, I knew that couldn't be it. Rebecca always specifically requested no turndown service upon check-in at my dad's request. It was easier to make the same request for all of the rooms she booked.

I ran to the bathroom. If there were fresh towels, that meant it was the maid service. I'd chalk it up to miscommunication with the check-in staff.

The bathrobe I'd hung neatly on the back of the door still neatly where I'd left it. The hand towels I'd thrown on the counter were still on the counter. And the bath towel I'd tossed on the floor after my bath was still there, exactly where I'd left it.

It wasn't maid service. But someone had definitely been in my room while Parker and I ate our pizza.

I had no idea if they'd taken something. I had no idea what they were looking for. But I was certain someone had been in there.

A tremor of fear raced up my spine.

"I know you're going to be opposed to this, but you're coming to my room for the night." Parker's voice broke into my thoughts. I was wringing one of the hand towels in my hands anxiously.

I nodded.

He was, after all, hired to protect me.

And as much as I didn't want to be near him, I needed him to do his job.

I needed him to protect me.

thirty-four

Parker's room was one floor down from mine. After I'd hurriedly gathered my belongings, he ushered me quickly down to his room. He bolted the door behind us and latched the swing lock.

"What's going on?" I asked as I stepped into his room. He set my suitcase on the dresser. I glanced around the room. It was smaller than mine, presumably not a suite, but it was still extravagant.

"I don't know." He nervously checked his phone when it started ringing in his hand. His nerves were fucking with my ability to remain calm.

"The curtains were open. She closed them before we left," he answered. His voice was stiff.

He handed me the phone. "It's your dad."

I sighed. "Hi."

"You okay, CC?" he asked softly.

"No, Dad. I'm not fucking okay. I'm freaked out. You two aren't telling me anything but lies."

"This is on a need to know basis."

"I'd say we're at the needing to know step right about now."

I heard him sigh audibly over the phone. "Look, I'm just glad you're here with us instead of home alone. I know you're mad, and I know you want answers, but I can't give them. Okay? Just try to relax. Stay with PJ. He will keep you safe."

"Fine. But for the record, I hate you both."

"I know. And I love you."

I hung up and threw Parker's phone at him. In a swift move that managed to irritate me for some reason, he caught it gracefully.

He watched me silently. Carefully.

A thought flashed through my mind, but it couldn't be.

I considered calling my dad back to see where his deceitful wife was, but I decided to keep my thoughts to myself for the time being. I was mad at my dad. I didn't want to talk to Parker. I didn't trust Jadyn. I had the sneaking suspicion she might have been the one who broke into my room. The question was why she would do that.

"Did Rebecca book this room?" I asked.

Parker nodded.

"Awesome." I opened the minibar and helped myself to a tiny bottle of Absolut. There were two more lined up behind it, so I took those out, too. If I was spending the night in Parker's hotel room, scared out of my mind that someone had rifled through my shit while I was out of my room, I was going to spend the time drunk… and apparently on my father's dime.

"Pass me that Jameson shit," Parker said. I handed him the three mini bottles of whiskey.

I twisted off the cap of the Absolut and took my first shot of the night. Those tiny bottles actually held about five milliliters more than a shot, but they were close enough.

I watched as Parker twisted off his cap, too. He offered his up toward me for a toast, but I rolled my eyes at him. This wasn't meant to be fun. I was stuck in a room with someone who I didn't want to even be around. I was too angry to consider making the best of things.

I twisted off the cap of the second bottle and drank it down in one big gulp.

I started twisting the cap off of the third, but Parker stopped me, grabbing the bottle from my hand. "Slow down, babe."

"Fuck off," I said, reaching for the precious liquid he'd taken from me.

He held me off. "Five minutes. Let the first two hit your system."

I huffed angrily and headed over to the bed, throwing myself down on it with a loud moan of frustration. I heard Parker chuckle.

I sat up in bed and faced him with a glare of fury. "This isn't funny, Parker. I'm scared. I'm mad. I'm frustrated. I'm pissed that I have to be locked in here with you. Nothing about this is funny, so stop your goddamn laughing."

I watched as he twisted the cap off his second bottle of whiskey and drank it down. He grimaced after he swallowed, and then he sucked in some air between his teeth.

"This isn't ideal for me, either."

"Bullshit. You love that I'm stuck here with you."

He moved across the room gracefully, stopping right in front of me. He stared down at me, sadness swimming in his dark eyes. His voice was tender when he spoke. "I wish you wanted to be here with me as much as I want you here. I love that you're here in my bed, but I wish it was on your own accord. I wish you were safe. I wish I didn't have to protect you. I wish your dad never would've asked me to do this. I never had regrets in life until the day you were hurt because of me."

He tossed the last bottle of vodka to me. "Do what you want." It landed with a thud next to my thigh as he turned and headed toward the small loveseat. He faced the window, his back to me as he stared out over New York City, and I sat in bed processing his words.

I picked up the bottle and stared at it. I wanted to suck it back, but I probably needed at least a few of my wits about me.

Because being locked in a room with Parker James was hard enough. If I was locked in a room with Parker James and I was drunk, who knew what sort of trouble I'd get myself into.

I glanced over at him. He was brooding as he stared out the window. He was probably feeling all of the same things I was, just in different ways.

He was scared. He was manly enough that he'd never admit that to me, but I saw the fear that flashed in his eyes when I'd felt that strange presence outside. The question was whether he was scared because someone was seemingly out to get me or whether he was scared that he'd lose his job and my dad's respect if he let anything happen to me.

I had to believe that he cared about me. The sincerity in his voice had been genuine when he told me that he'd fallen in love with me. I didn't doubt for a second that he loved me, because I felt it, too.

But I wasn't sure love was enough. Too many lies had been told. Too much of the truth had been left out.

Even now he was hiding things from me. He and my dad still had their secrets, and I wasn't sure I'd ever find out the whole truth.

The other predominant emotion I felt was frustration, and I saw the same emotion written all over Parker. He was frustrated with himself for hurting me. He was frustrated with me because I was so stubborn. And he had to be frustrated that he was stuck in a hotel room with me while his band was out sightseeing New York City without him. Touring with Black Shadow was a huge break for them, and he was missing out on the rewards that came with that.

For whatever reason—whether it was because he was on my dad's payroll or because he truly cared about me—he sat in a hotel room watching over me, making sure I was safe.

I glanced back at the bottle of vodka in my hand. What was the worst that could happen? We were locked in a room together.

Ultimately I decided to take my chances.

I twisted off the cap and threw back the vodka. The liquid burned its way down my chest. I felt it settle in my belly, warming me.

The first two were starting to hit me, and the familiar muddying sensation of tipsiness started to wash over me, obscuring rational thought. I felt lighter, some of the heaviness of the past day disintegrating.

I stood up from the bed. I opened my suitcase and grabbed a pair of shorts and a tank top to sleep in, and then I went to the bathroom to change. It was early to go to sleep, but it looked like I was locked in for the night. I figured I might as well get comfortable. I stripped out of my jeans and t-shirt and glanced at the back of the door. A fluffy bathrobe hung on the back of the door, just as it had in my room. I didn't want to tempt Parker, but all I wanted was the comfort of that fluffy bathrobe. I opted for pulling it on over my nightclothes. I emerged from the bathroom and set my clothes from the day on top of my suitcase. I felt Parker's eyes on me as I walked over to the minibar, pulling out the rum. Three shots of vodka wouldn't kill me. Rum on top of vodka wouldn't kill me, either.

"What're you doing?" Parker asked, watching me pull out three tiny bottles.

"Getting drunk. Why the fuck don't they stock these things with whole bottles?"

"You sure it's a good idea to mix vodka and rum?"

"You sure you want to ask me that?"

He shrugged.

I couldn't help my smile. "I see I'm starting to rub off on you."

He unscrewed the cap to the third bottle of whiskey. "You can rub off on me anytime," he muttered, and then he tossed back the liquid. "This tastes pretty good after the first two." I glanced up and saw him inspecting the bottle. He tossed it on the table beside him. "Good call on the full bottles. I think you might be onto something."

"Especially when money is no object. Let's order room service and charge it to dear old Dad. Vodka for me, whiskey for you."

He gazed sideways at me. "I don't think that's a good idea."

"Why not?" I challenged.

He stood and walked over toward me. The alcohol had helped dissipate some of the tension that crackled between us.

He took my chin in his fingertips, forcing me to meet his gaze. It was warm. It was sincere.

And it was worried.

"Because, Jimi. Someone got past every precaution your dad and I put in place and somehow got into your room while we were out. I'm not taking any chances."

He leaned forward and pressed a kiss to my forehead, and then he dropped my chin, took one of the small bottles of rum out of my hands, and turned back toward the window, reclaiming his spot on the loveseat.

But in the simple gesture of the split second when his lips touched my forehead, I forgot about the betrayal and the hurt. All I could focus on was how good Parker felt and how right my world turned when any part of him pressed to my skin.

As much as I hated everything about him, I was undeniably, irreversibly, absolutely in love with him. That was the moment when I finally admitted it to myself.

But that didn't mean that I could just forgive and forget. The stubborn streak that my dad loved to brag he had given me was too powerful.

I watched as he opened the cap and drank down the rum. He moved with an air of melancholy, and I knew that the sadness he felt was because of me.

I wished I could take it away.

I knew I could take it away. I knew exactly what I needed to do to see this man smile again.

And all it took was one more shot from one of those goddamn tiny bottles of liquor to force logic from my brain and give into the lust that was always simmering beneath the surface when we were in a room together.

After his first hit of rum, Parker stood and took one more bottle out of the minibar. Tanqueray.

The only thing I knew about Tanqueray was that it was in that Snoop Dogg song, "Gin and Juice." I assumed it was the gin to which he referred.

Apparently a shot of Tanqueray on top of three shots of whiskey and a shot of rum was a bad idea.

Or maybe it was a good idea.

It's all a little fuzzy.

I only put down one of the bottles of rum on top of my vodka. Sleepiness started kicking in, so I tossed the bathrobe on the floor and lay down on the bed. I was too lazy to pull the blankets over myself.

"Goodnight, Jimi," Parker said softly from across the room.

I didn't respond.

I turned over and looked at him. He was trying to get comfortable on the loveseat, but his body was too tall to find any possible comfortable position. He flipped over, sighed in frustration, and finally sat up, resting his head on the couch and narrowing his gaze back out the window.

It was painful to watch him, even more so because it was my fault he was uncomfortable. He didn't have to invite me into his room. He didn't have to give me his bed. I finally spoke up after a few minutes. "It's fine if you want to sleep in the bed."

His eyes moved from the window to me in surprise.

"I am crashing in your room, after all."

"I'll only ask this one time. Are you sure?"

I nodded. "It's fine."

I heard the slur in my own voice, but I ignored it.

He stood and closed the curtains. I turned away from him, refusing to look at him as he stripped out of his shirt and his jeans, turned out the light, and got into bed beside me.

I was suddenly wide awake knowing that Parker James was in bed next to me.

Every decision I made in that bed beside him would be fogged with alcohol. My first decision was whether or not I should speak what was in my heart.

But he spoke first.

"I'm so fucking sorry, Jimi." His voice was hoarse, quiet, and sincere.

No one likes a sad drunk, but his words of apology turned me into exactly that.

I no longer had control over myself as the emotions mixed with the rum on top of the vodka and a loud sob emitted from somewhere deep within me.

It wasn't the betrayal. It wasn't even the hurt from the lies.

It was the loss of Parker.

I could no longer take the pain of being apart from him, of fighting every instinct I had when I really just wanted to be with him, to feel him next to me, on top of me, inside of me. I craved him.

He turned in my direction when he heard me crying, and I felt his arm slip around me as the front of his body aligned to the back of mine.

A perfect fit.

I wanted to be strong. I wanted to deny him and ignore him. He wasn't good for me. He would only hurt me.

His lips were on my neck, and that was my undoing.

I was in self-destruction mode. Lust and instant gratification overcame the need to protect myself.

The scruff on his chin tickled my hot flesh. His tongue traced a path along my neck, and the tears slowed as my body automatically turned into him. His mouth crashed down over mine, his tongue hot and persistent and tangy from the gin.

I moaned, and one of his hands forced its way under my tank top to my bare breast. He was rough as he grappled at my breast, and then he tweaked my nipple. Hard.

I yelped out a startled moan, which turned into some erotic noise that I didn't even know I was capable of making.

And then suddenly he was over me, thrusting his hips toward mine as he kissed me in that erotic way he had, his hand running up the length of my torso as he pushed his body toward mine. We were separated by clothes as I kissed him with a hunger I'd never felt before.

I'd missed this. I'd missed him. I'd missed the way his body connected with mine, the way he fucked me so hard that I thought we'd break the bedframe and then the way he made love to me so gently that I never wanted it to end.

"Parker," I cried out on one particularly hard thrust. A growl rumbled up from his chest, and then he pulled away from me, panting. A low curse escaped his lips as he sat up. All I could see was his silhouette in the dark room.

"We shouldn't—" he started, but I cut him off.

"Don't stop." I reached for the hem of my tank top and took it off, throwing it to the ground, and then I pulled off my shorts and panties.

"I don't have a condom."

"I don't care. Fuck me, Parker. Now."

"Without a condom?"

"I'm on the pill. Can I trust you?"

He hesitated for only a moment. Then he nodded as he shoved his boxers off and to the floor and reared over the top of me again.

I felt the head of his cock between my legs. He slid it through my wet pussy, pressing it firmly against my sensitive clit. Then he dipped it lower and pushed into me.

The slick feel of his cock pumping into me with nothing separating us was incredible. It was like the first time all over again.

I dug my nails into his back, scraping my way as I held onto him, afraid the moment would end too soon.

"Holy fuck, you feel good," he groaned. He thrust up hard, balancing himself on one arm and running his other arm up my body.

Then he shifted and hit my G-spot repeatedly with his perfect cock, slamming into me and pushing me into a soul-crushing orgasm that had my entire body clenching him to me.

I screamed out in pleasure as he continued driving into me, and then I heard "Jimi" on a growl. He pulled out of me and jerked himself off. I felt the warm, sticky fluid on my stomach, and then Parker collapsed next to me for a few brief seconds. He pressed his lips to my neck, and then he stood and padded over to the bathroom.

He returned a moment later with a warm washcloth. He ran it tenderly over my pussy first, and then he wiped up the mess he'd painted on my stomach. His movements were gentle and slow, as if taking care of me was the only priority he had in life.

He tossed the washcloth on the bathroom floor and returned to the bed, kissing my lips softly once more before pulling my body against his.

thirty-five

"Come on, Roxy. We're going to be late," Damien said. He was wearing a black suit. It made his dirty blond hair look lighter than usual, almost a halo effect. His blue eyes were shining.

He *never* wore a suit.

I couldn't remember a time when I'd seen him that dressed up.

I stared at him in confusion.

"Where are we going?" I asked. I was sitting on the couch in the house I shared with him.

"Put on your black dress. The one that's your favorite. And hurry! We don't have a lot of time."

I followed his directions. I put on the black dress and the heels that made me feel like I had the sexiest legs on earth.

I curled my hair. I almost never curled my hair unless it was a really special occasion. Damien had only told me to hurry, though. He hadn't told me where we were going.

It just seemed special since he was so dressed up.

I stood at the mirror, fastening the diamond studs my dad had given me for my sixteenth birthday. They reminded me of Katie. I'd received those earrings on the second birthday I'd had without her, and somehow the sparkling diamonds reminded me of her sparkling personality, her beautiful presence in all of our lives.

But she was long gone.

I missed her every day, even after all this time had passed. I was sure I'd miss her every day for the rest of my life.

I hadn't been able to replace her presence in my life with any other girlfriend, so I stayed away from girls. I didn't need anyone, anyway.

I had Damien, and he was all I needed.

Just as much as he needed me.

"Roxy, you know that I need you, right?" Damien was standing behind me. He'd snuck up on me.

Our eyes met in the mirror. "I know you do, D. Just like I need you. Now are you going to tell me where we're going?"

He grinned at me in the mirror and shook his head a little, as if to say that because I was so stubborn, he had to ruin the surprise.

"Okay, Roxy. I'll tell you."

A butterfly soared across the room, and I looked at it as if it were totally normal.

I turned around to face him. His blue eyes had turned from bright and shiny to withdrawn and sad. The halo effect that had shown over him only a moment earlier had turned dark, almost like he had a cloud over him. It had to be the shadows in the room playing tricks on my eyes.

He looked sad as he gazed at me. "You look beautiful, Roxy. And if we don't get going, we're going to be late to my funeral."

thirty-six

I sat up in bed, my heart pounding as I gasped for breath.

The room I was in was completely dark except for a tiny sliver of light peeking through the curtains. Someone was in the bed next to me, and as I gathered my bearings, I realized that I was about to throw up.

I stumbled through the room toward the bathroom, making it to the toilet just in time.

I looked down at myself as my eyes watered. I was stark naked, kneeling over a toilet in a dark bathroom that was only lit by the glow from the built-in nightlight in the light switch.

I felt my stomach retch again, and then I felt my hair being swept back from my face as I continued to expunge the contents of my stomach.

Warm fingertips drew calming circles on my back, soothing and comforting me.

"I knew the rum on top of the vodka was a bad idea," Parker whispered. "You okay?"

I sniffed. I always cried when I threw up. "Yeah," I whispered, my voice small as I waited out another heave. It was empty. Dry. I'd gotten everything out.

I stood on shaky legs and rinsed out my mouth.

"Sit," Parker commanded, lowering the toilet lid and flushing the toilet for me.

He disappeared, and a stream of light from the other room flooded the bathroom. I leaned my head against the wall, a pounding headache searing through my brain.

It wasn't the combination of alcohol. It was the dream.

I was small and scrawny, but I could hold my liquor. I had my dad's kidneys.

But that dream had panicked me. It filled me with anxiety.

And the scariest part was that I hadn't even taken my sleeping pills. Those were usually the nights I had my vivid dreams. When I drank, I usually passed out cold and slept a dreamless sleep—or at least a sleep where I didn't remember my dreams.

So what was that dream telling me? Was Damien in trouble?

Parker reappeared with my toiletry bag and the clothes that had been tossed on the floor in our lust. He set the bag on the counter. He handed me the clothes, and I got dressed while he pulled out my toothbrush and toothpaste. He set it up for me and handed me the brush. I made a few passes around my mouth while he filled a cup with water.

I stood and spit, rinsing out my mouth a few extra times.

"Feel better?" he asked.

I nodded, my eyes drinking him in. His hair was messy and the snake on his torso stared at me.

He looked so damn good in nothing but underwear.

He held my gaze for a few seconds, and then he carried two waters to the bedroom, setting one on the night table next to my side of the bed and the other on the night table next to his side.

He turned out the light, and then we both fell back into bed.

He pulled me close against him again, and I felt warm and safe snuggled in his arms.

The next morning, I awoke when I heard rustling next to me. The bed dipped, and I watched as Parker got up and headed toward the bathroom. I heard the shower turn on. I was alone for a few moments, grateful that I hadn't remembered any other dreams except for the vivid one of Damien.

I got up and checked my phone.

Nothing new.

But that wasn't a huge shock. The only people who ever texted me were Parker and my dad.

It was a little before eleven. We had to get to Madison Square Garden by two, so we had a little bit of time to kill. Enough to shower and get dressed and maybe grab some lunch before we left.

I got up and pulled some clothes out of my bag, gathering everything I'd need to shower once Parker was done.

I sat in the loveseat by the window, staring out over the city as the dream from the night before replayed in my mind.

I hated those types of dreams. I knew it would be with me all day, clouding everything I did. I tried not to think about it, but that only made me think about it even more.

Parker emerged from the bathroom a few minutes later, wearing just a pair of jeans that hugged his hips perfectly. I stared as he rubbed his hair dry with a towel. A few droplets of water glistened on his chest, and I couldn't help but remember the night before when that chest was hovering over me, when his body entered mine and nothing separated skin from skin.

A tingle ran up my spine, but I stopped it in its tracks.

"Good morning," he said, his voice cautious. He threw the towel in the bathroom and ran a hand through his damp hair. "Feeling any better?"

I thought about telling him about the dream. I thought about admitting that it hadn't been the liquor. But all of that would just complicate things. It would just leave him with questions that I wasn't prepared to answer.

So I ignored his question and opted to tell him what was on my mind.

"Last night doesn't change things, Parker."

He chuckled. "Of course it does."

I shook my head. "I gave into something that I shouldn't have. You betrayed me, and I don't think I can get past that."

He walked over toward the window, toward me, and he knelt on the floor by my legs. I gazed down at him. "You have to," he said simply. "I refuse to believe that I'll never get to do what we did last night ever again. I refuse to believe that you don't feel as strongly about me as I do for you. I'm persistent, Jimi. I get what I want because I don't give up."

"It doesn't matter how strongly I feel for you. Betrayal negates all of that."

"I think someday you will see that everything I did was in your best interest. Someday you'll believe me. And I'll be right here, ready to wrap you in my arms the second that happens."

I sighed and stood, stepping around him and toward the bathroom for my shower.

His words rattled around in my mind. He was like a house fly. He was annoying and I couldn't figure out a way to get rid of him.

But he was absolutely right about one thing. I felt strongly for him, and the hatred I'd felt the day before was quickly morphing back into the love that I'd been developing for him since the night we met.

I lucked out. My dad wanted lunch with me. I was pissed at him, too, but he was my dad. I was stuck with him forever. I'd get past what he did eventually because he'd done it to protect me.

And I felt a little better after spending some of his cash on the minibar.

He invited Parker to our lunch date, but Parker opted to meet up with the Flashing Light guys since I was under my father's watch. I was grateful for the time away from Parker.

But to be honest, I missed him the second the door shut behind him when he'd left me with my dad.

"Where's Jadyn?" I asked after we were seated at some fancy French place near Times Square.

"I told her I needed to talk to you alone."

"Does she know what's going on?"

My dad shook his head. "She knows that Randy and I aren't friends anymore, but she doesn't know much else."

"Literally?"

My dad laughed. "She's an educated businesswoman, CC. Give her some credit."

"She did manage to snag the elusive Gideon Price."

I was rewarded with another laugh from my dad.

We both ordered soup, and I grabbed the baguette sitting on our table, debating whether or not to bring up my suspicious about Jadyn. I pulled off a chunk of bread and popped it in my mouth. It tasted perfect on my empty stomach.

"So I know you hate this, but I have to keep Parker with you at all times when I'm not with you. Keith, Vanessa, and George are additional alternatives if we're both tied up, which will happen on gig nights."

"I'm not a little kid, Dad."

"I'm well aware of that." He raised an eyebrow in my direction, and I squirmed.

It was like he could see right through me, like he knew what Parker and I had done the night before. I felt heat creeping up my neck at the thought of Parker's lips on my body.

I had to get control of my damn hormones.

I shoved another piece of bread in my mouth.

"The problem is that Randy has a lot of associates in New York. All over the country, really. None of us are safe, and

George has been working tirelessly to ensure that our trip is seamless. I can get Bruno back on you, but I feel more comfortable with Parker." My dad pulled off a hunk of bread.

"I'll take Bruno."

"You'd be okay with Bruno staying in your room with you? Sleeping on your bus?" He took a bite of his bread.

"Wait a minute. Sleeping on my bus? I thought you said Vanessa and Keith were alternatives."

"We made a few bus changes last night. You and Parker are sharing Shadow Two."

"Are you fucking kidding me?" I tossed my bread down on my plate. Tossed, threw. Same difference.

"Don't talk to me like that," he said sharply. "You know it pisses me off."

"You really want to talk about being pissed off, Dad?"

My dad laughed just as the waitress delivered our soup, giving me something to focus on besides this ridiculous conversation. But I had lost my appetite somewhere around "bus changes."

So in those moments when I would be able to escape to my bus, to travel to our next destination, to have the quiet peace away from this hot mess, I'd still be stuck with Parker James.

My dad and I went straight from lunch to Madison Square Garden. I completed my duties in record time, and then I hung out in my dad's waiting room with Jadyn.

We sat in the same room on the same couch together and stared blankly at the television. I wasn't even paying attention to the show that was on. I could not have cared less, really, what was on. I was too stuck in my own thoughts.

And I literally had nothing to talk about with my step-mommy. I could not think of a single thing to say to her that wouldn't come out accusatory and hateful. So I remained silent.

And then a commercial came on, and Jadyn started with small talk.

"So you and Parker are dating?" she asked. It rubbed me the wrong way that she'd even asked. I didn't want to talk about my personal life with her, let alone the complications of it.

"Sort of," I answered absently.

"He seems nice."

"He's a lot of things. I don't know that I would use the word 'nice' to describe him."

"Spoken like a girlfriend." She laughed at her own joke, like her wit just couldn't be matched. I shrugged.

"How's married life?" I asked, trying to deflect the conversation from me and my personal life.

"It's perfect. He's perfect." She started gushing, but I tuned her out. It sort of made me sick to think that she was married to my father. She was a gold digger, but I had to give my dad credit. If he was in love with her, that was his prerogative. He wouldn't have married someone if he didn't love her, and as irritated as I was with my dad, he deserved to have his daughter treat his new wife with courtesy. Even if I didn't trust one word out of her lying mouth.

My dad came in the room and sat on the middle cushion of the couch, right between us.

Mikey followed behind him, and he sat in a chair across the room. My dad and Mikey had been best friends my entire life, and I looked at Mikey like a second father. He didn't look like the fatherly type, but then again, neither did my own dad. Mikey had long black hair, and he always wore a bandana around his hair, Bret Michaels style. He had eyes so dark that they were almost black, and his skin was toned a beautiful olive color. Katie had been born his exact opposite—with her mother's fair skin, light hair, and blue eyes.

As much as I knew Mikey missed his perfect life before Katie had died and Fern had left him, he'd remained the same guy I had grown up with.

Johnny, Black Shadow's bassist, and Carlos the guitarist shuffled in behind Mikey. Johnny was the youngest of the men. He'd been only sixteen when Black Shadow had first formed, and he'd spent the first tour they'd ever gone on with a private tutor so he could finish his high school degree. The ladies tended to love him as he was incredibly attractive. He was the epitome of tall, dark, and handsome. He kept his hair cropped short, and he kept one of those really sexy, perfect beards. When I was a little girl, I'd nursed a crush on him, but now I just thought of him as one of my dad's friends.

And I always thought of Carlos as the jokester of the group. All four men were gentlemen, and all four knew how to have one hell of a good time. But Carlos told raunchy jokes, and he didn't care who heard them.

"You're all gracing us with your presence before the show? What's the occasion, boys?" I asked with a grin.

Mikey glanced over at my dad. Johnny and Carlos stared at the floor. My dad put his arm around my shoulders, and I felt nerves kick in.

"Someone attacked Keith last night. He's fine. He went to the ER and was released with a few bruised ribs." My dad looked anxiously at me.

I didn't know what to say. Keith? Why would someone attack Keith?

I thought they were after me.

Clearly Randy was stopping at nothing to rattle my dad. It was a clear message that he'd take out anyone close to Gideon Price.

My body started to tremble with fear, and I felt my dad's arm tighten around my shoulders. "It's okay. You're safe."

"Jesus, Gideon. Why Keith?" Jadyn asked, clearly vying for my father's attention.

I started to wonder how far back this feud between my dad and Randy went. Was it possible that my dad had married Jadyn just to piss off Randy?

Surely he wouldn't go that far.

Or would he?

Both my dad and Parker had admitted to me that there was a lot more to the story that I didn't know. Maybe Jadyn was part of it.

Flashing Light had just taken the stage. I had the sudden urge to get out of the stuffy dressing room with all eyes on me. I needed to get away from the drama and the fear.

I wanted to see Parker performing in front of a New York crowd. But I had no interest in fighting my way through the pit to catch my glance.

"Do you have a press pass?" I asked my dad.

He shook his head. "No, but I can get you one. Why?"

"I'm going to check out Flashing Light from the trench." The trench was the spot immediately in front of the stage, fenced off from the people in the first row of the pit. It was where security and photographers stood. My credentials only allowed me backstage, not into the trench.

"I can get you in the trench without a press pass." He reached into his pocket and tossed me his credentials. There were five or so plastic cards that looked like credit cards held together on a key ring, and they granted access to anywhere in the venue. "Be back with it before Pure Adrenaline takes the stage."

"And who is coming with me?" I asked, knowing it was inevitable. Vanessa was surely with her husband. Someone had to be responsible for watching over me.

"George."

"Fine. Where is he?"

"Right outside the door."

I stood, and my dad stood up with me. I glanced at Jadyn and saw the jealousy in her eyes.

He was my dad, for crying out loud. Her need for attention would have to wait.

My dad opened the door and checked the hallway. True to his word, George stood beside the door, his eyes trained on the long hallway in front of us.

"CC wants to watch Flashing from the trench."

George nodded, and that was that. George led the way, knowing the layout of the backstage of Madison Square Garden like the back of his hand. He led me through some long hallways, up an elevator, and down some more hallways, and then we walked out onto the floor.

I flashed my dad's credentials at the security guard blocking the trench entrance, and he let me pass. George was right behind me.

Flashing Light was in the middle of playing their current radio hit, a song called "Cash Out." I flashed my credentials at another security guard and took a spot right in front of Parker. George stood a few feet to my right.

I wasn't sure about the order of their set list, but I figured they'd play somewhere between five and ten songs. They had to be getting close to the end of their set.

I heard the opening bass drum. I recognized the beat of "Trial and Error." My eyes were fixed on Parker. He had stage presence in spades. He looked like the man who'd fucked me that first night when he was up on stage, not like the man who had made love to me the night before.

He looked like a goddamn sexy beast up there.

His fingers slid gracefully along the strings of his guitar. His hair was a mess. He wore his signature black pants and black shoes and black t-shirt. Sweat glistened on his forehead. He was lost in his music, and it was a sight to see. I drank him in.

I heard girls screaming behind me whenever he backed up on the mic. They loved him. They wanted a piece of him.

But he belonged to me.

I could deny it all I wanted, but my heart was in his hands as much as his heart was in my hands.

My eyes moved down to his shirt. I couldn't help but fantasize briefly about what was under there. And then I finally fixated on the shirt he'd chosen to wear that night. The familiar face and lettering finally registered.

It was a Jimi Hendrix shirt.

I felt hot tears prick behind my eyes, but I refused to let them fall.

Parker backed up vocals over the bridge and through the chorus of my favorite Flashing Light song. I listened to the words he wrote, to the words he'd imprinted on his skin.

He glanced down in my direction. Surprise flashed through his eyes as they met mine. His gaze didn't leave mine as he backed up Fitz's lead vocals. "We tried, we tried, we tried, But all we got was an error."

I couldn't help but think how appropriate this song was for us. We had tried, but we kept running into errors. I wasn't sure we could overcome them, and even though I was still devastated by what he'd done, the tingles that raced up my spine as his eyes locked on mine told me that I wanted to give it another try.

I had to get over the hurt, over the stubbornness that I felt. I had to figure out a way. As I thought about how good life could be with Parker versus how dark it could be without him, I knew I'd arrived at my answer. I just wasn't sure if I was ready to give in. The pain was too fresh.

I'd learned a little bit about him, but if we were ever going to make this work, I'd need the rest of the puzzle pieces.

"We've got time for one more," I heard Fitz tell the crowd after he introduced each band member. He glanced over at Parker. "You're up, man," Fitz said.

I heard the opening notes to a familiar song. It was a cover of "Sex Type Thing" by Stone Temple Pilots.

I watched Parker take the lead on vocals, and the crowd behind me started going crazy. I saw security beside me step up, shining a flashlight on someone in the crowd. My eyes never left Parker's. It was like he was talking directly to me as he sang about knowing how I wanted—and liked—what was on his mind. An intense heat passed between us from stage to crowd.

One of the things that set Flashing Light apart from other bands was the fact that they did different cover songs at every show they played. And tonight it was STP's song from the early nineties, the perfect song for Parker and me.

I knew without a doubt that he'd chosen it because it expressed so much about what was going on between us that he wasn't able to put into words. He was telling me through music, the one thing that he could use to fully express himself, to expose what was on his mind and in his heart.

But as I watched him take the lead on vocals, what scared me the most was the lyric about hurting me.

He'd already done that part. So how did we move past that?

How did I force myself to get over it?

The answer was simple, but it wasn't until a little later in the tour that I arrived at it.

thirty-seven

I cancelled my room for the next two nights at the Four Seasons. It seemed silly to pay for a room that I wasn't going to use. I wasn't sure that I was any safer in Parker's room, necessarily, but at least it would save us a few hundred dollars.

Not that we were hurting for money, exactly, but it was the principle of it.

After the show, I was completely exhausted. George ushered me back to Parker's hotel room. He sat outside Parker's room until Parker stumbled in a little after two in the morning. I'd left on a light by the door so he could see when he came in, and I'd fallen asleep a little before midnight without the assistance of sleeping pills. I wanted the ability to wake up alert just in case I needed to, and taking anything that could alter my consciousness in the middle of the Randy situation seemed dangerous.

The noises he made as he stumbled around the room told me that he was obviously intoxicated.

I didn't blame him. He deserved to let loose after a show and after the intense moments we shared as he sang that Stone Temple Pilots song to me.

That song that I'd forever consider "our song."

That song that wasn't romantic in any way but would always remind me of Parker.

I made out George's voice. "You okay, PJ?" I kept my eyes closed even though I was awake.

"Fine, fine," Parker sang.

"Goodnight," George said. I heard the door click behind him, and I heard Parker fumble with the lock for a moment. Footsteps moved in my direction.

I heard him singing some tune softly. I didn't make out the words until he was standing over me and I felt him brush the hair away from my face. "Jimi Price is in my head. Jimi Price is in my bed."

I stayed still, wanting him to believe I was asleep.

He seemed almost happy. I was happy for his happiness, but I wasn't ready to be happy along with him.

And I wasn't drunk.

One drunk person plus one sober person usually didn't create the best conditions for the type of conversation we needed to have.

Parker leaned down to press a kiss to my cheek. He smelled like a whiskey factory. "So beautiful," he sang softly.

He padded away from me and fumbled around in the bathroom for a few minutes, and then he returned to the bedroom, shut off the light, and got in bed beside me, wrapping himself around me. His arms around me felt good. Right. Perfect.

He sighed, and then he started talking softly. He was certain that I was asleep.

"I wish you didn't take your sleeping pills. You'd be awake now, and we could talk." When he said that, I shifted slightly. I was about to tell him that I actually *was* awake when he continued talking quietly in the dark to himself.

I couldn't stop listening.

"I wish I could tell you everything, Jimi. I wish you could listen and hear me and not be so mad at me and tell me that everything's going to be okay in that way you do with just your blue eyes. So fucking blue." He paused for a moment, as if envisioning my eyes in his head. His voice cracked slightly when he said the last part, and I could tell he was getting emotional. The night before I was the sad drunk, and now he was turning into one through his monologue.

"I wish I could confess to you how much it hurts me that I hurt you. I wish you knew about Kimmy and my parents and my past. I wish I didn't have to keep secrets because of the choices I made. I wish I never agreed to it, because it's making me keep secrets from everyone. I don't know if I can do this anymore, Jimi, and I wish you could hear me and tell me what to do. But most of all, I wish you could understand how hard I've fallen for you and how I would do anything to keep you safe. Anything." His voice was becoming hoarse and gritty with emotion.

"Promise or no promise to Gideon, I'd do this even if he took everything away. I'd do it because I love you so fucking much."

I wasn't sure if he was crying, but he was definitely emotional. I heard a sniffle, and then he repeated, "So fucking much."

His warm lips pressed against my neck.

His speech to himself in the dark had revealed nothing I was looking for but said everything that I needed to hear.

Everything.

I wanted to turn toward him, to cup his face in my hands. I wanted to know if his cheeks were wet with tears. I wanted to press my lips softly to his. I could smell the sharp smoky flavor of the massive amounts of whiskey he'd consumed mixed with the familiar scent of tobacco. Somehow that blend was comforting.

And because I wanted all of that, I did it.

I turned into him. His lips moved from my neck to my mouth, and he kissed me intensely, hard, with drunken abandon. He tasted as comforting as he smelled. Being wrapped in Parker's arms gave me a home away from home, a peaceful haven amidst the anxiety that the world outside our hotel room door held.

The kiss turned instantly heated.

Instantly.

I really had to stop sharing a bed with Parker. It was fucking with my emotions, and I'd never recover from him. He was ruining me, bit by bit. Just like I knew he would from the start.

I understood that he was there to protect my physical safety. But I hadn't realized how precarious my emotional safety was in his hands.

Before I could even think about stopping him—I didn't want to, anyway—our clothes were tossed aside and his cock was pushing into my pussy.

I'd have gambled on whiskey dick given his condition, but he was definitely up for the occasion.

He was thrusting into me as if his life depended on it, jackhammering away at me, and I held onto the headboard to brace us both so that he wouldn't fuck me right through the hotel room wall.

My body found its release faster than any man had ever made me come before in my life, and Parker followed soon after me. He collapsed by my side. He clung to me, and I to him, in the quiet afterglow, and we fell asleep naked and tangled in each other.

When we woke up together the next morning, still naked and still entwined, I repeated the same thing I'd said almost exactly twenty-four hours earlier. "Last night doesn't change things, Parker."

His response was the same, too. "Of course it does."

"We can't keep sleeping in the same bed."

His arms tightened around me. "I think it's all working out very nicely."

"I'm weak around you. I don't want to be. I want to be the strong woman I know I am. I want to be able to resist your temptation because you and I won't work."

"Give me a single reason why."

"Because you lied to me." I sighed and pushed his arms away from me, but he only gripped me more tightly.

"I told you on the bus that I wasn't going to say it again." His voice had cut from playful to serious.

"Say what again?"

He sighed. "You're a pain in the ass."

"Then let me go. And I don't just mean from your arms in this bed. Fucking let it go, Parker. And if you can't fucking let it go, at least give me some goddamn space."

He loosened his grip, but he kept his arms around me. "I'll let you out of this bed," he said, his lips finding my neck, causing goose bumps to rush down my legs, "on one condition." His breath was warm on my skin.

I held back a moan, just barely. "What condition?" My voice was a little more breathless than I wanted it to be.

"You don't ever—and I mean *ever*—try to talk me into letting you go. Because I will never let you go, Roxanna Cecilia Jimi Price. I'll fight for us. Maybe you don't see it yet, but this is right. And I'll wait around like a fucking chump until the day you accept that."

With those words, he fully let go of me, got up from bed, and padded over to the bathroom, leaving me a puddle of emotions in his bed.

The worst part of that whole encounter was that some part of me knew that he was right. Some part of me didn't want him to let me go, wanted him to fight for me, wanted him to wait for me.

Because if he kept fighting the way he had been? I'd come around eventually. It was really only a matter of time.

thirty-eight

The next night, I kept my distance from Parker. He was still essentially my bodyguard, but he didn't exactly have unlimited time to watch over me since he had a band to meet with and his own shit to take care of. My dad had put George on me, too, but that meant my dad was unprotected by his head of security. I didn't like that idea since I didn't trust Jadyn's intentions, so I tended to stick close to my dad as much as I could. That allowed Parker to get done what he needed, it kept my dad from having anxiety attacks when I was out of his sight, and it allowed me to keep an eye on Daddy's new bride.

I didn't watch Flashing Light from the trench during the second sold out show at Madison Square Garden, even though my heart was there with him. I needed some time away from him. Everything was happening too fast.

I did, however, want to watch my dad perform. Since he needed his credentials, I didn't have the option of watching from my favorite spot in the trench. Instead, I stood next to my least favorite person in the world, Jadyn Snow, on the side of the stage.

Her arms were crossed against her chest as she bobbed her head to the music.

I glanced out at the crowd during Black Shadow's first song. The audience surged forward as one, hands and middle fingers and devil horns held high in the air. Part of the chorus in the opening song called for the entire crowd to shout "Hey!" at the same time, and they did so with enthusiasm. New York really was a great city to experience a Black Shadow show.

The hair on my neck prickled as I felt someone's eyes on me. I focused on the faces in the crowd from my spot on the side of the stage. Some faces were drunk, and some were smiling. And then there was one…

One that was familiar.

My heart raced.

It couldn't possibly be him.

I squinted to try to see better, and when our eyes locked for one brief moment, it was confirmed. Damien Williams was attending the Black Shadow show in New York.

"Damien?" It was quieter behind the stage than on it, and Jadyn shifted next to me. She couldn't have heard me. Could she?

It didn't matter. It wasn't like she knew who Damien was.

"Damien!" I yelled, and then I turned to run after him.

I had about a million questions for the man who'd left me in the middle of the night without an explanation. For the man who'd taken my emotions when he left.

I wasn't interested in reconnecting. I had enough complications in the relationship department. But Damien had been an important part of my life for a long time, and I wanted hug him, to touch him. To know that he really was alive and okay.

But as I turned to chase after him, Jadyn grabbed my arm.

I turned toward her with a vicious glare.

"Where are you going?" she asked.

"None of your business." I ripped my arm away from her.

I turned back to the crowd to spot Damien again before I took off after him, but the face where his had been seconds before was replaced with new faces.

I scanned the area around where I'd seen him. I studied each face individually, focusing intently on every single one, squinting and narrowing my eyes to see better. But I never spotted him again.

Fucking Jadyn Snow. If she'd never grabbed my arm, I would've been able to run after him, to find him and to see him and to talk to him in person again.

Instead, I lost him.

I stayed on the side of the stage for the remainder of the show, studying the crowd and trying to spot him again. But he was gone. Again.

And I would never know if he'd really been there or if my imagination had just been playing tricks on me.

From New York, we headed to Boston, which was a short bus drive, and then the next show would be two nights later in Raleigh. The drive from Boston to Raleigh was a little over twelve hours, and that was if we didn't stop. We were set to take off in the early morning, so Parker and I would have some time to kill.

The Boston show went off without a hitch, and I decided to attend the party after the show, a laidback affair for the bands and crew after the stage was broken down. Sometimes the after party was held at a bar if someone was sponsoring it, but more often than not it was just a gathering back by the tour buses.

Vinnie had invited some women with "luscious tits" to check out the Flashing Light bus. Parker stood chatting with Mikey, Fitz, Garrett, and one of the guys from Pure Adrenaline who I had yet to meet. I thought about how much time Parker had lost out on with the guys because of me. The men of Flashing Light were an incredibly important part of Parker's life, but I hardly knew anything about them. I hardly knew anything about that part of who Parker was.

In fact, I really didn't know much about Parker at all.

I blamed myself, though. I'd been so busy being mad and holding grudges that I hadn't taken the time to get to know the man behind the guitar.

I meandered between the buses, finding my dad sitting on a camping chair next to Johnny and Carlos. All three of them had red solo cups in their hands, and I chuckled at the cliché playing out before me of rock stars getting drunk after the show. There were a couple of empty chairs next to my dad, so I plopped down in the one right next to him.

"Hey, CC," my dad said. Carlos and Johnny both nodded in my direction.

"How'd it go tonight?" I asked.

"After doing this for nearly twenty-five years, it's pretty amazing how it just never gets old," Johnny said. My dad and Carlos made noises of agreement.

"You see that kind of longevity for Flashing Light and Pure Adrenaline?" I asked.

My dad answered that one. "Flashing is one of the most talented young bands I've seen in a while. Both Fitz and PJ have the voices, and Vinnie and Garrett kill that bass. It's impressive."

"Pure's good, too," Carlos said. Johnny and my dad nodded, but none of them gushed about Pure Adrenaline the way my dad just had about Parker's band.

Vinnie jumped down from his bus, helping two women get down behind him. "You miss those days?" I asked, cracking a smile at my dad.

He shook his head and grinned wickedly. "Who said they're over?"

I laughed, and then I grabbed the drink out of my dad's hand and chugged down a few sips.

"Jesus, Dad! What the hell are you drinking?" I sputtered.

"Everclear and soda."

"Are you sure there's soda in there?"

He laughed. "I thought you had my kidneys, kid. Gotta break you in better."

Johnny and Carlos got a hell of a kick out of our bickering, and I didn't like that they were laughing at my expense.

I passed him his drink back and stood.

"Aw CC, don't go," my dad said, pulling my arm toward him. I rolled my eyes.

"I'll be back."

I wandered around the parking lot filled with buses, my eyes automatically moving over to Parker. He was still deep in conversation with Mikey. Just as I wondered if he was thinking about me, if he sensed that I was near or if he figured I was safe with everyone around, he glanced up and met my eyes. I saw a small smile reach his lips as his eyes returned to Mikey.

I felt George's eyes on me, too.

But I had the sensation again like someone else was watching me, too.

Despite the crowd around me, I was alone. I felt the isolation in my heart.

But even as that thought struck me, I acknowledged for the first time that I actually was truly alone. I'd been on my own but hadn't really felt it. I cut people completely out of my life, and then Parker waltzed in and made me feel like I was part of the human race again.

I wanted to be near him again, to feel his arm around me. I wanted to feel like I wasn't alone, because even though he was giving me the space that he assumed I needed from him while I was safely under the watch of my dad, a piece of me was missing when I wasn't in his arms.

I wandered back toward my dad when the sensation that someone was watching me became overbearing. Just as I approached the three men who were still chatting, Jadyn came down from my dad's bus and walked up behind him, grabbing his shoulders between her hands to massage his neck. I almost barfed, but I managed to keep it down. I wondered for a second if it had been her who had been watching me.

Instead of sitting down to watch my dad's new wife throw herself over her husband, I bid everyone goodnight.

As I started to walk away, I heard my dad's voice. "Can I talk to you for a second, CC?"

I turned back toward him, and he stood, disentangling himself from Jadyn.

He took a few steps toward me, and I snuck a glance at my stepmother. She looked like she wanted to murder me for pulling my dad's attention away from her.

Another tick mark in the negative column for the new Mrs. Price.

My dad pulled me away from everyone so that we could have a private conversation. We were standing by the front of his bus, the bus all the way on the end, away from everybody. From where I stood, I could see just about everybody who was part of the tour. It was a good group of people, yet I was clearly an outsider among them.

"Are you doing okay?" he asked.

I shrugged silently.

"Can you do something for me?"

I raised my eyebrows.

"Can you just have a talk with PJ? He filled me in on what's been going on between you two."

I rolled my eyes. Yeah, right. I was sure that Parker told my dad that I couldn't seem to share a bed with him without fucking him. I was sure he filled my dad in on every dirty detail about how I ran hot and cold and wanted him to bang me one minute and wanted him to stay the hell away from me the next minute.

"What exactly did Parker tell you about our relationship?"

"I know that it was getting serious, CC. I know that he fell for you. I know that he didn't want to, that he tried to resist it, that he tried to stay away and protect you from a distance. I know that he's suffering right now because he's trying to give you space." He ran a hand through his jet black hair as he paused.

He looked me dead in the eye. "And I know you. I know you don't hold grudges. I know that you're trying to protect yourself from getting hurt, but I've known PJ for a long time. I have to appeal to you on his behalf."

My mouth dropped open in shock. "Are you seriously meddling in my love life right now?"

He sighed and rubbed at his jaw. "You're forcing suffering on both of you because you're being stubborn. Look at it from his perspective. Give him another chance to prove to you that he's worthy of you. There aren't many men in this world who I'd give my approval to, but he's one of the good ones."

My dad pulled me in for a hug, and I felt his warmth. I felt his sincerity. And it was time for me to believe that everyone around me simply had my best interests at heart. None of them had intentionally hurt me.

And maybe that chat with my dad was all I really needed to see things a little differently.

He headed back to his wife, and I wandered around a little longer.

I was between the Flashing Light bus and the Pure Adrenaline bus when I heard voices. They were off to the side and they were talking quietly, but it was loud enough for me to overhear. Obviously neither had heard my quiet footsteps between the buses.

I made out Vinnie's voice. He sounded angry. And then I heard Parker's voice, too.

"You're always running to her."

"Shut up, Vinnie."

"If it's because of Gideon, I'm fine with it. Just don't tell me you're in love with her."

"Fuck off." Parker's voice was light despite his words.

"So that's it. You actually want her."

"I don't have to explain myself."

"You're right. But I miss the old Parker."

"Sorry, man. But he's gone."

"She must have a magical pussy."

"Not that it's any of your business, but she sure does."

I chuckled quietly to myself and headed back to my own bus. I'd heard enough to tell me that Parker's feelings for me were genuine. What he was telling one of his best friends confirmed my dad's sentiments about him.

Hank stood outside the bus I was sharing with only Parker.

"Ma'am," he greeted me.

"Hi, Hank. I think I'm ready to call it a night."

He smiled, and then he punched in the code to unlock the door. He was like a pseudo-bodyguard.

I heard the door close behind me, and I walked around the bus. I settled in on the couch and flicked on the television. I flipped through the channels twice before shutting it off.

I wished my mind was as easy to shut off as that damn television.

Parker and I had slept in separate beds since the Four Seasons in New York. It was at my insistence, but after the lecture my father had just delivered to me, I was certain I was really only punishing myself.

Parker had given me the space I needed, although he'd been nearby pretty much all the time. It was comforting, but I was making it awkward. If we were actually together, it would have been so much different.

But we weren't.

Because I wouldn't let us be.

I thought about heading to the back of the bus to use the queen-size bed. It looked much more comfortable than the tiny sleeping compartment that had given me a stiff back after only one night.

Plus the bed meant I didn't run the risk of sitting up too fast and hitting my head on the ceiling.

But if Parker saw me there, he'd see it as an invitation. I just wasn't sure if I was ready to give him that opening.

I wasn't sure what I was waiting for, exactly, but I wasn't ready to let him back in. I wasn't deliberately trying to be stubborn, but every time I thought about letting him back in, my mind wandered back to the lies, the omissions, the deceit.

The only difference was that now an equal part of my mind was reminding me that while he had initially done it to please my father and to get his big break, the feelings that he'd developed were as real as the feelings I had for him.

It wasn't fair of me to deny us both what we needed— what we deserved.

I headed toward the back of the bus. Fuck the tiny sleeping compartment. I was going to sleep in the queen, and if Parker saw that as an invitation, then so be it.

I wasn't going to admit to the huge part of me that *wanted* him to come back and snuggle in beside me.

Except he didn't view it as an invitation. I felt the bus moving, which meant it had to be sometime after five in the morning. I sat up in the darkness. I was alone in bed. I'd left the door open, so Parker must've closed it. He must've wanted to grant me some privacy.

I had the sudden need to see him.

I headed toward the living area on the premise of needing a bottle of water from the refrigerator. I heard voices toward the front of the bus, but I couldn't make out what they were saying, so I crept a little closer.

"…drove a tour through the Grand Canyon once when I worked for a charter company," I heard Hank say.

"We didn't travel much, but the Grand Canyon is definitely my favorite trip from my childhood." Parker was discussing vacations with Hank.

Hank was focused on the road ahead, and Parker was sitting on the floor next to him. A glass partition and a lowered seat separated the driver from the rest of the bus, so typically Hank had no idea what was going on in the bus behind him. He didn't need to. That became pretty important depending on who was riding on each bus, but between his seat, the CB Radio he used to communicate to the other drivers, and the nondisclosure agreement the bus drivers all had to sign, we could be fairly certain that whatever was said on the bus would remain private.

I found it adorable that Parker was talking to Hank like they were old buddies. I'd seen too many musicians treat the bus drivers like pieces of trash. It was one of those moments that showed me that despite the pain he'd inflicted on me, he was actually a good guy under all of the issues that had blossomed between us.

Parker must've seen me out of the corner of his eye, because he turned and his eyes met mine. His looked warm. He looked younger sitting there somehow. Maybe vulnerable.

He looked boyish and sweet as opposed to the usual carnal sex-god that I saw when I looked at him.

Those eyes that usually looked upon me with heat and lust were gentle.

That did it. Seeing this other side of him when I was so close to taking him back pushed me over the edge and into his arms.

If I fell, I knew Parker would be there to catch me.

Yes, he had hurt me. But I had to believe that life was about second chances. I'd hurt people before, too. No one is without sin, and I counted on the forgiveness of the ones I loved. If I couldn't grant that even after Parker had been trying to prove himself to me, I'd be even worse than the lies.

Parker stood, his eyes never leaving me. I felt like he was searching me, like he could see through my exterior to the inside of me that had been warming back up to him. "Hank, you have fun up here doing your thing." I heard Hank laugh.

He smiled broadly at me as he walked toward me. "Hey, you," he said softly.

"Hey." I rubbed my eyes sleepily. He reached out and tousled my hair. His actions were tender and loving.

He stood awkwardly. He was unsure. It was interesting to see him off-balance. He wasn't sure if he should pull me into his arms or if he should leave me alone.

So I took the guesswork out of the equation.

I walked into his arms, wrapping myself around him.

It took him a few seconds of stunned silence before he enveloped me. His lips were in my hair, and then they were on my face, and then they were on my own lips before I even knew what hit me.

I kissed him back, passion overtaking both of us as I finally gave into the very thing I'd been fighting—except when we found ourselves in a bed together.

His kiss was full of hope. This one was different from the heated animalistic ones that led to sex.

This one was filled with reverence and love and optimism and beauty. His mouth opened slowly to mine. His tongue moved sensually against mine, holding a promise of truth and emotions.

I pulled back to look at him.

His dark eyes met mine. Some lust had crept into his, but the unfiltered hope I saw there was enough to prove to me that he had true intentions. I'd been hard on him for long enough.

It was time to forgive and move forward.

"I think it's time for us to talk," I said.

thirty-nine

"Who's Kimmy?" I asked.

I glanced over at the clock. It was a little before six in the morning. Too early for this conversation, surely, and we had twelve more hours together on the bus before we arrived in North Carolina, but the question had been playing on my mind since the night of his drunken confessional.

His eyes were full of surprise at my question. "What did you say?"

"I asked you who Kimmy is."

"My sister." I breathed a sigh of relief that it was a relative and not a love interest. Surely he'd had girlfriends before me, but I wasn't really ready to hear about them quite yet. "Why are you asking me about Kimmy?"

"You mentioned her the other night. You actually mentioned quite a few things when you stumbled in drunk that night in New York."

He gave me a look of alarm, and then he chuckled. "So this is how you want to start this big conversation we need to have?"

I shrugged. He laughed.

"Same old Jimi." He pulled my hand toward his mouth and brushed his lips over my knuckles. "God, I've missed you."

"I know."

He chuckled. "Who's Damien?" he asked, countering my own question.

I froze. I supposed if I was asking questions about people in his life, he had every right to ask questions, too. I just wasn't prepared to dredge all of that back up.

"An ex." I kept it simple. "Why do you ask?"

"Your dad had mentioned something about Damien to George in one of our meetings. He didn't elaborate and I just wondered who he was."

"He left without an explanation in the middle of the night. Apparently my dad knows more." Parker shot me a look of sympathy, but I didn't want it. "I'm over it, Parker. I've moved on."

"With me."

I nodded.

"My dad knows the specifics of why he left, but he won't tell me. If you want to know more, you should talk to him since you two are so close." The last part came out more bitter than I'd meant it to.

Parker sighed and then completely changed the direction of our conversation.

"That first night we were together, do you remember that?"

I nodded. "I don't think I will ever forget that night. You were so…" I trailed off, searching for the exact right word. "Dominant."

"When I shoved my dick down your throat, you were scared. Did you like that?"

I froze, unsure how to answer that. "Uh… that's two questions." I stared at the floor, my cheeks burning.

He chuckled.

"Honestly?" I asked, my eyes finally lifting to meet his.

"I always expect you to be honest, Roxanna."

"You never call me Roxanna."

"I can't believe it's actually, really your name. You'll always be Jimi to me."

"I'm not sure how I feel about you yelling out 'Jimi' when you're dick is inside of me."

He chuckled, and then his voice turned serious again. "Answer my question."

"Yes." My voice was barely a whisper as I glanced over his shoulder. Part of me was worried that Hank would overhear our conversation even though I knew he couldn't, but the other part of me was trying pretty much anything to avoid eye contact at my reprehensible admission.

"Yes?" he asked, his voice much louder.

I looked down at my lap, nodding once.

"I was writing a song about fears right around that time. It was the fear I saw in your eyes when you looked around like someone was watching you. Half the time it was me watching you, but you couldn't have known that. I was just doing my job. That was before we met. But that night, I was in the moment, we both were, and I couldn't stop myself. When I saw that fear in your eyes, it turned me on. But when I was able to save you from that fear, to strip away that fear... It was a thrill."

"So you've got some hero complex?"

He shrugged. "Maybe. I like saving people. I like protecting people."

"Hence the tattoos."

He nodded.

"Who else have you protected?"

"We're not talking about me right now."

I pouted, and his lips lifted up in a tiny smile.

"So you like causing fear and then eliminating it?"

"Not causing it. That first night we were together, I wasn't trying to scare you. Part of it was the pleasure of that mouth of yours, but the other part was testing your limits. I've never deliberately done something to cause you fear. But I do seem to enjoy saving your ass."

"Because you were hired to."

His fingertips came under my chin. He forced me to look at him. "That might be how it started. But that's not at all where I am now."

"But let's call it what it is. You get off on saving me. It doesn't matter who causes the fear."

"I wouldn't say I get off on it. I don't want you to be scared. But if you are, I want you to know that I'm here. And what we do in the bedroom should never be scary. As soon as I told you to relax that night, you did. You enjoyed it."

"That night in the break room when Vinnie snuck up on me, you saw the fear in me then."

He nodded. "I did. Vinnie's harmless, but you didn't know that. You were terrified. You looked like you wanted to claw his eyes out. And when I held you, when you trembled in my arms…" He closed his eyes for a moment at the memory. A shudder of desire passed through me as I watched the look on his face.

He stood up and pulled me up with him, right into his arms. I rested my cheek against his chest, and we stood in the exact pose we had on the night he was referencing. His heart was racing against my cheek. "God, you were terrified of Vinnie. And you were so fucking grateful that I walked in when I did." He kissed the top of my head.

"Did…" I paused, not sure if I could really form the question. "Did you put Vinnie up to that?"

Guilt flashed through his eyes for just a second, but he played it off well. We both sat back down.

"Be honest, Parker."

"I didn't put him up to it. He doesn't know about my deal with your dad. No one does. We've both been really careful about that. Vinnie really is just that big of an asshole. But I did use it to my advantage. I caught you in a vulnerable spot and used it to gain your trust."

"More lies."

He looked sharply at me, and then he sighed. "I never lied."

"You told me you weren't going to tell me that again."

"Then stop questioning its validity. You trusted me because I saved you from Vinnie. You trusted me when I saved you from my own dick down your throat." He grinned wickedly.

I smiled back. When he looked at me with that glint in his eye, and when I thought back to that first night between us, I couldn't help but smile.

"And you trusted me that night we ran into Randy."

"Wait a minute. You knew he was going to be there?"

He shook his head. "No. I took you to that place because it really does have the best cheeseburgers in LA. I had heard a few details about Randy, but not much. Your dad had shown me his picture, said he lived in Culver City, and told me that he was a threat. I thought if Randy happened to see us together, he'd believe that we were a couple and he would never question why I was always around you. He'd never link me to your dad if he saw me with you first. I still don't fully understand what he's capable of."

I nodded. It was like a giant puzzle finally coming together.

"Do you want to tell me why you were so scared of him that night? Did you know about the shit between Gideon and him?"

I shook my head. "I didn't find out about any of it until my dad invited me to come on the tour. He told me about my ex's connection to Randy."

"Your ex Damien?"

I nodded. "And no, I don't want to tell you why I was scared of Randy."

"Tell me anyway," he demanded.

"He hit on me one night when I was a teenager."

"What did he do to you?"

"Nothing. He was just a slimy, drunk old man. He freaked me out a little, but I got away."

"Fuck," he muttered.

"I have a question for you now."

He nodded, looking at me expectantly.

"Where were you really during those weeks when you said you were writing?"

"I was writing."

"But you stayed away from me."

"I was writing. But I was also doing everything in my power to find a way to protect you while staying the fuck away from you. I was falling for you, and I was terrified you'd reject me, or you'd find out your dad hired me to protect you and you'd want nothing to do with me. And I was right."

"You were. But I think I'm starting to get it."

He looked at me with that same sense of boyish hope. "You think so?"

I nodded, and he smiled. He stood, and we walked together to the queen-size bed in the back of the bus.

And then there was no more talking.

forty

Washington DC was a little more than halfway between Boston and Raleigh, and that's where we stopped for lunch. My dad and Mikey had scheduled an appearance at some bar just outside of DC, so the rest of us scattered around the outskirts of town to find some place to eat. Parker and I ended up with George over our shoulder at some barbecue restaurant while Hank refueled, and then we were back on the road. The only thing the stop did was force us to get out of bed, but as soon as we got back on the bus, we headed right back to our compartment in the back. Parker slammed the door shut and pounced.

Once we'd gotten our shit out in the open and cleared the air, I felt about a thousand times better. I was where I needed to be, which was safe in Parker's warm, protective, and loving arms.

Our bus pulled into Raleigh and we were forced to emerge from our bus bed haven. We checked into yet another Four Seasons Hotel. I didn't even bother with my own room this time since I knew I'd be sharing with Parker anyway. I was beyond disappointed I had to tear myself from Parker, but he had stuff to do. Namely, he had a band meeting to review their Boston performance, and since he'd been on the bus with me instead of the rest of the band for over twelve hours, they had quite a bit of work to do.

My dad was conferring with George, which left me alone—or so I thought until I opened my hotel room door and saw Bruno sitting outside of it.

"Where would you like to go, ma'am?" Bruno asked. I hadn't had the chance to see him up close when he'd been following me around in LA. He was older than George. He had some salty white in his dark hair. He was serious, but his dark eyes were kind. They were eyes that I immediately trusted.

I shrugged. "Nowhere in particular. Just wanted to get out and stretch my legs a little. Maybe to my dad's room?"

I hadn't actually planned on going anywhere, but there was a conversation I unexpectedly wanted to have. I'd been so obsessed with everything Parker that I hadn't had time to focus on my relationship with my dad's new wife. The sudden need to take control over this part of my life propelled me down the hall.

Bruno knocked on my dad's door, just a few rooms away from my own.

Jadyn opened the door, camera-ready as usual. I didn't know anyone who wore as much make-up as she did in real day-to-day life. It was as if she could be photographed at any time, and she always had to be ready. I supposed it was likely that she would be photographed considering she was the new wife of an internationally acclaimed musician, but it still made me wonder what she was hiding.

I hadn't trusted her from the very beginning, but I didn't really know her all that well. My dad must have had some reason for marrying her. He loved her. He planned to have her in his life for a long time to come, so I supposed I should give her a chance.

"Is my dad here?" I asked through her glare. She hadn't invited me in, but I stepped in. Bruno stepped in behind me, and I heard the door latch shut.

She walked over to a wet bar and topped off her wine glass. "He's with George. And we have dinner plans after his meeting."

Bruno took a seat at a conference table. Having him there for this conversation should've been awkward, but instead it was comforting. It was like someone was on my side. It propelled my confidence forward.

I sighed. "Can I talk to you about something?"

She set the bottle down and picked up the glass. She shrugged in my direction with indifference, and then she walked over to a loveseat situated across the room. I paused and took in the room for a minute. It was about four times the size of the room I shared with Parker, and I thought our room was the lap of luxury.

Even though I'd grown up around extravagance, I still appreciated it when I saw it.

Apparently the new Mrs. Price had already grown accustomed to it. She curled her legs underneath her, hooker heels and all, right on the loveseat.

As she sat there, I realized she hadn't offered me a drink. It wasn't really a big deal, except it was. It was manners. It was trying to get along—or at least trying to make a decent impression—with the daughter of your husband.

Apparently she didn't give a fuck about that.

I sat on a chair across from her.

"Why don't you like me?"

She glanced in my direction with surprise at my candor, and then her eyes diverted to the window.

"I never said I don't like you," she said flippantly.

"You didn't have to. You act like I'm a nuisance."

"I didn't mean to. I'm sorry you feel that way."

Her lack of a real apology echoed in my head. She wasn't sorry that she had treated me poorly. Instead, she was sorry that I felt like she had treated me poorly. It was a fine line but a huge difference.

"I'm sorry you act that way."

"That's a little dramatic."

"Look, my dad and I are close. I get that you want time with him, but I need you not to look at me like you're jealous every time he talks to me. I don't mean to sound condescending, but I'm his daughter. I will always be his daughter. You're his third wife in ten years. You do the math."

Jadyn looked over at me, and I could have sworn I saw a flash of admiration before it was wiped away and replaced with daggers. I saw Bruno shift in his chair out of the corner of my eye, but I kept my eyes leveled on my stepmother. Mother. Monster. Whatever.

She was just about to respond with something that would most likely cut me down to size when there was a knock at the door. I looked toward the door; Jadyn looked toward Bruno.

He stood to answer it, checking the peephole first. He let the visitors in, and I stood when I saw Vanessa and Keith.

Keith looked a little worse for the wear, and Vanessa had lines of anxiety around her dark eyes and fanning out from her red lips. I hadn't seen either of them since the attack.

I ran over to Vanessa and pulled her into a hug, which was completely out of my character yet instinctual.

She burst into tears, and I rubbed her back as Keith hobbled past us to the chair I'd just vacated. "How're you doing, Keith?" I asked as he passed by.

"Alright. Been better, but I'm getting there. It's always the worst a few days after, you know?"

"And how are you?" I asked Vanessa softly, pulling out of our hug to look at her.

Jadyn hadn't moved.

"I'm okay. I'm scared, Roxy."

"I know. I am, too. But we have George and Bruno, and don't forget about Hank and the other drivers. You know our crew's great."

She nodded, and a fresh wave of tears rolled down her cheeks. "I know. We never should've left."

"Where did you go?"

"Just out to dinner. But we broke away from the pack. We didn't bring anybody with us. He was jumped from behind." She wiped her eyes and headed over toward her husband. She knelt beside him, patting his knees.

"Did you see who did it?" I asked.

They both nodded. "He was short. He was wearing a dark cap and dark clothes," Vanessa said. "I've never seen him before, but I'd recognize him if I ever saw him again."

"What was the point?"

Vanessa shrugged, but this time Keith spoke. "We don't know. He took off with my wallet. The police said it's a mugging. Said it's not common for that part of town, but violence doesn't discriminate."

I rolled my eyes. "Sounds really helpful."

My dad and George emerged from some other room.

My dad's eyes connected with mine, and I saw real worry in his.

He was usually better at hiding his emotions. He was good at putting on a blank face. He'd mastered the art of acting. He had to. He was a person just like anybody else. He had feelings that ranged from happy to sad. He had good days and bad. But it didn't matter what was happening in his personal life, because people paid upwards of a thousand dollars at a chance to see Black Shadow live, so he had learned to hide whatever was going on inside in order to perform the best show he knew how.

But he wasn't hiding the anxiety he felt from me. Maybe he'd done it on purpose to give me a wake-up call, or maybe he'd forgotten to mask it in front of me. Either way, he'd just come from a meeting with his head of security. The news couldn't be good if he had emerged looking like that.

Jadyn finally stood. "Can I get you anything, Gideon?" she asked.

What started as a semi-confrontational meeting with Jadyn had become a small party by that time, so our one-on-one conversation was over. I was sure that it would linger between us, though. I'd gone with the intention of finding some answers, but instead I just managed to burn a bridge.

forty-one

I'd performed my list of duties at the Walnut Creek Amphitheater the next day, and I'd grabbed dinner at the catering table. Between time with Flashing Light and meetings with George and my dad all day, I hadn't seen Parker since breakfast. I felt like I should have been in those meetings with George and my dad, too, because whatever they were talking about concerned me. They made me feel like some weak and pathetic woman who wasn't allowed in on the big manly conversations.

I knew my thoughts were dramatic, but I didn't care.

It was a hot and humid June day at ninety-five degrees, so I headed back to the bus to freshen up and change clothes before the pre-show rituals, Bruno ever at my side. He did afford me some privacy to change my clothes, at least.

My dad had a meet and greet a scheduled for a quarter to seven. Flashing Light was scheduled to go onstage at seven. I wanted to watch Parker from the trench. I loved the nights when Parker took lead vocals on their last song, which was often. I hadn't had the chance to watch them perform since Parker and I had made up, so I couldn't wait to watch him perform "Trial and Error." Somehow that song never got old, especially as I thought about the way my tongue traced across the letters tattooed on Parker's torso.

I reached into my pocket to check the time on my phone. It wasn't there. I realized that when I'd changed jeans, I had left my phone in the sweaty pair on the bus. "Fuck," I muttered.

I headed toward my dad's dressing room. Parker was just leaving as I walked in. He paused, grabbed me by my upper arms, and pressed a hard kiss to my lips.

"Make sure you check your texts," he murmured so softly into my ear that I almost didn't hear him. He seemed nervous. I realized then that in the past few weeks, I'd never actually seen him right before he was about to take the stage. I was always tied up doing things for my dad.

Parker headed toward the Flashing Light dressing room for their pre-show traditions, and I informed my dad that his fans were waiting for him for a meet and greet.

"Fuck," my dad muttered. "I need to talk to you, CC."

I glanced at the clock hanging in the room. "It'll have to wait."

He nodded once, and then he and George headed up toward the fans.

I sat in the empty dressing room, wondering for just a moment where Jadyn was.

I didn't care, exactly, but I was curious. Too many strange things had been happening, and I wondered if her whereabouts were accounted for.

"Shit," I muttered to no one in particular.

"Do you need something?" Bruno asked. I'd forgotten that I wasn't alone.

"I need my dad's credentials to get into the trench for Flashing Light."

Bruno nodded. "Let's go get them." He typed out a text, presumably to George, and then we headed toward the meet and greet. I stood and watched for a few minutes before approaching my dad.

The clock was inching toward seven. I walked behind my dad and waited for him to finish signing a t-shirt before I knelt behind him. "Credentials?" I asked, and he reached into his pocket and passed me his all-access card.

I kissed his cheek and left him to his fans. Bruno stayed with him, and George followed me down. Apparently Bruno wasn't a fan of loud rock music, and George could take it. He was used to it.

We entered the trench just as the house lights went down. My heart started pumping in anticipation as I saw silhouettes, and then the stage lit up and there stood Parker.

Everything seemed to stop for a moment as I drank in the sight. He was perfection up on that stage. Women behind me screamed. Fans yelled.

I watched his eyes scan the crowd, but they didn't land on anyone in particular until they landed on me.

His eyes lit up, as if he drew his energy from the woman watching from the trench, and then the notes of their opening song sounded through the amphitheater.

I grinned as I bobbed my head to the beat.

It seemed like no time at all had passed and suddenly they were playing the closing notes to "Trial and Error." The entire show had been perfection.

Fitz always made the band introductions right before the last song, and the last song was always the cover. He was in charge of talking to the crowd, of regaling something personal or of getting them excited for the upcoming acts. He introduced Vinnie first and then Garret, and then he nodded toward Parker.

"And this is Parker James, who has something he wants to say tonight!"

I looked up at Parker, who looked nervous as fuck. In fact, as I looked at him, I could not remember a time when he'd looked more nervous in his life.

"We're going to close with a song that makes me think of someone very special to me. She's right here in front, just like she has been almost every night," he paused and searched my eyes out, "and I want her to know how much I love her. Roxanna, this one's for you."

The band launched into a cover of Motley Crue's "Without You."

Tears filled my eyes as I listened to the words of the song. He sang to me with his whole heart. I felt it from where I stood. I gazed up at him, the light hitting him in some perfect angle that lit up his whole face. As he sang about how he would love only me until we grew old together, I couldn't help but think how different my life was just a few months earlier. He'd walked into Vintage and made me feel all of these things again after I'd written off getting close to people. He'd become the center of my life in such a short time.

As much as I wanted to hate him for the deceit, I couldn't help that I'd fallen for him—that we'd fallen in love with each other.

Love begs forgiveness.

So I forgave.

And now here we stood, our entire future before us.

Nothing hit that point home more than Parker's words when the song neared its end and he stopped singing and started talking, the band still playing the melody as he spoke.

"Roxanna Cecilia Price, my Jimi, I want to spend the rest of my life showing you that I can't live without you. Will you marry me?"

to be continued in
Vintage Volume Two

acknowledgments

I always have to thank my husband first. He listens, makes suggestions, and supports so much that sometimes he thinks he's the one writing the books. Thanks for always being my first beta reader and for being my very own rock star. And to Sadie, my fuzzy best friend, thanks for the cute puppy dog eyes and for lying next to me while I write.

Louisa Maggio, you designed the perfect cover to represent Roxy and Parker. I am in love with the cover and still haven't stopped staring at it.

Thank you to Team LSD. Your support and friendship means the world to me. I particularly want to thank the lovely ladies on my street team who also beta read *Vintage*: Kelly, Katie, Anna, Crystal, Jen, April, Johnnie-Marie, Alissa, Sheri, Stephanie, Jenna, and Tiffani. In case you didn't see it, both Katie and Anna also appeared in this book…Katie in her quest to be killed off in as many books as possible, and Anna, who won a contest to make an appearance in my next book.

A huge thank you to Bryan Wickmann for the behind-the-scenes look at an actual tour bus. Seeing what goes on behind the stage during a huge concert was a once in a lifetime opportunity, and I'm forever grateful you took us on a tour and offered to answer any of my questions. And thanks to my brother, Brad, for taking me to see Bryan after all these years!

Thanks to the creative and talented authors who gave me beta feedback: Madison Street, Jenni Moen, and Josie Bordeaux.

I owe a debt of gratitude to the many bloggers who spend countless hours doing everything they can to support and promote authors, especially indie authors like me. A huge thanks to Kellie Montgomery for being an all-star in every way and for running the exclusive cover reveal on Eye Candy Bookstore. Thanks also to Kylie and Beth at Give Me Books and Debra at The Book Enthusiast for the release day blitzes.

Thank you to all of the readers who take the time to get lost in the world I created. Time is a precious commodity, and to know that you spent yours with me touches my heart. I hope you found your time well spent and that you will consider leaving a review of Vintage.

Lastly, thank you to all of the creative people in this world who continue to inspire my writing. Whether it's a good book that I just couldn't put down or that one song that I listened to on repeat, thank you for creating something out of nothing and sharing it with the world.

XOXO,

Lisa Suzanne

about the author

Lisa Suzanne started handwriting her books on yellow legal pads after she took a creative writing class in high school. She still has those legal pads full of stories, but now one of them is published under the title *How He Really Feels*. She currently works as a full time high school English teacher, and her favorite part of the year is summer. She has been blessed with the world's best dog, a supportive family, and a husband who encouraged her to publish after reading one of her novels. She likes the advice of Ernest Hemingway's famous quote, "Write drunk. Edit sober."

Web: http://www.authorlisasuzanne.com
Facebook: https://www.facebook.com/AuthorLisaSuzanne
Twitter: https://twitter.com/LisaSuzanne24
Instagram: http://www.instagram.com/authorlisasuzanne
Goodreads: http://www.goodreads.com/AuthorLisaSuzanne
Pinterest: http://www.pinterest.com/lisasuzanne24
Google+: https://plus.google.com/u/0/+LisaSuzanne/posts

also by Lisa Suzanne

HOW HE REALLY FEELS (HE FEELS, BOOK 1)

Julianne and her boss embark on a sexy affair that's everything Julianne ever dreamed of... except she can't tell anyone about it due to the company's strict "No Dating" clause. What will happen if anyone finds out about their secret relationship? And how will Travis, her lifelong best friend, react when Julianne begins a relationship with someone who isn't him?

WHAT HE REALLY FEELS (HE FEELS, BOOK 2)

Will Travis ever figure out What He Really Feels, or will he be stuck on his first love forever? Will he find his happily ever after?

SINCE HE REALLY FEELS (HE FEELS, BOOK 3)

Julianne and Nick know they should form a united front, but knowing what to do and actually doing it are two very different things. Will Travis's presence in their life pull them together or push them apart? Find out in the passionate and emotional concluding book of the He Feels Trilogy.

SEPARATION ANXIETY

We all get one true love in our lives, and it's up to us to find it. Fate will act and try to push us together, but ultimately it's up to us to recognize who that one person is when he's standing in front of us. If only my husband would stop getting in the way of the man with whom I was meant to be.

SIDE EFFECTS

She isn't interested in commitment. She doesn't want a relationship. The confident Quinn is never nervous around men, so what is it about preppy Reed Porter that has her questioning everything? And what will be the side effects of attempting to juggle two men at the same time?

SECOND OPINION

What do you do when the person you love breaks your heart… twice? Grant's solution is avoiding relationships until someone makes him want a future he thought he'd written off. Ultimately, he has to decide what to do when the past makes her way back into his present.

Printed in Great Britain
by Amazon